W9-BZU-686

The Rest Is Silence

CARLA GUELFENBEIN

Translated from the Spanish by
Katherine Silver

Harwinton Public Library
Harwinton, CT

Portobello
BOOKS

Published by Portobello Books 2011

Portobello Books
12 Addison Avenue
London
W11 4QR

Copyright © Carla Guelfenbein 2008

English translation copyright © Katherine Silver 2011

First published in Chile as *El resto es silencio* by
Editorial Planeta Chilena, S.A. in 2008

The right of Carla Guelfenbein to be identified as the author
of this work and Katherine Silver's right to be identified as its
translator have been asserted by them in accordance with
the Copyright, Designs and Patents Act 1988.

This is a work of fiction. The characters, incidents, and
dialogues are products of the author's imagination and not to
be construed as real. The author's use of names of actual persons,
living or dead, and actual places is incidental to the purposes of
the plot and is not intended to change the entirely
fictional character of the work.

A CIP catalogue record is available from the British Library

2 4 6 8 9 7 5 3 1

ISBN: 978 1 84627 231 8

www.portobellobooks.com

Text designed by Patty Rennie

Illustrations by Carolina Schutte

Typeset in Bembo

Printed in the UK by CPI William Clowes Beccles NR34 7TL

CARLA GUELFENBEIN was born in Santiago, Chile, and lived in England for eleven years, where she took degrees at the University of Essex and Central St Martin's College. Returning to Chile, she worked as fashion director for *Elle* magazine, until she decided to become a full-time novelist and screenwriter. She is the author of three best-selling novels, which have been translated into twelve languages; this is her first to appear in English.

KATHERINE SILVER is an award-winning translator of Spanish and Latin American literature. Among her most recent translations are works by César Aira, Horacio Castellanos Moya, and Daniel Sada. She is co-director of the Banff International Literary Translation Centre in Canada, and lives in Berkeley, California.

For Micaela and Sebastián

So tell him, with the occurrents, more and less,
Which have solicited—the rest is silence.
                      Hamlet, Act V, Scene 1, William Shakespeare

PART ONE

White Silence, Black Silence

1 ↗

Sometimes words are like arrows. They fly back and forth, wounding and killing, just like in wars. That's why I like to record what grown-ups say. Especially when somebody says something and then suddenly, like magic, everybody starts laughing at once.

All I can see down here are lots of legs, moving around. Every kind of leg: camel legs, rabbit legs, flamenco legs, monkey legs, legs of other animals who have names I haven't learned yet. There are three women sitting at my table with knees as thick as elephants' legs, and a man wearing golf shoes, and a giraffe who quickly takes off her golden sandals. Even though they're all talking over each other and it'll be hard to get anything worthwhile, I turn on my MP3 player and voice recorder and start recording.

"Did you notice Tere and her husband came in separate cars?"

"No, I didn't, but I'm not at all surprised."

The ocean breeze lifts the tablecloth. In the garden, the bride and groom pose for the photographer with Grandfather's aviary in the background. My cousin Miguel is smiling like he has a stick stuck lengthwise in his mouth. I see Alma among all the colorful dresses. She's moving her hands and sketching shapes in the air as she speaks. She has red hair and the same name as the biggest telescope in the world. A.L.M.A. is mainly used to study star formations. My best friend, Kájef, and I found out that it can analyze organic particles like carbon, and that will solve the Great Mystery of how life began. It's amazing how many things A.L.M.A. can see. On the other hand, Alma, Papa's wife, is a little absentminded. But I don't care, because she doesn't mind that I'm a little slow and a little clumsy. Sometimes we do things Papa doesn't approve of. Like today, for example, she was the one who convinced him that my cousins would laugh at me if I wore that suit I usually wear on special occasions, even though we both know they'll laugh at me no matter how I'm dressed. It's not that my cousins are mean; they just always seem to be in a rush, like people going on a treasure hunt a long way away, somewhere I'm never invited.

"I'm telling you, no, they don't even know each other."

The woman's voice is hoarse like a frog's. I lift the recorder a little.

"I thought they were friends. Look, there she is, with the bride and groom, in front of the aviary."

Of all the birds in my grandfather's cage, the ones I like best are the golden pheasants.

"Are you crazy? Never! You know how Marisol is."

A pair of men's shoes stop in front of the table I'm hiding under.

"Carmen, what a pleasure to see you!"

It's Papa, with that doctor voice he never leaves behind. If he finds me here, recording grown-ups talking, he'll get angry. He says it's "an invasion of privacy," but I don't really understand what "privacy" is. The way I see it, what's private is what you do and feel when you're alone. These conversations don't seem private to me.

One of the women jiggles her foot back and forth; you'd think she had a pebble in her shoe.

"Please don't get up," Papa says.

I hold my breath and clutch the recorder.

"It's been a long time, Juan," the woman says.

4

"Five, six years?"

"At least."

"You look fabulous, Carmen. I'm so glad you came. Where's Jorge?" Now Papa is speaking in his calm but cheerful voice, the one he uses when someone asks him for medical advice.

"He left me a couple of years ago. His secretary," the woman explains, then laughs. *"Don't worry—I'm happy. Good riddance, I say. He was useless."*

"If you say so," Papa answers.

"We all say so," another woman adds quickly. Sounds like somebody pricked her with a pin.

A few minutes later, Papa's shoes move away. Good thing he didn't find me. Papa and Alma are going to stay here and I'm going to go back to Santiago with one of my uncles. "We need a break from you guys," Alma told me in a sweet voice and with a big smile. It still didn't seem fair.

"Juan got remarried, didn't he?"

"Yes, to a much younger woman."

"She's a bit pale and skinny for my taste," the golf shoes add.

Grown-ups wear signs on their foreheads that say things like, "You are the most boring person I know," or, "You stink," or, "I would love to kiss you." Of course, from under the table, I can't see those signs. I'm getting tired of being here, curled up in a little ball, but at this point it would look suspicious if I just stood up and walked away.

"The bride is the one who really looks smashing," they start talking again.

"You mean Julia? Yes, though she's a dark little thing. Her family's from the south. Nobody knows who they are," the giraffe says, modulating her words like she is chewing on a ferret.

"Anyway, it's a good thing Juan got remarried; Soledad's illness was so tragic and sudden."

5

"*Illness? Ah, the lies we swallow*," says the elephant woman.

"*What are you talking about?*"

"*Oh dear, I shouldn't have said anything. Sorry. Please, let's change the subject.*"

I can't see the elephant's little sign, but as far as I can tell, she wants to keep talking about it.

"*You can't leave us hanging now.*"

The elephant is quiet for a second, then says, "*Soledad didn't die of an illness. She committed suicide.*"

"*Didn't she have an aneurysm?*"

"*That's what they told everyone to avoid a scandal, but Soledad committed suicide. I know it for a fact.*"

I feel a pain in my chest. The recorder slips out of my hand and bangs on the ground. Mama got sick when I was three. She got sick all of a sudden, they told me, and then she was gone.

"*It's one of the best-kept secrets of the Montes family.*"

"*But Soledad was so gorgeous, and she always seemed so upbeat, so content with her life.*"

"*Well, appearances can be deceptive. Just because she looked happy doesn't mean she was. In fact, she'd been hospitalized for a few months before she committed suicide, at Aguas Claras.*"

"*I don't believe it. I volunteered there once. That was no place for Soledad. It did have beautiful grounds, but the rest of it was awful.*"

At first I remembered Mama all the time, but one day I discovered that no matter how hard I tried I'd never stop growing, or forgetting. The two go together, and there's no way to pull them apart.

"*They didn't want anybody to find out. If they'd put her in the Clínica de Europa, they'd be sure to run into somebody. Actually, it was right around the same time that María Elena's daughter was hospitalized, at the Europa, of course.*"

My memories of her feel like scenes from a movie. There's one image that always comes back. We're lying on the floor of an empty room, just me and Mama. She's holding me in her arms. We can see the sky through a skylight in the ceiling. Sometimes I close my eyes and imagine I'm there, but I always end up wishing it was real.

"*Poor Juan.*"

"*He must be a little to blame, don't you think? After all, she was his wife.*"

"*Don't talk nonsense. Juan's an angel.*"

"*Speaking of blame, did you hear about Toti's ex?*"

If Mama killed herself, it's because she didn't love me. I hold my breath and count: Ten, nine, eight, seven ... I'm sure I can go back, back to before I hid under this table ... six, five ... the elephant would say anything to impress her friends ... four, three, two ... My head is spinning and I feel a thousand stabs in my belly, as if a propeller were turning round and round inside my guts. I can't stand it anymore. I make a dash for it. I slip and fall. I bang my knees and my hands.

I've come to the very end of the garden, where it plunges down into the sea. The light in the sky is white. My cousins are playing ball at the top of the hill, the highest point in the garden. I sit down on the grass. I hug my knees and bury my head in my lap. I stink. I don't know exactly when my guts exploded. Now I'm really in trouble.

Sometimes I know what it feels like to be unhappy, to wait for night-time so I can hide under the sheets, close my eyes, and escape forever to Kájef's barge. Is that how Mama felt?

2 〰〰

The younger guests have started dancing. I take off my high-heeled sandals and walk along the gravel path into the garden. When I get to the grove of Peumo trees, I lie down on the grass. It's a warm afternoon, and the waves crash gently against the seaweed barrier. Past the house, I can see the distant outlines of a group of golfers on the golf club's large lawn. I remember the first time I stepped foot in this place, the Montes family summer residence. Now, seven years later, the enchantment and fear I used to feel have completely disappeared.

I can picture Juan's father perfectly, the caustic aristocrat sitting in his Louis XV armchair, with his high forehead and aquiline nose, and that indolent way he has of lifting his eyes and looking at me. Though always gracious, Don Fernando displays the aloofness of someone who never fully acknowledges the people around him. The baby I brought with me to that first meeting, only a few months old and obviously not the fruit of my recent union with his son, must have made him uncomfortable, though he gave no indication that it did. His attitude, both casual and cold, formed the perfect backdrop for the house and all its furnishings. Back then, I had difficulty imagining a single spot in the entire property, which seemed so frozen in time, where I would feel comfortable; but from the very first moment I arrived, finding that spot was the thing I most longed to do.

After lunch, we took a walk through the park. Juan pushed Lola's carriage and we strolled with Don Fernando along paths lined with boxwood hedges and past fountains that reflected the sky's fickle colors. Every once in a while Juan looked at me and smiled, trying to gage my reactions. So many aspects of our lives separated us, made us different, but at the time I wasn't willing to think about them.

When we got back to the house, Don Fernando said he wanted to show me his library. Juan said he had to make a few phone calls and asked to be excused. I followed Don Fernando all the way down a wide hallway lined with display cases of ceramic pottery, until we reached the library—a room with high ceilings, heavy beams, and stone walls. After showing me his pipe collection, Don Fernando climbed a stepladder and took down a photo album from a shelf. His voice sounded hollow and peremptory when he handed it to me.

"Open it."

Inside I found countless photographs of Juan, from adolescence to young adulthood. His travels, his friends, the sports he played, his metamorphoses. It wasn't the images in the photos that would remain etched in my memory, however, but rather the white spaces in between, spaces from which dozens of photographs had been removed.

"They're the pictures of Soledad," Don Fernando explained. "They knew each other as children."

The thoroughness with which someone had erased all trace of Juan's wife was disturbing. Under Don Fernando's attentive gaze, I pored over each and every page in that album. That afternoon I asked myself a question that would keep returning: What lay under Juan's façade of calm and respectability? Just like the white spaces where there had once been photographs of his wife, there must be other aspects of his life that would remain invisible to me: hidden desires, fears, obsessions. Perhaps I too would one day become a blank space in a photo album.

The only question Don Fernando asked me that afternoon, and which struck me as quite strange, was if I was of Jewish descent. I said I wasn't. He indicated his approval with a smile. I added that if I went far enough back, I might find a Jewish ancestor, as one could in many families. Don Fernando twirled his silver-shanked cane in the air and said that the Earth was round before Columbus but that men had lived perfectly well thinking it was flat until then. His little parable baffled me. Was he implying that even if I did have Jewish blood, I could carry on perfectly well as I was as long as I didn't know about it?

Later, when Juan joined us, I didn't mention that I'd seen the photo album. I still haven't, not even to this day. Maybe I'm afraid of discovering something painful, something that would come between us. A few years later—I can't now recall under what circumstances—I did tell him about Don Fernando's strange question. His response was rather curt; he said his father was old and said such things just to get attention. His explanation wasn't very convincing, but I preferred not to dwell on it. As for Soledad, the only photograph of her I've ever seen is the one Juan jealously guards in his desk drawer.

Before we left for Santiago, Don Fernando opened a bottle of champagne and toasted us. My relationship with Juan wouldn't have been possible without his approval. I mentioned this once to Juan, but he denied categorically that anything would have changed between us. He said that his father's opinions held no sway over him, and that the only thing that mattered was the feelings we had for each other. With time, though, I've come to realize how significant his family's opinions are to him. I've also come to understand that Don Fernando's attitude toward me—and the rest of the family's—was no whim. My Slavic features and the bit of sophistication I'd picked up in Europe counted in my favor. If I'd been dark, short, and from the provinces, it would have been much more difficult for them to accept me. The times also played a big part. Nowadays, people who consider themselves enlightened think that overlooking class and cultural differences is highly desirable, even if, privately, they still deplore such differences. Don Fernando must have seen the advantages of our union. By accepting me, he could appear open and modern to his contemporaries without really taking any risks. Right from the start I proved to be docile enough to adapt to his customs and lifestyle.

On the main terrace, couples saunter by and greet one another. The men laugh and pat each other on the back, perhaps reminiscing about their shared childhood, the schools they all attended, the various paths they'd taken on their way to adulthood. Some guests are still having after-dinner drinks and eating dessert, their faces sweaty, determined to have a good time, no matter what. Juan, sitting at a table with three of his brothers, slips a few inches down in his chair so he can stretch out his legs. Suddenly, he plucks his cellphone from his pocket and holds it to his ear. He stands up and walks a few steps away. He nods a couple of times. A few minutes later, he turns onto the path leading into the garden, and starts to look around; I think he is looking for me. I watch him, not letting him see me. If he finds me on his own, it means our bond persists. Tommy and I often play telepathic hide-and-seek. He doesn't know he has an unmistakable smell, a child's smell, like Lola's, but more intense. Juan doesn't see me, and I'm not going to help him.

He walks up to his father. Sitting alone and watching his guests' every move, Don Fernando holds his cane upright and keeps tabs on everybody's behavior so scrupulously it's impossible not to feel intimidated. Juan places his hand on his father's shoulder and kisses him on the cheek. Is he saying goodbye? He couldn't be. We agreed we'd spend the night in Los Peumos. We need some time alone. Just to break the routine—if only in a small way, to create a narrow opening where desire can slip back in. Each day it becomes more and more difficult to find that first gesture, the one that sets in motion the mechanism of desire. My hopes are resting on tonight, and I know that if we fail, we won't be able to blame the children, our daily distractions, our tiredness. Juan brings his cellphone back up to his ear. He paces, gesturing with his free hand. I stand and start walking toward him; then I see Tommy's tiny figure at the other end of the garden. He's alone, as usual, swinging a branch around in the air. I continue walking down the small slope and along the gravel path toward the terrace. As I approach, Juan is saying goodbye to one of his brothers; he looks preoccupied.

"What's going on?" I ask, as I put on my sandals.

"There's a heart for that little boy," he says, looking at his watch. "It's already on its way."

"But, Juan, you told me that you'd let Sergio take care of it if that happened."

"I'm sorry, Alma."

I search for something in his stern expression that shows genuine regret but don't find it.

"Do you really think saying, 'I'm sorry,' will cut it?" I ask scornfully. "You made a promise. We've been planning this for weeks."

"I have to go," he says. "It's my responsibility."

"Sergio's been waiting two years for you to give him this opportunity."

"Not this time."

"You'll never do it. Your greatest joy is opening the door to the operating room and seeing those faces looking at you as if you were God, isn't it?" I press my lips together to stifle my rage. "I'm sorry—I didn't mean to say that."

"It doesn't matter," he says. His voice is cold and measured.

He runs his hand through his hair, pushing it off his broad forehead. One rebellious lock falls back over his brow. He takes a deep breath. "He's twelve years old, like Tommy." He sounds agitated but controlled.

"Don't give me that. Sergio is as capable as you are of performing this operation; he wouldn't ask to do it if he didn't feel he was. I want you to stay because it's important for us." I speak in a whisper, the way he prefers me to when we are around other people.

Juan looks up at me impatiently. "Alma, please don't pressure me. You're only making things more difficult." His face shows irritation and anger.

"That's just what I want to do, isn't it? To make things more difficult for you . . . At least then I get a reaction."

"I have to go. Have you seen Tommy?" I hear him say.

"He's over there," I say, and point. "You can tell him you're leaving."

"I will."

He gives me a kiss and brushes my cheek with his hand, like the reasonable and good man that he is. As I watch him walk away, I can just make out Tommy's gaunt silhouette on the grass, as usual fighting an imaginary enemy.

3 ↗

The enemy forces sent an emissary who looks just like my father. I must resist, ready my weapons, but mostly I have to believe that Good will always triumph over Evil.

"Hey, champ," I hear him call to me from a distance.

They did a good job. They've even taught him our own private language. Luckily, my powers to perceive danger are superior. I raise my weapon and assume a defensive position.

"I have to return to Santiago. They called me from the hospital. You're going to go home with Alma and Uncle Rodrigo. Come and say goodbye, Tommy."

He can't fool me. Never again. Of course, I want to hug him. I want to hear him say that Mama didn't kill herself, that it's just one of those stories adults tell that get stuffed full of monsters and evil deeds as they pass from mouth to mouth. The man who looks like my father picks up a weapon and raises it in self-defense.

"As you wish. If you want to resolve this through hand-to-hand combat, I'm your man," he says.

I raise my stick and strike it against his. This is the first time I've ever attacked anyone who wasn't in my head. I hurl myself against Papa a few more times. Luckily, I put an extra pair of jeans in my backpack, just in case a miracle happened and my cousins invited me to join them on one of their adventures. Even so, I'm afraid the smell has stuck to my body and Papa will find out. He doesn't even try to defend himself.

"That's enough for now, Tommy," he says with a smile that isn't quite a smile. "You know you're not supposed to exert yourself."

The little sign on his forehead says, "You know you're weak and you'll never be able to defeat me." I lunge at him again. I have disobeyed. The man crosses swords with me. Our weapons remain in the air, pressing against each other. We stand face to face. I'm short of breath. I look at his square chin, his lined forehead, and I try with all my might to hide how difficult it is for me to breathe. Even with my eyes closed, I can picture every inch of his face. I usually imagine him as a wise and powerful warrior, the warrior that I will one day become, with the help of my friend Kájef, but now I don't know what I'm seeing. Papa lied to me. My eyes sting; I blink hard. I must keep fighting.

"Tommy, we'll have to continue this another day. I have to go now." He throws down his stick and walks up to me to say goodbye.

"Who do you have to operate on now?"

"A boy. His name is Cristóbal Waisbluth. We were waiting for a heart for him and now we've found one. He's on his way to the hospital right now."

"That means somebody's in a coma, right? Is that a child, too?"

"I don't know yet. It could be an adult's heart. I'll tell you tomorrow. Take care of Alma for me. Promise?"

He holds my chin, kisses me on the forehead, and quickly walks away with his jacket slung over his shoulder.

When you're waiting for a heart, what you really hope for is that somebody will die so you can live. That doesn't seem so weird. My life would be much better if Lola, my stepsister, disappeared. Also, when I started loving Alma, I had to let Mama die a little. I couldn't have little pieces of my heart spread out all over the place.

I pick up my stick and smash it to bits with my foot. I haven't finished destroying it when I notice that the sun is about to disappear into the sea. While it keeps sinking very, very fast, I think about this being the only moment when we humans can see the Earth turning. That's why I like it, and because of the green flash you sometimes see as the sun sets. Alma says it's really just an optical illusion, but I'm not so sure about that. We convince ourselves it's right there in front of our eyes because we want it to be. I'm really good at that; I make up stories, even memories. Otherwise, how's it possible that I can remember Mama's death?

Growing up is like climbing a hill carrying a big sign round your neck that says, "Forget." Sometimes I hold my breath so I can stop time. I can walk backward or forward, just like I can count from one to a hundred and then from a hundred to one, so I don't understand why time can't go back to then, to when Mama was still alive.

4⧗

Through the windshield of the cockpit the heads keep getting smaller. I try to catch a glimpse of Alma's red hair even though I know it's impossible. I didn't mean to quarrel with her. My departure wasn't premeditated; it's just the way things turned out. From up here, everything becomes insignificant: Alma's grudges, Tommy's peculiar behavior, my father and his little temper tantrums, my brothers and all their problems. Altitude—like the passage of time—emphasizes the most pleasant parts of life. I think about the battle Tommy and I waged. I've never seen him show such spunk, so normal for boys his age. He's finally growing up.

I can't help thinking that something special connects me to Cristóbal Waisbluth. He and Tommy were born with the same anomaly: a rare kind of heart disease called hypoplastic left heart syndrome. The difference is that Cristóbal's heart didn't respond as Tommy's did to the Norwood procedure, nor to the two other recommended surgeries.

Emma, his mother, reminds me of Soledad. Not physically: Soledad's body was almost childlike, whereas Cristóbal's mother is sturdy without being heavy-set, a woman who seems born to deal with adversity. Both women confronted the birth of a baby whose left ventricle was smaller than normal and therefore incapable of maintaining circulation to the entire body. A baby who could die at any moment.

Neither Soledad nor I was ready for this card life dealt us, but I had an escape and Soledad didn't. It was right after Tommy was diagnosed that I decided to specialize in cardiac surgery. There was always a problem to solve, a procedure to carry out, more research to do. Somehow, my work, and my pragmatic nature, protected me from having to delve too deeply into my emotions, but Soledad lived those moments intensely, and it was probably then that she began to feel that her efforts to rise to the occasion were futile. During Tommy's first few months, Soledad spent most of her time in the hospital. Once, she spent three days and nights without budging from his side, not even to take a shower. Her mother was the one who finally forced her to take a break.

"Do you want to die, too?" she shouted at her.

"My son is not going to die, Mama. I want you to get that into your head. Not as long as I'm alive."

The fierce glint in Soledad's eyes terrified both of us. She seemed capable of forcing anybody to do anything to save her son's life. If only we'd known then how much darkness her words were hiding.

Surgery is scheduled for an hour from now. I'm beginning to feel restless. In this state I am acutely aware of both my self-control and my utter lack of control over the situation. I never forget that something unforeseen can happen at any moment; it's what those with faith call divine force, what fatalists call destiny, and what others call chance.

As I approach Santiago, the lights of the first houses sketch straight and curved lines across the dark surface of the Earth. During the day the capital mostly looks chaotic, but at night it becomes as tidy as an architect's drawing. And somewhere among all those straight lines, at some precise spot in this city, less than two hours ago, the girl whose heart was donated was in a car accident.

5 ≋

Juan's airplane pierces the frayed clouds, turns into a dot, then disappears into the sky. Miguel and Julia waltz round the dance floor as their friends applaud. A pale young man with sharp features approaches and begins to dance in circles round them. He snaps his fingers in time to the music and purses his lips like a trumpet player. He has a desperate look on his face as he embraces them and drops his head onto Julia's shoulder. Miguel pushes him away with his elbows, trying to break free, but the boy, his fists clenched, seems to be holding on to them even more tightly. Trapped between the two men, Julia tries to lift her head to get some air. The blind energy of the applause swirls around them. A roar of female voices chants, "The kiss! The kiss!" Suddenly, a man approaches, takes hold of the boy, and separates him from the couple.

For a split second I think I'm just imagining it, but I'm not. This isn't the first time I've thought I've seen Leo. The young man cries out and staggers away, swaying back and forth as he punches his fists into the air. Leo follows him. He moves the same way he did before: His shoulders swing gently from side to side, a suppleness that is oddly both composed and hesitant. He's wearing a dark, loose-fitting suit. They stop at the bar. While Leo talks, he brings his hands to his head; it looks like he's having a difficult time reaching the young man. He still has that slight build, and his hair is short and curly. I can't quite make out if that look of disdain still hovers over his lips, around that austere, swarthy face, those gray eyes, and those black spirals in the depths of his pupils. Leo and the boy disappear from my sight. I look toward the sea. A silvery light emanates from the nearest rocks, as if an internal glow were rising through the water's surface.

Memories flash before my mind's eye. Everything that happened since the last time we were together. The abrupt end of my adolescence.

Until I was sixteen years old, I imagined the world as an empty house filled with water, a building of some kind rising as if out of the ocean floor, its blinds drawn, surrounded by melancholy. In one of the rooms, hidden from the light and everybody's sight, lived a fish. I was that fish.

At the time, I was living with my mother in a tiny, run-down apartment near the center of town. Papa had taken his first trip down south to look for a place we could move to, and Maná—the name a guru had given my mother—and I managed as best we could. Our meager income came from the meditation classes Maná gave to wealthy women and from what I earned on weekends as a bagger in a supermarket. This didn't prevent Maná from coming home every afternoon with new friends or staying up with them until all hours of the night, playing the guitar, listening to music, and smoking pot. I would close my bedroom door, enter my house of water, and go to sleep. It wasn't hard for me. Inside there, neither the smoke nor Maná's lovers could touch me. Sometimes I was so deeply submerged in my house that when somebody spoke to me, I couldn't understand their words.

Things weren't much different at school. I saw how the other girls looked at themselves in the mirror, in the windows of the classroom and the hallways as they walked by, how their skirts got shorter and shorter, their lips redder, their eyes more deeply set. I had no trouble understanding what was behind the determination I saw in them; I'd seen that same look a thousand times in my mother's eyes. But I was living in my house of water and my own skin was impermeable to those new currents coursing through their bodies.

One of my classmates invited me to a party. In exchange I promised to do her homework for two weeks. When we arrived, it was in full swing and the girl quickly disappeared from sight. The agreement didn't include her keeping me company. It was a modern house; it had a long hallway with glass walls. In every room, kids were talking quietly, sitting in armchairs, and smoking like grown-ups. In the living room, couples were holding each other close and slow-dancing. I decided to stay in a room filled with books. There was a lively conversation going on there and I thought nobody would notice me. I found a book about butterflies and sat down in a corner and started leafing through it.

Leo was sitting in a dark red velvet armchair holding a glass of Coca-Cola. He had some kind of romantic air. His gaze seemed to be turned inward and have an edge of irony, and he was obviously older than the others. The people he was sitting with were talking enthusiastically, but he didn't seem to be listening. Every once in a while he nodded in agreement. During one of those gentle descents into reality he must have caught sight of me. I was staring at him. When our eyes met, I smiled, imagining that his distance from the world was similar to my own. I can still see his brief pause, that fraction of a second when his eyes were still lost, then his fabulous smile. He brought his hands to his neck and pretended to strangle himself as his still-smiling face turned into a scowl. I let out a laugh and the others turned to look at me with surprise. Leo leaped out of his chair.

"You like butterflies?" he asked me, pointing to the book I held on my lap.

"Yes, I do, actually."

"I hate them," he admitted, laughing.

Again, his smile. It turned his taciturn, even weary expression into one that was lively, full of energy. He seemed to have the face of both a child and a grown man. The way it switched abruptly from one to the other was simultaneously unnerving and compelling. I found it difficult to take my eyes off him.

"Now this, for example, I like a lot," he declared, pulling a book out of the bookcase above my head. It was *Lady Chatterley's Lover*.

"My mother loves that book!" I exclaimed with childlike excitement. As soon as the words left my mouth, I blushed and looked away. "I do, too," I added without lifting my eyes. Some instinct made me quote the line "Ours is essentially a tragic age, so we refuse to take it tragically."

He turned the pages carefully, seriously.

"So it seems you've read it," he remarked, raising his eyebrows. "That must be why I noticed you."

"Am I that transparent?"

"Well, it's not every day I see a beautiful girl like you sitting in a corner with a boring book about butterflies when she could be dancing with anyone she wanted."

I laughed again.

"What's your name?"

"Alma."

"I can't believe it. This must be part of a plot."

That's the kind of reaction my name often provokes. I look away.

"Don't take it the wrong way, please. I mean it," he said. He held my face and forced me to look at him. "Really. I'm serious.

It's not every day that I meet someone named Alma who can quote from *Lady Chatterley's Lover*. Please don't take it the wrong way."

My cheeks began to burn under the touch of his fingers. His hand slid down and caught my arm, his thumb brushing the side of my breast through my blouse. I felt pressure in my lower belly. I wanted to stand up. I felt pins and needles up and down my spine. It was so intense I could barely breathe.

"You don't have a drink. Do you want something?" he asked with the hint of a smile.

We walked to the kitchen. He took out a beer for me and refilled his glass with Coca-Cola. I offered him a sip from my can.

"I can't drink. I just got out of rehab."

His words moved me. They seemed to expose him and forge a bond between us; the others, with their happy lives, were outside, far away. We stayed in the kitchen for a few minutes listening to the chatter and exchanging knowing looks. Our smiles, full of irony, implied that we were the only ones there capable of recognizing human folly for what it was.

After a while, we went out to the garden and sat on the grass to get away from all the hullaballoo in the house. Leo lit a cigarette. There wasn't even a hint of a breeze and the smoke rose in a straight line, then vanished into the darkness. He talked about the rehab clinic, about the Bosch print hanging in his room, about a friend who had died from an overdose. He told me about the hole he had dug at the far end of the garden. Every afternoon he dug it a little deeper until it was deep and wide enough to sit in. He went there every afternoon, until one day he found it had been filled in with dirt.

"Why did you do that?"

"So I'd have a place that was mine," he stated, completely serious. I could hear the despair in his voice, the hunger that had taken him there to begin with.

24

The answer seemed so obvious I regretted having asked. He looked at me sideways, a touch of shyness in his glance, and I imagined that his words hinted at much more complex emotions. He took a drag on his cigarette, threw it on the grass, and crushed it under his shoe. Then he asked me to tell him about myself. I told him my father was looking for land in the south where we could go to live in peace and quiet.

"Peace and quiet," I mused. "I wonder what he means by that. It sounds to me like getting buried alive." I tried to sound light-hearted, but my voice carried a tinge of the anxiety my family's precarious situation caused me.

Leo laughed. It was difficult to imagine a guy with a laugh like that in a drunken stupor. We kept talking, him more than me. Under the sway of his voice, everything seemed simpler and brighter, even shapeless things like fear. It was hard for me to leave my house of water, but little by little our shared enthusiasm gained the upper hand. We both became more animated and talkative, sharing opinions, asking each other questions; perhaps we were discovering that words were the only tools we had to coax our life force out of hiding.

"I have to go," he informed me. "Part of the agreement with my parents is that I get home before one in the morning." There was a glint of insolence in his eyes.

He offered to take me home, but I told him it wasn't necessary. I was ashamed of where I lived. We gave each other a hug goodbye.

I left once I was sure Leo had gone. I walked for hours, trusting my sense of direction and my instincts to guide me home. For once, I wasn't afraid; the feelings overwhelming me were stronger than any fear. When I arrived, Maná was sleeping with her door open. A man was snoring by her side. I quietly closed my door and re-entered my house of water.

6 ♐

Alma is walking toward me. She's carrying a plate with two pieces of cake in one hand and a bottle of Coca-Cola in the other.

"I'm hungry. How about you?" she says. "I stole this from the kitchen."

We sit down facing each other, the plate and the bottle between us. One couple is dancing barefoot in the garden. My cousins are leading a line dance on the terrace.

"Oops, I forgot the forks," she says, as if she's apologizing. Then she raises her eyebrows and brings her hand to her mouth. We both smile because we know she did it on purpose.

We look out at the sea. Red and yellow clouds rise from the water like aquatic soldiers ready to conquer the sky. We eat with our hands. Alma licks her fingers and so do I.

"Papa left again."

"He had a very important operation."

I nod without looking at her. I don't want her to see my eyes because then she'll see that I'm unhappy. Alma always sees everything.

"It's his work, Tommy. Come over here." She stretches out her arm and pulls me toward her, letting me lay my head on her lap.

I lie on my back. There's a big silence, one of those that fills space up instead of emptying it. The soldiers dissolve in the dark blue sky. The battle is lost, night approaches, and an almost invisible piece of the moon appears from behind the clouds. I know that the moon in front of us is full; we just can't see all of it. That's what happens with most things. We only see one part. For instance, neither Papa nor Alma has noticed that when my nanny, Yerfa, thinks nobody's watching, she takes a sip from a little bottle she carries around in her pocket.

"Did you know that the naked human eye can see only about three thousand stars and that there are more than a billion in our galaxy alone?" I ask Alma.

"Is that true?"

"One hundred percent. There are more stars in the universe than grains of sand on all the beaches in the world."

"That's hard to imagine."

She stretches her neck and looks up, as if she were trying to get a glimpse of one star in particular. She runs her fingers through my hair, tucking the longer strands behind my ears and brushing them from my forehead. Kájef is going to be amazed when I tell him I waged a battle with Papa. I'll also tell him that Alma and I were looking at his sea. He'll like that. I won't tell him she cuddled me like I was a little boy.

"Your hair is even softer than Lola's."

I'd have preferred she hadn't mentioned her. Lola is seven, she's tall and strong, she likes to play soccer, and when she gets the ball, everybody watches her, her pirouettes and fancy footwork. Lucky for me she stayed in Santiago with her grandmother, Alma's mother, and I won't let the thought of her ruin everything. Especially because Alma is telling me with her hands,

27

It means "I love you" in sign language.

Alma learned it when she lived in Spain. We're not that good at it, but we're good enough to send secret messages to each other without Papa finding out. It's too bad Alma taught it to Lola, too.

"Ah, so here's where you're hiding out," I hear a man's voice say behind me.

I lift my head to see who's butting in on us. It's some guy carrying his shoes.

"Hi." He bends down and shakes my hand. "May I join you?"

Alma says yes. I would have sent him packing, shoes and smile and all, to the other end of the ocean. Alma's body gets really tense, as if a ball has just dropped on her head. The guy keeps staring at her, then gives her a kiss and holds her arm. I get up and switch on the recorder in my pocket.

"You've changed so much, Alma. You look beautiful, really."

Alma bobs her head up and down like a chicken. Adults look so defenseless when people say nice things to them.

"This is Tommy."

"Hi, Tommy. I'm Leo, an old friend of your mother's."

Nobody calls Alma my mother because everybody knows she isn't.

"I knew you would be here. Matías warned me," the guy says.

"How do you two know each other?"

"Matías, the bride's father, and I all went to the same school."

"Oh, yes, that's right—he told me he was invited, but he hates weddings."

"He told me you are an amazing film editor and his best friend."

"What else did he tell you?"

"Well, just about everything I wanted to know."

"Then I'm at a disadvantage, because all I know about you is what I read in the papers."

28

"*Which isn't much.*"

"*Not about your personal life, at least. I read somewhere that you were living in Bogota and teaching at the university there.*"

Alma's smile is plastered on her face, like that time we saw the tail of a comet.

"*I'm still there.*"

Now she opens her mouth; it seems like she's about to say something, but instead she rubs her braid against her cheek.

"*And you, Tommy, what grade are you in?*" the guy asks.

"*Sixth.*"

"*Are you one of those kids who sits in the front or the back?*"

"*That's relative.*"

"*What do you mean, 'relative'?*"

I raise my eyebrows to let him know his question is stupid and doesn't deserve an answer.

"*I understand. Maybe I'd better keep quiet.*"

I nod. The guy, still smiling, turns to Alma.

"*Matías told me about the movie you are both working on. You wrote the script together, right? I remember you loved reading. You must be good with stories.*"

"*Fabulous, better even than you,*" Alma answers without taking her eyes off him, as if challenging him to play a game of war.

They both smile. I get the impression they're hitting it off pretty well, which means he'll hang around longer than I want him to. At least I'm recording. Alma gestures for me to come closer to her. I obey. She rubs her hand back and forth across my chest, as if she were pointing to my lungs.

"*What was going on with that guy you were talking to?*" Alma asks.

"*Oh, so you saw me. Why didn't you say hello?*"

"*I don't know. What was up with him?*"

"*He's my nephew, my younger brother's son. A year ago, he was Julia's boyfriend. I thought he was over it, but the poor thing is taking it hard.*"

29

"*His heart is broken,*" I say, just to say something. "*That must hurt a lot.*"

"*Maybe you've felt that before?*" the guy asks me.

"*A bunch of times,*" I answer as if I'm an expert.

"*How do you deal with it?*"

"*I play war.*"

"*You like war?*"

"*Yeah, because when I play, my head fills up with war.*"

"*You know, that's what happens to countries, too.*"

I say that I don't know about that.

"*It's really simple. When a country has serious internal problems, and the rulers don't know how to solve them, they invent a war with another country. That way, the people forget their own problems.*"

"*Yeah, I figured that out years ago, when I was at the most three years old.*"

"*And you, what do you do when that happens to you?*" he asks Alma.

Without answering, she gives him a look that doesn't seem very friendly.

"*Which do you prefer, to suffer or to die?*" I ask them, thinking about Mama.

"*To suffer,*" they both answer in unison.

They look at each other. Alma holds her braid, squints, and then lowers her eyes. I know those are just details, but that's how you find out and understand the most important things. Just ask Sherlock Holmes. I wish I had magical powers and could turn Alma into a groundhog or a beetle so this guy would think she's disgusting.

I lift my hand like magicians do. They both look at me. I lower it and say, "*Not me. It's better to die in war. Suffering turns warriors into cowards.*"

Mama chose to die. Her grave is in the Los Peumos Cemetery,

30

not far from here. She's got a golden cross, which isn't really made of gold, just like all the graves of the Montes family.

"*Or it makes them stronger,*" Alma says, and musses my hair.

"*You want to dance?*" the guy asks, looking at Alma.

She looks at me. Maybe she thinks I should decide, but the truth is, I'm starting to get bored. That's why I say, "*I'm going to go see my grandpa.*"

"*You sure?*" she asks me.

"I'm sure."

On the way I turn off my recorder. It's not that I'm jealous. Why should I be? Still, as I walk toward the terrace, I think I shouldn't have left them alone together.

7 〰

We walk onto the dance floor. The lights blink intermittently, in syncopated time, and the silhouettes moving against the background of the night make the scene look vaguely theatrical.

"I like your son. I don't know, but he's got a certain look in his eyes, like an old man, and the things he says . . . It must be fascinating to live with him."

"It is."

"How long have you been married?"

"Eight years. Tommy is my husband Juan's son," I correct him.

We walk over to the bar and I ask if he wants a glass of white wine.

"I'm still not drinking. I've remained loyal to Coca-Cola," he confesses.

We make our way through the couples swinging their hips to the beat. We put down our glasses. Leo follows my steps awkwardly as we dance. He watches me intently, full of curiosity.

"And your husband?"

"He had to leave for an emergency operation. He's a surgeon."

A few minutes later, I ask him, "And you, are you married?"

"Nope. I haven't found a woman with the patience to put up with me. Anyway . . ." His voice goes down an octave and gets muted. He shakes his head, as if he's already gone one step too far.

"Anyway, what?" I ask. For a fleeting second we hold each other's stare. Time has made his features stronger and deeper. He has a few gray hairs at his temples.

"Anyway, I'm no good at it; long periods of monogamy make me feel like a dishrag," he adds, recovering his bantering tone. He puts his arm round me. His open hand presses against my bare back.

"Alma," I hear him whisper in my ear as we dance.

I look up and our eyes meet.

"I think I behaved very badly that night, didn't I?"

The blinking lights make it impossible for me to see the expression on his face or gage the sincerity of his words. Mostly, I'm amazed that he remembers.

"Nothing irreparable," I reply, trying to sound indifferent.

"If I did, I'd like to ask you to forgive me. I know it's a bit late, but better late than never. I . . . I didn't know what I was doing."

Images get delicately pieced together, then deposit themselves in memory, but they don't remain stable there; they continue to change along with the feelings that accompany them, until one day it becomes difficult to know how much truth they contain.

I see Leo leaning on the hood of a car parked in front of my school. I see him bring a cigarette to his mouth, then crush it under his foot with determination, as if something very important were at stake. We greet each other; then I just stand there next to him, waiting for him to say something. In my memory, Leo's gaze is fixed and his brow is knitted.

"Looks like that asshole isn't coming. We were going to go up to La Pirámide. Want to come with me?"

We jumped in his car and drove up Cerro San Cristóbal, that

green mountain sticking up in the middle of Santiago. When we reached the lookout point, Leo stopped the car. He took a folded piece of paper out of his pocket, unfolded it, then placed it on his knee.

"Want some?" he offered me.

I accepted, even though I despised the drugs my parents took. I hated how they always reeked of marijuana and alcohol. I was afraid of anything that distorted their sense of reality and distanced them from me. I inhaled the white powder twice, once through each nostril. He did the same. The last flickers of sunlight were disappearing in the darkness when I took his hand, brought it under my shirt, and carried it to one of my breasts. I remember the sticky surface of the seat behind my back, the weight of his body against mine, his penetration, the pain I hid behind my laughter, my quick and furtive search for the blood that fortunately never came. Then his cigarette smoke reaching down into my stomach and making me nauseated, which I cured with another snort, our silence, his eyes glued to the roof of the car, as if he had shut down emotionally. Leo didn't realize it was my first time, and I wasn't able to tell him. I was paralyzed by fear and the certainty that what had just happened meant nothing to him. A short while later, we got out of the car and sat by the side of the road, looking down on the dark city.

"You like to read, don't you?" he asked.

"There's nothing I'd rather do."

"Me too."

"Why?"

For a moment Leo seemed to be gathering his thoughts.

"I think it's because when I read, I enter a world that runs parallel to my own. That's also why I like to write."

I listened to him carefully, hoping he would keep talking. Suddenly, he turned to me and lowered his eyes. Without looking up, he took a deep breath and said, "Please don't have any illusions about me, Alma. You are a child, and I'm a mess."

"But I'm sixteen years old," I argued. "And believe me, I've seen more than you can ever imagine."

"I'm twenty-three and involved with another woman." He shrugged his shoulders and lit a cigarette.

I felt dizzy. By the time I'd recovered some sense of myself, everything had changed. I was back inside my house of water, and his voice was echoing outside it.

"You are going to be an excellent writer," I asserted emphatically.

"What makes you so sure?" His face looked both incredulous and hopeful.

"Because you know how to lie."

While I move my body to the music's cadenced beat, I hear Leo whispering in my ear, "On San Cristóbal, at La Pirámide, maybe that's where everything got fucked up. Maybe you were the one and I didn't realize it."

"Don't let your imagination run wild, Leo," I warn him lightheartedly. "I'm married to a wonderful man and I have two children I love deeply."

"Are you happy?" he asks, recovering his composure.

"Do you really believe in that?"

"I don't know. I've never been *happy* happy, but I expect others have had better luck than me."

"Yes, I am," I tell him, and don't look away, so he won't doubt that I'm speaking the truth.

"Well, I'm glad for you, really I am, even if in some ways I hope it is not complete happiness."

"You are perverse."

"No, no, on the contrary. You know, as our friend Tolstoy said so well, all happinesses are the same, and boring; misfortune, on the other hand, comes in thousands of shapes and sizes."

"He didn't say they were boring, just that they were all the same."

"Same thing. There's nothing more boring than uniformity."

"You want me to tell you something?" I challenge him.

Leo nods.

"I'm content to feel lonely as infrequently as possible, just like everybody else, and to know that there's nothing more I can do. That's not a very lofty ambition, but you know what? I'd bet that even the most extraordinary people, in the end, have similar goals."

Leo impulsively pulls me toward him and presses me tighter.

"It feels so good to hold you," he whispers in my ear.

We remain like that, moving rhythmically, tight in each other's grasp. For a brief moment all the conventions vanish. Suddenly, he pulls away.

"You want another glass?" he asks. He looks at me almost with disdain; he's obviously uncomfortable about what has just happened.

"Too bad you can't drink," I say. "We'd probably have a much better time if we were drunk."

8 ♐

When I wake up, I think about Mama and a big hole opens up in my stomach, a hole as big as a crater a hundred miles wide left by the biggest meteorite that ever fell to Earth.

I take out of my Hold-Everything Box the only picture of Mama I kept when Papa got rid of everything of hers. I don't know why he was in such a hurry to forget her. I'd rather remember, because that way I understand things better. The problem is, I don't always know where to put my memories, or how important to make them. The same is true for my discoveries. But at least this time I'm sure. It's really serious that Mama killed herself. So serious that Papa hid it from me. I think about the Antarctic rifts. On one side of the rift is everything I know, and on the other . . . No matter what, when your mama dies, half the people you love most in the world are dead, and that shouldn't ever happen to a child.

I record, "*I think that when Papa is staring off into space and seems like he isn't listening to anybody, he's thinking of Mama.*"

In the picture, Mama is wearing a party dress. Her dark eyes remind me that our pupils are the openings that connect the Outside with the Inside. Her eyebrows are raised, like they're saying something, but I've never managed to figure out what she's trying to tell me or if her eyes look sad or happy. Sometimes I ask her not very important questions, just in case one day she sends me a sign. Like, for instance, if I'm going to do well on a test, or if some kid will ask me about the stag beetle I carry in my backpack. But she never talks to me.

I hear the front door close. It must be Papa leaving for the hospital. For a moment, I wish I was that boy he operated on so we could spend this Sunday together. I jump out of bed and go to the bathroom. I don't remember putting on my pajamas. Alma must have done it when we got home late last night from the wedding. I pull up my T-shirt. My stomach is almost as white as the tiles on the walls. I look at the scar across my chest. I lower my trousers. The miniscule bulge I have between my legs isn't a very encouraging sight. I don't like Alma, or anybody else, to see me naked. That's why when I swim in the pool in summer, I wait for the sun to go down and for the garden to be deserted. When I'm in the middle of the pool, I see my clothes on the side and I imagine that they are my skin and bones. Sometimes I go way down to the bottom, and when I look up, I can make out the figures drawn by the fading light. The silence echoes in my ears under the water and I become as powerful as Neptune. I imagine Alma finding me and me showing her the world at the bottom of the pool.

When Alma came to live with us, she bought me a tape recorder and told me I could make music with it.

"What do you mean, 'music'?" I asked.

"It's easy—look." She turned it on and made a sound on the table with her fist; then she hit a pen against a vase; then she told me to clap really loud. She played it back, and it was really good. "That's how you can make music. You just put sounds together, or words, whatever you want."

When I asked her if it was sensitive enough to pick up the sound of a burp, she walked away laughing and her laughter echoed all through our very quiet house. Then I ran upstairs, and before Papa ruined everything, I brought my Hold-Everything Box and spread all my treasures out on the table. He'd never seen them before, but he pretended he had. I helped him a little, saying things like, "Remember when we found this lava rock at Lake Llanquihue?" We never went to that lake together—nor to any lake, to tell the truth—and Yerfa brought me that rock from the south, but if Alma had found out that Papa and I hardly talk to each other, she would have left us. I know how scary silence can be when you aren't used to it.

I turn my voice recorder on again. "*'Ways to Kill Yourself.' One: hang yourself. Two: eat rat poison. Three: shoot yourself in the head, the mouth, or the heart. Four: throw yourself in front of a moving car. Five: sink to the bottom of the pool and breathe until your lungs fill with water. Six: jump off a building or a very tall tree. Seven: cover your nose and mouth until you suffocate. Eight: stop eating and drinking. Nine: slit your wrists. Ten: fall asleep in the snow. Eleven: stick your head in an oven and turn on the gas.*"

It was last year when I started recording things that popped into my head. The first time was while we were reading Genesis in school. That's when I found out that God created the week to make some order out of the chaos. He divided time into seven days, and He named each day, and He decided that we'd rest on Sundays. My teacher said that to name something is to give it a shape our minds can understand and absorb. Now I know there are at least eleven ways to commit suicide and one of them was the way my mama, Soledad, did it.

Alma will take us to Maná's house. That's what we call Lola's grandmother. Alma is checking one last time to make sure all the doors and windows are locked, and Lola is jumping up to see herself in the mirror in the entryway. Each time she jumps she makes one of her horrible faces.

Just when we're about to leave, I say, "I'm staying."

"No way," Alma says. "It's Yerfa's day off. You can't stay here alone."

"The Falcons Squadron is doing its air show today and Maná doesn't have a TV."

"Don't make things difficult, Tommy," Alma says in a weary voice.

"I promise I'll just wait here for Papa. I'm already twelve years old. I can make a ham and cheese sandwich, I can play, and I can watch the Falcons."

Alma looks at me. She picks up her hair and wraps it round her hand without taking her eyes off me. She knows Papa wouldn't approve. We both know it. He's always worried that my heart will stop beating.

"OK," she agrees. "But promise me you won't leave the house. I'll be back before six."

Lola puts her head out the back window of the car and makes a face at me. I can't believe it. I did it! I never thought it would be so easy! The second they disappear, I go inside. I've never been alone before. I get a bag of potato chips out of the cupboard and shut myself up in my room. I look out the window. Baby Hippopotamus Meanie, the kid next door, is looking for something in his front garden. He often scratches his big belly, spits, and makes pee-pee in the planters on his terrace. Once, I saw him throw a hamster out the window. He's got a round, red face like a baby's. When he sees me, he gets up and waves. I open the window, but I don't know what to say. Someone's calling him from inside the house and he disappears. He moved here three months ago. Alma knows his mother, and we agreed we'd go visit them one day. She also gave me his phone number in case I feel like calling him.

I'll go find Kájef. Papa prohibited me from talking to him, so now we have to meet under my blankets.

I close my eyes. "Kájef," I whisper. Kájef doesn't come. What happened to him? Now we have the chance to play during the day, so I can show him my phosphorescent swords, my space ships, and especially my red airplane, the model plane Papa gave me, like the ones the Japanese flew during World War I.

I turn on my computer and check my email. There they are, as usual.

```
fagot dwarf shit-hed do us all a favor and get lost
u wimprag.
```

No matter how I look at it, upside down and backwards, I can't figure out what to do. If I tell Papa or a teacher at school, it will only make things worse. They'd accuse me of being a tattletale. Anyway, you can't force a kid to like another kid. That's why I'd rather think about other things, like, for instance, Mr. Thomas Bridge.

I open his blog. Mr. Thomas Bridge is an English sailor. Six days ago, he found a girl, a boy, and three adults on a little islet near Lennox Island in Cape Horn. Their island is so tiny it doesn't even show up on the maps. Mr. Bridge says that it's probably a family of Alacaluf Indians and they're living just like their ancestors did in the Neolithic era. Word has spread and journalists and scientists have come there from all over the world, but none of them has yet landed on the island. Mr. Thomas Bridge, with his long hair and blond beard, speaks into the camera. He looks worried. He says he wishes he'd never found them, because if we interfere with their lifestyle, we'll endanger the last Alacalufs on the planet.

The phone rings. It's Alma. "What are you doing?" she asks.

"A little of everything."

"I bought you that Chinese chicken with cashews you like so much."

"Great."

"We'll be back home soon."

"Don't you worry about me."

"You sound like in the movies."

"That's the idea," I say, and we both crack up. "OK, see you soon."

"Goodbye, darling," she says in English, and we hang up.

I copy the conversations I recorded at Miguel's wedding onto my computer and then I go down to Papa's office. I think about the photo of Mama I first saw a long time ago in one of his drawers. It's the only thing of hers he kept. Sometimes, when he and Alma have gone out, and Yerfa is busy, I take it out of the drawer and look at it. Like I do now. Mama is sitting on a park bench in front of a great big tree, holding a piece of paper in her hands. She's wearing a loose-fitting dress, like an apron, and her hair is short and messy. This time I don't put it back; I decide to take it up to my room and put it in my Hold-Everything Box along with the other one.

After watching the Falcons acrobatics air show on TV, I draw a castle, wait for Kájef, then sit down in an armchair in the living room. I miss Alma, Papa, and Yerfa. I even miss Lola. I think Papa's right: I should make a friend. I take out the little piece of paper where Alma wrote down the number of my neighbor B.H.M. I memorize it, then close my eyes and wait for Kájef to come for me.

9 ⌛

Back at the hospital, I find Emma sitting at the far end of the corridor. Her husband must have gone to the cafeteria to get something for breakfast. They both spent the night here. Her hands are folded on her lap and her legs are slightly apart; she looks bereft.

"I already thanked you, didn't I?" she says without looking at me.

At dawn, when I finished the operation, I found Cristóbal's father jamming his fist repeatedly into his knee. When he saw me, he stopped, but his feeling of impotence was written all over his face and body. Emma, on the other hand, still had that same, totally focused look on her face, as if her son's life depended on her summoning up all her energy.

"You should go home to rest," I suggest, knowing she won't, that she'll stay right here, watching the nurses coming and going, until her son wakes up. I take her hand and explain that Cristóbal will be on the respirator and in a semi-conscious state for another few hours. "You know, you've been very strong," I add.

I see a quick glimmer in her eyes. She motions with her hand for me to leave, then turns to look out the window. I get up, squeeze her shoulder, and return to the recovery room where her son is.

After making sure that Cristóbal's post-op recovery is following a normal course, I drive over to the airport and board my plane. A few minutes later, I'm flying over the roofs of the city. My plan is to be back at the hospital by the time Cristóbal wakes up. Then, as soon as I see him open his eyes, I'll return home.

I remember perfectly the moment Tommy woke up after his last operation. He was three years old. His face had changed. He seemed to have seen things during his journey that we, waiting for him on shore, could never even imagine. Soledad also sensed his transformation, and the tears began streaming down her cheeks when she realized she could never accompany her son to all the places he had been. I remember her pressing her face against Tommy's and closing her eyes. I took her by the shoulders. My feeling of impotence, knowing I was incapable of alleviating her pain, became more and more palpable as time passed. Since then I don't even try to comfort people close to me with hugs or any other physical sign of affection. It was quite unusual for me to have taken Emma's hand this morning. I felt moved by her demeanor—she sat up so tall, her head turned, looking out the window—the way it seemed to mingle tragedy and dignity.

As I approach the airport, I see the neighborhood soccer field where children and adults are running after a ball. The tranquility of the surrounding streets brings me back to a sense of normality. I prepare for landing. It's just another Sunday afternoon. An eighteen-year-old girl died in an accident and a young child has a new heart. Before I start to feel too pleased with myself for my part in this whole thing, I search through my memory for some Buddhist-like proverb about the impermanence of life and how futile our efforts are to hold on to it.

10 〰

On the way to Maná's house, I stop at a Chinese restaurant to get takeout. I drive through the empty streets of the neighborhood where she has been living for the last two years. It's a quiet area, with small, one-story houses and plazas whose tall, leafy trees seem to take a stand against the neglect around them. My mother opens the door wearing a skirt, below which I can see her bare feet, leathery and weather-beaten from all her treks around the world.

"Alma, Lola, what a surprise!" she exclaims, waving her hands and making her bracelets jingle.

Her straight gray hair, which she cuts herself, is plastered to her head. Even though she's never made any particular effort to win over her granddaughter, Lola runs up to hug her. Maná forgets her birthdays and arrives late for Christmas dinner, she has never shared her child's world, and the few times she's gone out with Lola, she's taken her to meditation sessions, but Lola's affection for her grandmother is unconditional. That's pretty much how it was during my childhood. I can see myself running after Maná down some hallway in a temple, or perhaps that's a dream, eternally running after my mother while she takes long strides toward her own salvation.

"I brought Chinese food—vegetarian, of course."

"Fantastic!" she exclaims, squinting her almond-shaped eyes.

We go inside. Maná pours out two cups of green tea and a juice for Lola. We sit at the wooden kitchen table. Maná observes us with a smile that spreads across her face, which is lined with fine wrinkles. She lights a cigarette, and her cat, Malinche, jumps onto her lap. In the meantime, I serve up the food on whatever plates or bowls I happen to find in her chaotic kitchen.

Maná's houses are always crowded with useless objects, like fossils, canes with carved handles, or pokers for a fireplace she doesn't have. She regrets having never held on to possessions all those years she lived like a gypsy. That's why she picks up things at garage sales and flea markets, things that seem to have been worth a lot to somebody and whose silence seems to tell some story.

Maná is smoking more than usual. I mention this.

"I have to die of something," she explains.

I don't think I've ever heard her mention death before. She always behaves as if she has the same opportunities she had when she was twenty. Her slogan is "Everything is possible." And that's how she lives—always ready to embark on a new adventure, especially if it's related to the spirit or to sex. I don't want to ask her about her most recent boyfriend, a writer with a big belly and a thick mane who observes the world with a smugness he must summon from having published a couple of novels over twenty years ago. I don't know what he's doing with my mother. In spite of being a good reader, Maná is far from his "been-there-done-that" type. Actually, her capacity to be astonished by absolutely anything could be interpreted by someone who doesn't know her as a sign of stupidity. Maybe he's with her for the sex. Maná knows a lot about that.

Lola discovers a basket with five kittens under the counter. Their eyes are still closed.

"Can I pick one up?" she asks excitedly.

Malinche springs up, hisses, and shows her claws. Maná laughs.

We go out to the garden carrying our feast on a couple of trays and sit down at a table with peeling paint under a walnut tree. Maná brings one of the kittens wrapped in a colorful shawl so Lola can hold it. If it weren't for the past, for the memories that keep welling up, everything would be perfect.

When I was a little girl, I always wanted to have friends who were living the kind of life I have now. It wasn't easy, because most of the time we lived on communes far away from any city. It was in one of those communes that I got my first glimpse of who my mother really was. That was also the moment when I first saw the impotence in my father's eyes, the capitulation, even the despair. With time, all that became more obvious, and eventually I couldn't see him in any other light.

At the end of the school year, we children produced a play. We worked out the story, then performed it for the grown-ups. No kings or queens were allowed in, no authority figures who had subjugated people throughout history. We used all the meager resources at our disposal and planned every last detail: the costumes, the stage set, the music, the lights. Papa was sitting on the ground, in the first row, next to Maná. I could watch him through the entire play because I was a tree and stood to the rear of the stage. He and I began to carry out a silent dialogue. We winked, smiled, made faces, tilted our heads from side to side. I was so enthralled by the communication we'd established that a boy had to push me off the stage at the end. That night at dinnertime, Papa and I excitedly discussed the play. He told me I was an excellent actress and that when we moved to the city, I could go to a school where they taught theater. Maná didn't look up from her plate.

"You want us to leave here," she said. She looked defeated and, like a weak light bulb, as if she was about to flicker and go out.

"That depends on you," my father responded.

47

"It's stronger than me," Maná said, and she sat there with her head bent, a posture that seemed somehow rehearsed.

Papa's face turned a grotesque red. His eyes were bulging, but he didn't move, perhaps waiting for Maná to take back what she'd just said, to change the direction they both knew her words were heading.

Suddenly, he shouted at her with violence and despair, "What the hell are you talking about? That's total crap. You are an adult woman and responsible for your actions, not some stupid chick in heat all the time."

"Don't talk like that—Alma's here," Maná warned, her voice breaking.

"You decide," my father said with finality. He got up morosely, like an old man, and left the house.

My next memory is of my mother sitting on the deck, her legs stretched out and slightly apart, her arm hanging down by her sides, her eyes closed, sobs pouring out of her throat. I can see myself as a child, watching her, knowing that her tears had nothing to do with me, that her suffering had something to do with a man who wasn't my father. By the following week we were crashing at the house of some friends of Papa's.

Maná is teaching Lola how to use chopsticks. Between the two of them they've managed to spill a good part of the food on the table. They are laughing, that same irresponsible hilarity I remember hearing as a child. Sometimes I enjoyed it, but at other times I knew it foreshadowed a long night listening to my parents' laughter while they changed the LPs on the record player again and again, never agreeing on anything, but delighting in the discrepancy between their musical tastes, everything concluding in the sounds of panting and moaning, which I could hear no matter where in the house I was. I try to believe that these memories, though not always pleasant, imbue the present with more depth, even if they do sometimes hurt.

Maná invites Lola to come with her to the kitchen to make coffee. I lie down on a blanket on the lushest part of the grass. The breeze touches the leaves of the walnut tree, producing a refreshing rustling above my head. Some blues music from the neighbor's house breaks the peace of the afternoon. When Maná returns with the coffee, I'm half asleep. Lola climbs on my belly. Maná has brought a book. At least this is one way we have always connected: sharing the pleasure we get from a well-told story. It's a beautiful edition of *Emma*.

"A friend gave it to me. Take it. You'll enjoy it more than me. What's up with Juan?" she asks, finally.

"He had to do an urgent heart transplant, on a little boy," I answer without looking at her. "The same age as Tommy." I wish I knew more details so I could give more weight to Juan's absence.

"He came home last night after we were asleep and left this morning before we woke up," Lola adds.

My mother lifts her eyebrows, as if to interrogate me.

"That's normal. It's his work, Maná."

I feel like calling her "Mama," just to snatch away from her that beatific state that spreads a thin sheen over her dissatisfaction, but I hold my tongue. She hates to be called that. "Maná" situates her in a place without bonds, a timeless place. I look at the weeds growing anarchically along the fence.

"There's a bowl of milk in the refrigerator. Why don't you take it out and give it to the cat? She must be hungry," she says to Lola.

"You guys want to get rid of me. Don't think I don't know that. I'll do it only because I love the kittens," Lola informs us with one of her big-girl faces.

Once we can no longer see Lola's soft silhouette, Maná asks me, "Is something going on?"

"What makes you think that? Anyway," I say, "if I did have a problem, why would I tell you?"

"Because you've got nobody else to talk to," she replies gently, without acknowledging my defiant tone. It's what she always does: avoid any kind of confrontation.

"What do you know?"

"I know that you are my daughter, however hard that may be for both of us," she observes in the same tone and with a coquettish smile.

In spite of her age, my mother remains seductive; that almost infantile glimmer still shines out of the sliver of her eye visible under her half-closed lids. This quality continues to disgust me in a way that is not remotely filial, that made me run away from her fifteen years ago.

"It's a little late for me to start telling you my problems." I try to remove any trace of reproach from my voice. "We can talk about what we're reading, spend a Sunday afternoon together, watch Lola grow up. It's far more than a lot of mothers and daughters share."

"Much more," Maná agrees.

The rays of the setting sun shimmer behind the branches of the walnut tree. I could tell her that I saw Leo yesterday. Now would be the chance—after all these years—to unleash the storm, to talk. But it's an opportunity I'm not going to give her.

The third time I saw Leo was when I caught a glimpse of his sleeping face on the pillow in my mother's bed. It was after one of her wild parties. From my room, I could hear people coming and going all night long. I fell asleep to the sound of their voices and the beat of the music. The next morning, I got up early to go to school. Before leaving, I looked into my mother's room. As usual, the door was open. The first thing I saw was Leo's dark, curly hair, then his face. That look of disdain had disappeared from his mouth and a dark shadow hovered over his upper lip. His torso was naked, and his arms were folded under his head. My mother opened her eyes. She took a deep breath, like she did when she meditated, perhaps contemplating what her first words to me would be, because I just stood there in silence, staring at them, my cold gaze never flinching. Leo kept sleeping. My mother got out of bed naked, closed the door behind her, and hugged me. She swore, crying, that it would never happen again.

As far as I know, Maná never found out that I knew Leo, and all these years I've wondered if he ever discovered the connection.

That was the day I realized I could no longer live with my mother. I wrote my father a letter and asked him to send me the modest inheritance my grandfather had left me. I wanted to go away; it didn't matter where—anywhere but there. Papa told me he had used that money to buy the small piece of land where we were soon going to live. I shut myself up in my room and barely came out. I spent the summer sleeping. Maná no longer held parties in our apartment. She carried on her life elsewhere. Whenever she showed up at home, she'd knock on my door and try to talk to me, but most of the time I pretended to be sleeping. At the end of the summer, Maná and I moved to Papa's cabin, near a coastal town in the south. They kept fighting then having their noisy reconciliations. Everything in my life had come to a standstill, everything except the implacable and secretive construction of my house of water. That summer, one of my father's sisters came to stay with us. I had lost fifteen pounds. She must have realized that my only hope was to get away from there. She bought me a ticket, and in August of that year, I flew to Barcelona.

The day I left, my mother and father came to say goodbye to me at the airport. I can still see them so clearly: Maná pacing back and forth, her bracelets jingling, eking out a few tears to complete the image of herself as an actress playing a tragic role; Papa, meanwhile, was lugging my suitcase, his back hunched over, his eyes darting, and his hand-knit sweater from the island of Chiloe hanging baggy and loose over his increasingly shriveled frame. That image remained frozen in my memory like those daguerreo-types that capture the essence of a family. I can see them standing next to each other, holding hands, watching me walk away, all of us knowing that this was the end of our little unit. It had been me, the eternally absent one, who had had the guts to break the bonds that were destroying us. That single idea accompanied me throughout my entire trip and filled me with hope. I had escaped from my parents and emerged as a separate individual. I now had proof that I did not lack character like my father, and I was resolved to never be like my mother.

And while I watch Maná, a beautiful fifty-something woman, smiling at Lola, who has appeared at the window holding a kitten in her arms, I think that I have achieved my goal. I'm not like her. Even so, I still feel the same rage that overwhelmed me that morning when I found her lying next to Leo, for no matter what Maná does, she always—with her jangling bracelets and those rags she picks up at the cheapest rummage sales—comes out ahead of me.

11 ♐

I open my eyes. Papa is standing above me, staring at me with an expression I can't puzzle out. Gray rays are shooting out of his eyes, and he is biting his lip. The sign on his forehead is written in an incomprehensible language:

□♎♌♑♊◆♓□♌♍♎♊●□

I sneeze. I wish I were like the kids in movies who always say something intelligent at just the right moment.

"I stayed here watching the Falcons," I say, and I feel like the S.K.W. (Stupidest Kid in the World). If I tell him about the Alacaluf family, he'll think I'm talking about Kájef and mixing up reality and fantasy again. I know that Kájef doesn't exist. I invented a friend so I wouldn't feel guilty about keeping him all to myself, away from the world, like you want to when you love another person a whole lot.

"I see," he answers without taking his eyes off me.

The sign now seems to say, "I know I should scold you but I can't, for a reason that's difficult to explain." My father doesn't scold me often. He just screws up his mouth and shakes his head back and forth, which is his way of silently letting me know that he's not going to waste either his breath or his energy trying to make me be what he'd like me to be—that is, what I should be.

This time he doesn't even do that.

"How's Cristóbal?" I ask.

"He's OK."

We can hear Alma and Lola in the hallway. When they come into the living room, I see that Papa and Alma look at each other without smiling.

"Don't you guys want to know how it went?" Alma asks, taking off the scarf she has tied round her neck.

"How'd it go?" I ask them.

"Incredible!" Lola exclaims. "Maná has five newborn kittens and she let me pick them up. Well, not all of them, just one, but it was sooooooo cute," she says, and cradles her arms as if she were holding and rocking one, the whole time making her spoiled-little-girl faces.

A while later, we're in the kitchen and it's just like every Sunday night: Papa is cutting the sausage for the pizza, Lola is showing us her latest pirouettes, and I'm hating her while I talk about something I saw on TV or found on the Internet. This time I get to tell Papa about the Falcons and their air acrobatics: the Cuban eights, the tailspins, the vertical quarter-turns. I move my hands around to show him the shapes they make, but I know Papa is thinking about something else. My eyelids start opening and closing without me being able to stop them. Alma asks him whether he wants some pizza and he doesn't answer. When Papa doesn't say anything, it's like somebody just turned off the light and everybody is standing around in the dark, lost in their own corner. That's why Papa's silences are black. White silences are different; they're full of light. I draw a circle and a square on a paper napkin. I'm not going to label them because then they'd know I've drawn a white silence and a black one.

"If you're angry at Mama, you should be angry at Tommy. He forced her to let him stay home," Lola declares, then stares at us

54

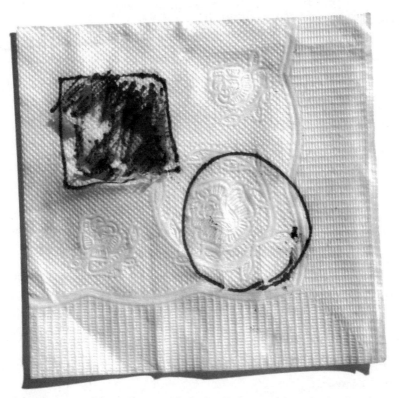

with that stupid smile, as if she's done another little leap and deserves an applause.

The pizza is ready, and Alma and Papa still aren't talking to each other, and I hate my stepsister. With her sixth sense not to miss out on an opportunity, she turns on the TV. The grown-ups don't complain, so we watch an episode of *Avatar* while we eat.

When we finish, Alma comes with us to make sure we put on our pajamas and brush our teeth. Once I'm in bed, she gives me a kiss and in sign language she says, *Good night*.

"Good night," I answer.

After I hear her go down the stairs, I sneak out onto the landing. Alma left the door ajar and if I strain my ears, I can hear their voices in the living room.

"Are you going to talk to me now?" Alma asks.

"Why should I? You know what I think."

"He needed it, Juan. Tommy needed to stay alone for once."

"I can't quite believe you did what you did. You know Tommy can't be alone, ever. At any moment his heart can stop beating. Of course, you know that, but you—"

"Juan, please listen to me."

"You have no idea."

"It's important for him to feel independent. There are hundreds of things he can't do, but he can stay alone for a few hours. Nothing's going to happen to him; the fact is, nothing did happen. Your anxieties are making it impossible for him to grow up. Anyway, breaking the rules together is a way to love him, to be close."

"So now you're criticizing me. Isn't that a bit much? Look, Alma, I've raised Tommy the best I could. I'm sure I could have done better, but nobody, not even you, is going to tell me how to do it. Breaking the rules, like you say so nonchalantly, could cost him his life. This is not a game."

"I know."

"It doesn't sound like you do. Sometimes you're exactly like your mother, imagining that if we only do what our infallible hearts tell us to do, everything will turn out just fine."

"If all you want to do is attack me, I think I'll leave."

Papa doesn't answer, but I can imagine him shaking his head in that tired, bewildered way of his.

"And the boy, how is he?" Alma asks before going out the door.

"Now you ask."

"I'm sorry."

I hear the living-room door close. I run to my room before Alma gets back upstairs. I don't hear her steps, but I can hear her go into Lola's room. I never should have asked her to leave me home alone. She just wanted to make me feel good. To tell the truth, I don't even like the Falcons that much.

12⏳

I switch on my bedside lamp. I wish Alma and I hadn't quarreled, but I have a harder time controlling myself when I'm tired and tense, especially when it's about Tommy. When Alma came to live with us, my only stipulation was that I would be in charge of him—of his upbringing, the restrictions on him. Of course, it's difficult for her to fully understand his condition, even less what lies hidden in the depth of his memory, but we shouldn't have fought. I picture her curled up next to Lola and I feel like holding her in my arms. I've never asked myself how intense the love I feel for her is; all I know is that it's strong enough to keep us together, and I assume Alma feels the same way. One thing I am sure of is that we both need a certain amount of time alone to be able to enjoy each other's presence.

"How much do you love me, Juan Montes?" she asked me a few months ago with a challenging smile.

We were walking through the park in Los Peumos, looking over my father's recent renovations. Alma had picked a flower and was quickly pulling off the petals, reciting the loves-me-loves-me-not we all learn as children. At that moment, it seemed like one of those questions that doesn't make sense to answer, especially after so many years, when the day-to-day experience ends up being much more eloquent than any words. Without answering, still lost in my thoughts, I looked at her. A few seconds passed and then we heard Papa's voice calling us from his aviary. By then it was too late. Now I wonder if my silence opened up a fissure in her mind and doubt has snuck in. I wanted to wrap my arms round her then, as I do now, but she took off toward the aviary.

I can't fall asleep. I keep thinking about Tommy. There's a look in his eyes, direct, though somehow distant, that always unnerves me, as if he were observing us through a crack in a wall that surrounds him. Whenever I see him withdrawn, I get anxious, wondering what he's thinking about, that world going on inside him that I can never know or touch. Sometimes I wish he'd be naughty like other children so I could scold him for something concrete and then I'd be able to get a sense of the boundaries he moves within.

I hear Soledad's voice in my ear: "Now Tommy will grow up, and we can buy him a real bed." That was after his last operation. At three he was the size of a one-year-old and he still slept in the crib Soledad had inherited. I can see the noon light shining in through the windows in Tommy's room, his toys, new and shiny, on the shelves. A world arrested, waiting to come alive. I remember the look in Soledad's eyes, seeking my corroboration, a quiet "Let's go!" that would finally start things up. I also remember the way I avoided her gaze, incapable of giving her the assurances she was asking for. Tommy would never be a normal child. That was the truth Soledad wanted me to deny.

After the operation, Soledad devoted all her time and energy to Tommy. Totally absorbed in his every need, she never left him, never took her eyes off him. His nanny, Yerfa, lived with us, as she does now, and I urged Soledad to take some time off, begin to develop a life of her own, find something to do outside the house, but she insisted that the only place she wanted to be was with her son. There would be time for all the rest later. I suppose her behavior was understandable, and even if I didn't agree with her, I knew her well enough to know that she wouldn't change her mind. I'm not trying to justify myself, to relieve the guilt I might feel for everything that happened later. In spite of her apparent fragility, she was always a woman of character. She was, to a certain extent, responsible for most of the important things in our lives: the fact that we married, that we moved to this neighborhood, that I got a job in the most prestigious hospital in the country, and so many other things that defined our life together, none of which ever gave me cause for complaint.

Tommy's recovery was slow but constant. That year, I was named chief of the Cardiac Surgery Unit. This meant I'd have to work much harder and that I'd have less time to spend with my family. So when Soledad suggested opening an art gallery, I thought it was a brilliant idea; she'd studied art history and had excellent taste. She found a space not far from our house, rented it, and with the help of an architect friend began to transform it. She did everything with Tommy. She'd tell me how she'd put him in his stroller and go out to buy supplies, haggle with the architect or the contractor, visit artists, and discuss the latest trends in art with her old schoolmates. Tommy, with his easygoing temperament, went everywhere with her and never made a fuss.

The word "happiness" has always sounded false to me. It's too categorical and emphatic, and at the same time too trivial and imprecise. Nonetheless, in retrospect, I think we were happy—at least until the alarm bells started going off.

The first time was almost imperceptible. Soledad arrived home one night after eleven with Tommy asleep in her arms. I was waiting for her in the living room, about to burst with anxiety. She quickly ran upstairs and shut herself in Tommy's room. When I knocked on the door a while later to talk to her, there was no response. I figured she'd fallen asleep, so I went to bed. Late at night, I heard noises coming from the living room. I stood at the top of the stairs and asked her what she was doing. She said that everything was fine and she'd be up soon. I needed to be in top shape the next day for one of my first open-heart surgeries, so I went back to bed without giving the whole thing much further thought.

In the morning, when I woke, Soledad was asleep next to me. I got up without waking her. When I went downstairs, I saw that she'd rearranged all the furniture in the living room. She'd moved everything around, and the new arrangement made no sense at all. Still, I didn't make a big deal about it. Somewhere inside me I must have known that to even formulate the necessary questions, I'd have to start seeing what was hidden behind the fragile façade of our lives.

I get out of bed and walk into the hallway. Ever since I met Cristóbal and his family I've been unable to avoid certain memories. They lie in wait until I'm alone; then they launch their assault. I open the door to Lola's room. In the semi-darkness I see Alma's sleeping face, her curly hair on the pillow, and next to her I see Lola in profile. I stand there looking at them for a few minutes, then return to the bedroom.

13 〰

When I stuck those phosphorescent planets on the ceiling in Lola's room, I thought they'd be a path she could follow to reach her dreams when the lights were off. I never thought I'd be the one trying to lose myself in their twinkling. I hug Lola and bring my face to her hair to smell that acrid scent of a sleeping child. She mutters something in her sleep. She turns round, stretches out her arm, and throws it over my chest. For a second the anxiety loosens its grip. I close my eyes and realize I won't be able to fall asleep.

A wall's being erected between me and Juan, a transparent one that allows us to see each other but not touch. Even now, in the darkness, I can see the tension in his face, his quick and irritable movements. Silence has as many nuances as speech, and I sense that Juan's are part and parcel of a rage whose depth and origin I know nothing about. Maybe, like me, he's tired of the same thing, over and over again, of looking ahead and seeing a path already traced in the sand. Maybe, like me, he misses the time when anything was possible, when the future was unpredictable. Maybe all the things Juan appreciated when he first met me now annoy him: the way I move, express myself, caress the children, drink, bite my nails. This thought comes to me with increasing tenacity because that's how I have begun to feel toward him. Apathy, unfriendly words, indifferent gestures, they've all become part of our daily lives, so much so that one night, after one of our quarrels, I even felt physically repelled by him.

Without our connection, my life, other people, all of it seems so far removed, as if I were observing everything through a thick fog. What once seemed meaningful has become banal. It's not a dramatic feeling, not like I'm drowning or in despair. It feels weightless, like a vacuum. This tendency toward indifference is always lurking, and it's only ever affection and desire—or the illusion of them—that keeps it at bay. Sometimes I even start to think that everything is in my own head: affinities, certainties . . . Maybe I am seeing only what I need to see in order to give meaning and consistency to a life that would otherwise be futile; it's all happened so slowly I've ended up believing the story I've been telling myself.

Lola turns, opens her eyes, and smiles.

"I knew you were here," she says, her breath smelling of the remnants of dreams.

She cuddles up to me, and a few minutes later is fast asleep again.

The only way to restore our tranquil existence is for me to let the script play itself out, not trip it up, not bring up doubts or try to challenge it. Just get up in the morning and ask for nothing more than this world we have created together and share with Lola and Tommy. I would have to give up—as I imagine all other couples do when their passion fades—my longing for that urgency to touch, for our bodies to be so close that sparks fly and sex becomes inevitable. Maybe that would be enough. Then I could find my way back to the cautious happiness that was mine until recently. But I don't want to. And that—she—is what disturbs me: that fearless woman who is watching from afar as she destroys what she thought would be the rest of her life.

14⌛

Almost seventy-two hours have passed since Cristóbal Waisbluth's operation. This morning, we finally took him off the respirator and reduced his dose of sedatives. I've just checked on him and he appears alert. Emma was sitting at the foot of his bed, reading out loud the messages his classmates have sent him. She looked up at me when I walked in and anxiously asked me to tell her every-thing she should do when she took Cristóbal home.

Then she looked at me sideways and added, "I know your son made it. I want to know what you did."

"Yes, of course. Let me think it over; then we'll talk," I answered.

"I want more than that. I want you to write down everything you did to save his life."

Her face turned red; then she immediately pulled herself together. She bent her head and started reading again. I promised to give her a list of recommendations that don't usually appear in the post-operative care manuals.

It's quite unusual for someone to talk to me so directly and peremptorily. Patients and their families tend to be very polite, even somewhat deferential, and though I don't expect that, I suppose I've grown used to it. I suspect Emma mulled it over for a long time before speaking to me, and she must have had a hard time finding the right way to express her concerns.

Now that I'm back in my office, I'm writing down details of my life for the last twelve years that I can give to Emma. And while I type on my keyboard, images rise before me, making a mockery of my efforts to pretend they don't exist, that they were never there, that I am not, after all, a receptacle of memories.

After that night when she rearranged the living-room furniture, Soledad seemed to retreat ever deeper into her inner world. So when she announced that she was going to invite a group of artists and art critics for lunch, I thought it was a sign of improved spirits. She spent the week planning the event, down to the very last detail. On the day itself—a Sunday in the middle of winter—she got up early and began working. I can still see her slight, agile body moving with renewed vigor, preparing the food, setting the table, and arranging winter branches in vases for decoration.

The first guests arrived exactly at one: a woman who took off one layer of clothing after another until she was almost naked, and her companion, who never took off his black coat. She sat on the edge of an armchair with her elbows resting on her knees and did nothing but look from side to side, while he kept his hands in his pockets, stretched out his legs, and stared out the window, as if he were contemplating something immensely important. Fortunately, they both ate heartily of the abundant hors d'oeuvres. Soledad wore a pleased smile and at no point seemed anxious that none of her other guests had turned up. I tried to catch her eye so I could ask her discreetly, but she never looked over at me, focused as she was on her guests. I soon learned that the woman carved miniature wooden animals and that he was a proofreader at a publishing house without a name, and, it seemed, without publications. That was the extent of the conversation about "art." In addition to the attention she paid her guests, Soledad was constantly attentive to

Tommy. She brought his colored pencils and paper, and coaxed him into playing at her feet. Tommy had a cold and wasn't feeling well. When we sat down at the table, our guests once again exhibited prodigious appetites, though still not sufficient to finish even a quarter of the food Soledad had prepared. She talked constantly, as if she were afraid that if she stopped for even a second, the fragile edifice holding her up would shatter and she would collapse. It struck me then that perhaps Soledad needed to be playing a role— any role whatsoever as long as she could make it believable—to avoid succumbing completely to madness.

When we finished, the woman put back on her multilayered wardrobe, and then both of them, a little drunk, took off walking down the street. I thought that Soledad would finally collapse or there would be an opportunity to talk about what had happened. Instead, she turned to me, her eyebrows raised and a wide smile on her face, and moved her head back and forth as if to express some kind of silent joy. Then she gave me a kiss and led me to bed. This happened so rarely those days that I offered no resistance. After making love, we remained in bed, lying there without speaking, like two statues felled in a riot, defeated in tandem.

"What happened to the others?" I asked cautiously.

Soledad raised her head and looked at me, perplexed.

"Did you invite them?"

"I really don't know. And please don't ask me again." Her voice was shaking. Her eyes were vacant, as though she were somewhere else, a place where not even my touch could reach her. It occurred to me that maybe it would be good for us to go away together, somewhere sunny, a vacation; I was still clinging to the belief that her behavior was temporary and that a change of air would bring her back.

★

65

My secretary, Carola, informs me that Alma called while I was out on my rounds and said she'd like to come with me to the board of directors' dinner. How long have I been wandering through that darkroom of my memories? I dial Alma's cellphone. It's busy. Just as well. As Tommy says, she always sees things. I'm afraid these two separate worlds will collide in my head. Last night, I dreamed that when I turned round in my bed, I fell overboard from a ship in the middle of the night. I looked up and saw hundreds of feet of steel rising up before my eyes. Soledad and Alma stood at the highest point, laughing. I shouted, but they couldn't hear me. The ship, festooned with lights, vanished—the music, the voices, the laughter, all irretrievably gone.

One night, after a long operation, I came home and found Soledad out on the street, barefoot and washing her car. It was below freezing. I stood in front of her holding my briefcase. The moon lit up her childlike features.

"It's eleven at night," I said to her.

"I know, but tomorrow I have a very important meeting with a Spanish artist." The water from the hose was wetting her feet.

"You can take it early to a carwash," I said.

Without answering, she continued scrubbing the windows compulsively.

"You're not wearing shoes," I told her. "You'll catch a cold."

"What are you talking about, I'm not wearing shoes? You think I'm crazy?"

This was not, could not be, Soledad and me carrying out this incoherent dialogue. We weren't that kind of people. I took the sponge out of her hand and wrapped my coat around her. She made an initial show of resistance, then gave up. She looked at me, totally defenseless. She had suddenly understood what she was doing and felt ashamed. We entered the house and her body went limp, falling heavily into a chair.

Before leaving for the dinner, I finish jotting down on a piece of paper a few things for Emma; then I copy out in my own handwriting the printed list of post-operative instructions we give our patients. I leave it on my desk; a sense of my own vileness overwhelms me as I close the door.

15 〰

I've spent the whole afternoon in the editing room working on a couple of scenes and I think they're turning out well. The phone rings and I jump up to answer it. I called Juan several times to say that I wanted to go with him to the annual board of directors' dinner, but he hasn't called back. Yesterday, when he got home late, I pretended I was asleep. He got undressed and climbed into bed without turning the light on and without touching me. He lay there by my side, barely breathing. I don't know what's going on in his head, and I'm starting not to care.

It's the mechanic telling me that my car won't be ready this afternoon. I listen to his explanations while looking at the frozen image of a little girl on the monitor. The moment I hang up, the phone rings again. I hear Leo's voice.

"Hi," I say.

"How are you?"

"I'm working."

"Did you get back to Santiago OK the other night?"

"Yes, of course. Juan's brother brought us. How are you?"

"I'm good. I'd like to see you, Alma."

"That would be great."

"We could have a coffee, a meal, I don't know . . . Today, if you can."

There's some kind of wicked synchronicity in the way things are playing themselves out, but Maná's the one who believes in that, not me.

"I'd love to," I say, "but I have a ton of work to do. I'm going to be staying here till late."

"I hoped you'd say yes." I can hear the disappointment in his voice. "I'll leave you my cell number, in case you have second thoughts." He tells me his number and I write it down on a piece of paper. "I'm working, too. Call me whenever you want."

"Really, I promised Matías I'd finish a few more scenes."

"That's fine. Don't worry. You've got my number."

His voice has a determined edge that confuses me. I can't tell if it indicates an imperious character or an irrepressible desire to see me. We hang up. I keep working. The offices are slowly emptying out. The last person to leave is Lorena, Matías's secretary. Through the narrow window in my editing room I catch a sliver of the darkening sky. I'm not hungry. I make a cup of coffee in the kitchen. On the way back, I stop in the hallway. It's dark and the wooden floor creaks with every step I take. I hear a whisper in the silence, as if the world inside me has spilled out and is taking over the outside world. A sensation I've had before—but had forgotten—constricts my throat: I want to see Leo. It's a longing that takes my breath away. I quickly start searching for reasons to call him, and then the opposite: reasons not to call him. I pick up the piece of paper on which I wrote down his number and dial.

"Alma?" he says, without hearing my voice.

"Yes," I respond, suddenly ashamed.

"You had second thoughts?"

"I finished sooner than I'd expected and I'm hungry."

"Great! Shall I come pick you up, or do you want to meet somewhere?"

"I have some old footage I think you'll find entertaining. You could come here to watch it and then we can go for a bite."

"Perfect. I was at the studio the other day with Matías."

"And you didn't come to see me?"

"You'd already left . . . Alma, it's great you called. I want very much to see you."

"So, I'll expect you," I say, my voice a little cold, as if to counteract his excitement.

While I wait, the anticipation of seeing Leo fills me with euphoria and unease. The memories get all mixed up in my head; they hurt and upset me. When he finally arrives, I am confronted with that look in his eyes, both happy and determined, which softens his angular features. He seems so carefree, so far removed from everything I'm going through.

He gently touches my shoulder and gives me a kiss on the cheek.

"Come in," I invite him as I start walking toward the editing room.

I sit down in front of the computer and search through the folders where I have the videos I want to show him. Matías appears on the screen. He's nineteen years old and he's making funny faces on a busy street in Barcelona.

"He hasn't changed a bit, has he?" Leo remarks with an affectionate laugh. "He's the same old oaf."

"Take a look at this," I say.

Now I'm the one making faces. I'm wearing a red cap that makes me look like Little Red Riding Hood and I'm reciting a manifesto about our aesthetic principles. I'm wearing the clothes of the era: an unorthodox mixture of Doc Martin shoes, a motorcycle jacket, a silk scarf round my neck, and leather gloves. My voice can barely be heard over the street noise.

"I was seventeen years old."

"I like you better now," he says, then takes his eyes off the screen and turns to look at me admiringly.

"And you, what were you doing back then? You were still in Chile, weren't you?" I give him a slightly aloof smile, just to let him know that I'm not won over by flattery that easily.

"I was back in rehab, going through detox." He shrugs his shoulders and screws up his face without losing his lively expression. "You know who saved me?"

I shake my head.

"A girl who tried to commit suicide twice. She wanted to be an actress and we read Ibsen plays together. She was pretty good. She played Hedda Gabler, and I did all the masculine roles, the judge, her husband, Lövborg."

"Were you in love with her?"

"When you're desperate, you don't fall in love. At the most, you use another person," he says. His smile seems sincere, but it also seems to contradict his words, which he clearly lives by.

"Poor thing, she was probably crazy about you."

"She was desperate, too. That's usually what brings people together," he says without taking his eyes off me.

Maybe he's tracing a line we can walk down without getting hurt, or maybe he's spelling out the nature of his attraction to me. I feel his full lips brushing against my neck. In the room's darkness, the light from the screen splashes the walls with a blue glow, like water touched by the sun. I caress his neck. His hand makes his way under my clothes and descends to the base of my spine. When I close my eyes, I see a fish, lackluster and blind, swimming at the bottom of my house of water. Suddenly, a ray of sunlight hits its scales. Aroused by the brightness, the fish quickly rises to the surface as my back arches under Leo's skillful touch. When I look at his face again, I see that he has an even more mischievous expression and I can't help smiling. I take off my shoes and straddle him. He touches my breasts under my shirt. His eyes are shining, triumphant and seductive. He traces the borders of one of my erect nipples with his index finger, pressing harder with each circle he makes. Now his hand covers it and presses while he unzips and lowers my trousers with the other hand. A laugh escapes his lips. He grabs me round my waist with both hands, then penetrates me.

We've arrived at my house, at the foothills of the cordillera. Leo has brought me here in a taxi.

"So this is where Princess Alma lives," he jokes when he sees the house through the car window, with its Tudor-style beams, its ivy-covered walls, the two huge chimneys.

"Thank you for bringing me," I say.

The light in the portico shines on the leaves. The neighbor's dog barks and bares its teeth through the fence. Leo puts his arm round my waist and pulls me toward him.

"Am I going to see you again?" he whispers in my ear.

Behind his smile, I again see that streak of uncertainty, that crack in the façade that attracted me when I was a teenager.

"I don't know."

"I want to see you."

I kiss him on his forehead and get out of the car. Leo gets out, too. I tell him not to come with me to the door. I suddenly realize how reckless it was to allow him to accompany me home.

I get undressed and take a shower. A light shines in the window through the slightly open curtain onto Juan's sleeping face. I get into bed and press my body against his. I can feel the warmth of his back against my belly. I hug him; he turns and wraps his legs round mine without opening his eyes. We make love for the first time in a month. I imagine it is Leo's body. When we finish, we pull apart. Juan kisses me on the cheek. He lies on his back, staring at the ceiling, and I turn my face to the wall.

16 ♐

That's my red airplane, the one from World War I, soaring through the sky. And that's me flying it. Papa and Grandpa are sitting behind me. I check the time on my Breitling Emergency watch. If we have an accident, its 121.5 MHz microtransmitter will send out a signal for 48 hours over an area of 160 kilometers. I hear Papa's voice. He's telling me not to be afraid, but I'm not afraid. I know I can spin, rise in a straight line to the very edge of the atmosphere, and cross it, keep going and going, until I start seeing planets, satellites, shooting stars brushing against the windshield. That's what I've been doing for a long time: flying. All I have to do is close my eyes and I'll find infinity, like it's inside me. A dog barks in the heavens and the sound spreads across the fields, over the rooftops, the tiny roads, the lighted windows, and as my airplane speeds through the night, the barks get louder and louder. It's Capitán, Baby Hippopotamus Meanie's dog, who's barking.

I get up and look out the window. The city lights reflected in the sky are so bright that there aren't any stars. Alma and a man are getting out of a taxi in front of the gate. Where's Alma's car? Is that the man from the wedding? Why did he bring her home? He gets back in the taxi and it drives away. I hear Alma climbing the stairs and going to the bedroom. I stand there watching the empty street through the crack between the curtains. I remain alert, but now all

I hear is the sound of darkness. Sometimes, without wanting to, I imagine Alma leaving us, like Mama did. I don't like having that thought because Yerfa says that fear brings bad luck.

The day's first light is blue. The gate is open, and the outside light is on. It wasn't a dream. Alma came home with another man. I want to edit out that whole scene, like she does with her movies. Erase it from my memory. But when something new and important gets into my head, there's no way to get it out of there. No matter how hard I try to forget, there are little monsters who keep reminding me it's still there. Not long ago, I explained it to Alma and she told me that the little monsters are called your conscience. I asked her if they ever go away and she said they don't, but we learn to live and just pretend we don't see them. I wanted to know why I can't do that and Alma told me that maybe I was one of those very few people who, instead of closing their eyes, confront the monsters and fight against them until they defeat them. That's why I've been thinking that if I can discover ten things about Mama, everything will become clear. Why ten? Because God gave us ten commandments to live by, because we have ten fingers, because ten billion kilometers are one light year, because Yerfa says I should count to ten before I say or do anything that I might later regret.

At the bottom of my bed, an ice storm is pouring down on Kájef's canoe. He's asleep.

"Tommy, come have breakfast," I hear Yerfa say outside my door.

Yerfa is almost as short as I am. She has a big, round body and very straight hair, pure black. She hardly ever laughs, but we've always been together and I love her. I open the door.

"How many times have I told you not to lock yourself in? What if there's an earthquake?"

Yerfa notices I've been crying. She brushes her fingers across my eyelids, then shakes her hand. "You have to shake off your sorrows," she always tells me.

"Your father's already up. Go say good morning to him if you want, then come downstairs."

Yerfa can read my mind.

"Papa, it's me, Tommy," I announce as I knock on the door to his bedroom.

Nobody answers. I enter. I find Papa in the middle of the room with a towel wrapped round his waist. I'd like to tell him that Kájef is resting in his canoe, but I can't talk to him about Kájef. Alma is sleeping with her face to the wall. The pollen-filled air hangs heavy just outside the half-open window. I don't want to sneeze.

"You didn't knock again," he whispers so as not to wake up Alma.

"Yes, I did, but you didn't answer. I thought something might have happened to you."

"What could happen to me here in my room, Tommy?"

"Nothing."

"Exactly." Papa has big rings under his eyes, and the usual lines around them look deeper than ever. "What have you been up to?"

I sit down carefully on the edge of the bed. It's so high my feet don't touch the ground. Or I could put it another way: I'm so short—as tall as an eight-year-old—my feet don't reach the ground. Papa takes some gray trousers and a blue shirt out of the closet.

"You haven't told me what you did yesterday."

"I was reading."

"As usual."

I want to tell him that nothing anymore is as usual. I know that Mama killed herself and that Alma arrived home with a man. I'd like to tell him all of that, but the words are trapped inside me,

76

like the birds in Grandpa's aviary. Papa gets dressed and goes to the bathroom. A while later, he comes out with his hair combed back. He adjusts his tie in front of the mirror. He takes a deep breath, half closes his eyes, and straightens his collar.

"You don't have school today?"

"The teachers have a professional development day."

"Why don't you call our new neighbor and invite him to come play? Please don't spend another day shut up alone in your room."

I follow him down the stairs. Lola left her stuffed seal on a stair. Papa picks it up.

"Papa . . ." I start to say.

I'm scared Alma will leave us, but I know that if I tell Papa what I saw yesterday, it will just make everything worse. I start blinking really fast. Papa looks at me.

"Nothing," I say.

We keep going down the stairs. He stops in the hall. We're standing in front of one of my drawings: *The Minotaur's Labyrinth*. Alma says it's the best one I've ever done. I like to give my drawings names. In front of the Minotaur I wrote, "Minotaur." In front of the rays I wrote, "Rays." In front of the sun I wrote, "Sun," and so on. Sometimes I switch them around and on an ant I put, "House," and on a tower, "Bird." And then when I look at some of my drawings that have the names mixed up, the things themselves transform. The tower becomes a little bit of a bird, the house a little forest.

"Tommy, why are you following me?"

"Just to be with you."

He musses my hair like he usually does when he doesn't know what to say. He hands me the stuffed seal. He keeps staring at me with those doctor eyes of his and then he hugs me.

"You can't stay home?"

"Impossible. What would my patients say if I didn't show up?"

77

When I was very little, I used to think that if I could stop time, Papa wouldn't ever leave again. One Sunday morning, I carried out my mission. I broke his watch. Obviously, time didn't stop, and I got myself a good scolding.

"You know you're my champ, right?"

I answer that I do.

17 ≋

Juan is fixing his tie in front of the mirror on the closet door. Tommy is with him. I am pretending to be asleep. My head hurts. When they both leave, I drift off again, succumbing to exhaustion.

Gentle knocks wake me. The bright noon light pours in through the window. Outside, beyond the walls of the room, spring is simmering. I can barely open my eyes, the light hurts so much.

"Señora Alma, are you OK? You didn't ask for breakfast, and you told me you needed to leave early," Yerfa asks through the half-open door.

"I don't feel well, Yerfa."

"I'll make you some *matico* tea. Don't you get up, now."

I think of Leo. I know I'm not going to be able to keep away from him, and I feel like I'm suffocating. This is desire. It wields a power over us we don't even want to resist. The memory of his face lying on the pillow next to my mother sweeps into my mind, like dust in the eyes, painful because it is so tiny. I hate the irony that after trying so hard to avoid it, I've returned to exactly where I was when I left Maná. I hate her—now more than ever—for having taken this road ahead of me, for having spoiled everything with her excesses, for making me feel so abandoned. I close my eyes and fall back to sleep. The pain vanishes. When I wake up, the room is deep in shadow. It's eight at night. Juan hasn't come home. I've always believed that if it weren't for him, I'd still be in the state of hopeless despair I was in when we met.

Whenever any Chileans showed up at Restaurante La Goleta, where I worked, I would do my best to avoid them. It's not that I had any aversion toward my compatriots; I just didn't want to feel obliged to engage in conversation and answer their questions about my life in Barcelona. I was twenty-three years old and trying to graduate from film school. I worked as a maître d' at nights, took correspondence courses in literature, lived with a musician in an apartment furnished with junk, and the only person I confided in was Edith, the owner of the restaurant. In short, I had a full and exhausting life, like so many others, but to the kind of Chileans who usually came to that restaurant, it must have looked pretty miserable.

Juan was no exception. I didn't know many men of his type, nor did they interest me very much. He looked so respectable, and his manners, both tactful and solemn, were the sort that seem inherited, passed down through the generations. According to what he told me later, he noticed me the moment he entered the restaurant. In spite of my pristine black uniform—which I made an attempt to wear with as much dignity as possible—I reminded him of a teetering, long-legged fawn who seemed at any moment about to fall flat on its face.

I was seating an Italian couple when I heard the shrieks. My co-workers and I dropped everything and ran to the kitchen. Edith's hands, neck, and part of her chest were in flames. Her mouth was open, but no sound came out of her throat. Roberto, the sous-chef, screaming with horror, was pressing his apron against her body. The rest of the staff were running around frantically. Suddenly, Juan appeared at the kitchen's swinging doors.

"Get down on the ground," he shouted at Edith, and quickly rushed over to her. "Now roll back and forth," he ordered as he took off his jacket and wrapped it round her burning chest and arms. "I need a rug or a coat, and water."

Someone threw him a blanket. Juan immediately wrapped it round her and doused her with water.

"What's her name?"

"Edith," I told him.

"Edith," he repeated in a gentle voice, "can you hear me? You're going to be OK. I am a doctor and I'm going to take care of you."

He moved Edith's gray braid to one side and brought his ear to her nose to make sure she was breathing.

"Did someone already call the ambulance? I'm going to need some pillows, or something to put under her, clean cloth, maybe some tablecloths. Tear one of them into strips," he said, addressing me. Those were his first words to me.

With the pillows, he raised her chest about thirty centimeters off the floor.

"This will make you more comfortable, Edith. Can you hear me?" he said as he felt for her pulse.

He took the singed blanket off her body and covered her with one of the white tablecloths. He made compresses from the strips and placed them between her fingers.

We all watched him and followed his instructions. He was clearly in charge, but he communicated discreetly, almost silently. When the ambulance arrived, Edith bore the pain stoically, her eyes glued to Juan's face, as if he were her only link to the real world. We accompanied her on the stretcher outside. Before they got her into the ambulance, she lost consciousness. Juan and Roberto got in a taxi and followed behind.

Once the customers, all in a state of shock, had left the restaurant, a couple of colleagues and I closed up and went to the hospital.

We found Roberto in the waiting room in the emergency department. A woman with bruises all over her face sat on a bench waiting her turn and stared blankly at the wall in front of her. A little boy in pajamas was curled up in a ball on her lap.

"She's come round. Looks like she's out of danger," Roberto told us. "The Chilean is in there with her."

"She was drunk, wasn't she?" I asked him in a whisper.

Roberto nodded. Edith frequently started early with the gin and tonics and kept at them all night long, until she was thoroughly plastered. It was dizzying to watch her frying fish in those huge pans, chopping onions and garlic, cutting up potatoes, her body swaying back and forth, and her vision getting cloudier and cloudier, all the while her hands moving with skilled precision, as though they belonged to somebody else. Sometimes, after the last customer had asked for the check, she'd collapse into a chair, as if some internal clock had been set for the exact moment she could succumb to her alcoholic stupor.

As soon as I started working in the restaurant, Edith became important to me. I didn't only need a job, I also needed rescuing, and that's what she did. Ignacio, the musician I'd been living with for two years, was a good lover, at times a good friend, but he was too preoccupied with his own problems to be able to help me with mine.

While Roberto and the two girls went to get some coffee, I sat down in a corner. I was thinking about Maná, and the images of the two women—Maná and Edith—got superimposed in my mind. They had both embraced life with an intensity that had left them battered and worn, damaged by the effort they made along the way.

A few hours later, Juan joined us. He introduced himself by only his first name and explained Edith's condition. The fire had burned the cartilage in her fingers and it would probably be months before she'd recover the use of her hands. Fortunately, her face had suffered no injury. There was nothing we could do, for now. It was three in the morning. His calm voice, his firm and deliberate way of saying and doing things, made me feel peaceful—in spite of the circumstances.

After everything that had happened, I didn't feel like going home. I wanted to go have a drink, and suggested that to the others. They agreed and we took a taxi downtown, then walked around for a while. Soon, Roberto and the two girls said goodbye. It was a hot early-summer night. It was so hot, in fact, that the humid air seemed to rise from the streets, and you could smell the sea. Juan took long but measured strides, and looked straight ahead of him. From time to time, I'd observe him out of the corner of my eye, trying to figure out if his silence and indifference were the result of an unhealthy shyness—which hardly seemed likely— or a simple lack of interest. The fact that we were both Chileans and that we had shared the accident didn't mean we had anything to talk about. I was sure he was a respectable man, married, and that he had little desire to strike up a conversation, no matter how superficial, with a stranger. I was embarrassed for having suggested we go for a drink. After we passed the third bar without stopping, I told him I was tired and that we should just say goodbye there.

"It's hard for you to go unnoticed, no matter how hard you try," he said. His eyes were suddenly bright and affable.

"What makes you think I try?"

"Mine was the only table you didn't come to, to ask how things were."

"You noticed."

I wasn't going to tell him that when I first saw him, I wrote him off as one of those men who spend their lives doing exercise and keeping fit, the type—on principle—I couldn't stand.

"I'm a doctor; I notice everything. Is that how you always treat your fellow Chileans or only boring types like me?"

"Both."

We laughed.

"Your name is Alma, isn't it?"

"How did you know?"

He brought a finger to his lips, turned the idea over in his head, then answered, "Along with the airplane ticket, the travel agent gave me a note with the name of the restaurant and your name."

"Really? Do you know who it was from?"

"I don't have the slightest idea. There was also a photocopy of a review of the restaurant from *El País*, which sounded great. That's why I came."

"So, it wasn't for me?"

"I did notice your name, but the truth is, I came because of the review."

"And look at the disaster you stepped into; you probably wish you hadn't."

"I've no regrets," he said, looking straight at me. Then, after a few seconds, he added, "I'm happy I was able to help Edith."

It's incredible, that ability we have to interpret another person's gestures; when we're engaged in a game of seduction, there are only two possible readings: one that encourages us to advance and the other to retreat. Juan's body language, however, was ambivalent. Anyway, by that time Ignacio had probably already been home for hours.

We caught each other's eyes again. I turned mine away, wanting to keep my thoughts to myself. The night air was dense and enveloping. The streetlamps flickered, making the streets disappear into the darkness for fractions of seconds. I asked him what had

84

brought him to Barcelona and he said he was attending a medical conference.

"But I don't want to talk about me. My life is incredibly boring. The truth is, I've reached that age when most of the interesting things have already happened," he said. "Tell me about you."

"Why do you say that about yourself?"

"I'm thirty-nine, I'm a widower, and I have a five-year-old boy."

"I think you're still young enough for unexpected things to happen."

"And old enough to avoid them all, if I possibly can. And you?" he asked, with a smile that showed real interest. "Your name has a story behind it, doesn't it?"

"You know the Place de l'Alma?"

"Paris. The Eiffel Tower. Across the river," he summed it all up rapidly, as if it were a guessing game.

"Well, my name has absolutely nothing to do with that square."

He laughed out loud. "So?"

"The *alma*, the soul, was one of my parents' most basic concerns. Everything had something to do with the soul, especially the most down-to-earth things."

Encouraged by his interest, I found myself talking about Barcelona, the parts I liked, my studies, how I ran from place to place, juggling all my activities. Juan, patiently and steadily, plied me with questions whenever I stopped or hesitated. And, like an old-fashioned gentleman, he didn't let me walk—in my gawky, meandering way—next to the curb.

People who go on and on about their own experiences, convinced that they are as fascinating to others as they are to themselves, have always seemed pathetic to me, but that night, talking was a way—undoubtedly a childish way—of prolonging the time we spent together.

I found myself chattering in that slightly elated tone, as if I were afraid of losing my listener's attention. We walked through the old quarter and up Las Ramblas before we stopped in a bar. We sat down and ordered some coffee. Juan whispered in the waiter's ear.

"Who do you live with now?" he asked me after a short silence. His gaze, though direct, was shy.

I let down my hair, which I'd had tied back in a rubber band, then pulled it up again. A seemingly pointless action, but it gave me the time I needed not to feel trapped.

"Alone," I lied. "And you?"

"With Tomás, my son, and Yerfa, his nanny." He spoke in a curt, clipped tone. He was obviously uncomfortable talking about himself.

We drank our coffee, and the waiter came to tell us that the taxi was waiting. We went out. It was a brilliant dawn.

"It's for you," Juan explained as he opened the taxi door. "My hotel is just a few blocks away."

I didn't want my discomfort at this abrupt ending to appear too obvious, so I sat down in the taxi and placed my hands on my lap. Juan, holding the door open, looked at me.

"Alma," he said, then paused, "sleep well."

I asked the driver to take me to the beach. I wanted to see the dawn colors spreading across the sea and the sky.

When I finally got back to our apartment, Ignacio was deep in a feverish, drunken sleep. Like most nights I got home from work, I encountered the telltale signs of a party; cigarette butts, empty bottles, leftover Chinese takeout, Ignacio's guitar and other musical instruments scattered around the room. I got into bed without getting undressed. I was disgusted by his labored breathing, his snoring, his drunken sighs that sounded like groans, and I had to get up. I went into the living room and looked around, realizing that even though I was the one who'd furnished the place, sparse as it was, it didn't belong to me. I went out to the hallway and climbed the stairs to the rooftop. I sat down on the asphalt, still warm from the sun. A pair of trousers hanging on a clothesline made me think of a drunken man dancing. How had I ended up on this desolate rooftop? I'd escaped from Maná, from Papa's weakness, from the fights, from my own loneliness, but I was still there, crouching in a dark corner. My best friend was lying in a hospital bed, and my boyfriend was one of those guys who makes a lifestyle out of his immaturity and aimlessness.

When I returned to the apartment, Ignacio was still sleeping. I opened my suitcase, the same one I'd brought with me to Barcelona, and stuffed it as full as I could. The rest, which wasn't much, I put into a garbage bag. Then I left for the hospital.

I found Edith on the ward, her arms, hands, and chest bandaged.

"It had to happen sooner or later, right?" She spoke haltingly.

"It had to happen," I repeated. I ran my fingers over her gray locks.

We were silent.

"I left him," I suddenly confessed.

"About time," Edith concurred, her voice barely audible. "Take the key to my apartment . . . It's in my handbag . . . Stay there. Later, we'll see what we'll do . . . You with your life and me with mine."

She closed her eyes. Her breathing was irregular. I thought about Ignacio and the drunken nights he spent trying to write a song, capture a tune, nights he spent hoping for the chance to finally prove his talent, the one that always managed to elude him. I felt sad.

That night, Roberto and the rest of the staff worked with more dedication than ever. The news had reached our regular customers and the place was packed; there was a somber but supportive mood.

The following evening, Juan stopped by and ordered a glass of white wine. I sat with him whenever I had a spare moment.

"I went by the hospital today," he said. "The doctors told me Edith is a very noncompliant patient."

"I'm not surprised," I said.

"I'm leaving tomorrow. If you want to, or feel like it, I thought maybe we could go get a bite to eat after your shift."

I noticed it wasn't easy for him to say those words. The speech wasn't part of the carefully written doctor role in his script.

"I have a better idea," I said, smiling. I jumped up, then came back a few minutes later and sat down in front of him.

"I'm ready to leave."

"Who will greet and seat the other diners?"

"Any of the others can do it. Nobody will miss me."

"Don't be so sure. I've no doubt that more than one customer comes here specifically for you," he said, making me feel good for the first time in several days.

Juan took me to a fashionable restaurant he'd been to with his colleagues. The minute we sat down at the table, we buried our heads in the menus. When I finally looked up, I saw that his straightforward expression had vanished. I suddenly found myself sitting in front of a total stranger with indecipherable thoughts passing through his mind. We barely spoke; we both sat for long stretches watching people at other tables.

At one point, he suddenly grabbed my fingers, squeezed them, and lifted them in front of his face. Then he smiled.

Except for that small gesture, our meal passed without any erotic overtones. That's why I was surprised that he put his arm round my waist when we got outside. He kept his arm there for a moment, looking at me somewhat despondently. He seemed incapable of taking the next step.

"Are you afraid of me?" I asked boldly.

"Of all women," he said, narrowing his eyes with a mischievous twinkle.

"You're right to be afraid of us—we're treacherous."

Then he kissed me, and I did not resist.

We walked a couple of blocks. When we got to the door of his hotel, we went in without saying a word. Once in his room, he asked if I'd like a glass of wine. I sat down on the bed with my legs crossed and he did the same in an armchair, all the time observing every move I made. I was afraid that my fear of acting inappropriately would be too obvious. Unlike most men I'd known, he didn't stuff gestures and words into those moments of preamble, which anyway always lead to the same place. The mere fact that I was there sitting on his bed rushed things in a way that probably made him uncomfortable. I didn't know why I cared so much what he thought of me. Juan was a man I'd met a few nights before, a man who would vanish from my life the following morning, a man I was attracted to and desired, as I had desired so many others.

I'd found myself in this exact same situation so many times, saying the same thing to myself, yet always believing, somewhere inside me, that this time would be different. Fortunately, I always managed to shake off any painful illusions and abandon myself to the erotic promise of momentary pleasure, but Juan—sitting in front of me without saying a word—made the natural unfolding awkward. I held my breath and undressed quickly, without turning the process into a game of seduction. I stood up. For a second I felt like an idiot; then it seemed as if I'd leaped into unknown territory, and there was something liberating and light in that leap.

"You're pregnant," he said. "Ten, eleven weeks?"

Juan's face was a mixture of tenderness, admiration, and desire. I'd taken off my clothes impulsively, but his gaze now made me aware of the energy emanating from my body. My swollen breasts and the small bulge in my belly were brimming with life.

"Twelve," I confirmed.

He put his arms round me and I clung to the lapels of his jacket and rested my head on his shoulder. We remained standing in that embrace for a long time. The silence surrounding us was laden with feelings that must have been as strange for Juan as they were for me. He was the first person to know my secret. I'd even managed to hide it from Ignacio.

When I woke up the next morning, Juan, already dressed, was watching me sleep.

"I have to meet a colleague before I leave. My flight's at noon. You are welcome to stay here, but I won't have time to come back."

Only then did I realize that his suitcase and a big box with a model airplane were standing next to the door. I sat up in bed, somewhat bewildered.

"I left my card on the bedside table." He gave me a kiss. With our faces still quite close, he added, "I don't want to lose sight of you."

"Me neither."

"My email address is on my card. The baby is due in April, right? What are your plans?"

That was the first question Juan had asked me about the baby and its future.

"Keep doing what I'm doing until it's born. I want to finish my studies, then return to Chile."

"Do you have somebody to help you with all this?"

He must have figured that since I'd spent the night with him, there was nobody waiting for me at home.

"Edith," I answered.

"Anybody else? Edith is going to be convalescing for a long time."

"You don't know me. I always get by," I said that without any irony, because it was true.

"Will you promise me something?"

I nodded.

"I want you to keep me informed. I know several doctors in Barcelona who can help you. With anything. OK?"

His concern seemed genuine, and it touched me. He gave me another kiss, picked up his suitcase, the box with the model airplane, and left.

I got up and ate breakfast with the television on. When I'd eaten everything, I ordered more coffee, toast, fruit, and cereal.

I went to visit Edith at noon. Her head was propped up on several large pillows, and her bandaged arms were on top of the white bedcover. I usually shared the gory details of my life with her, but I didn't mention Juan. I didn't want our sarcastic mirth to spill all over what had just happened. But what, really, had happened? I recalled our embrace, me standing naked in front of him in that room, my impression of being with a cautious and awkward lover who never forgot for a second that another life was gestating under my skin. So what was upsetting me? Perhaps it was precisely that. Juan seemed to understand the magnitude of that being I was carrying in my belly better than I did. I'd been hiding it for so many weeks that, despite its relentless growth, it had been fading out of my consciousness instead of becoming more concrete. By acknowledging the space it occupied between us, Juan had made it real. It didn't take me long to realize that although he wasn't talkative and sharp-tongued, his calmness and conviction seemed unshakable. I already missed the way he looked at me, without any covetousness whatsoever.

I said goodbye to Edith and walked through the streets of Barcelona, which were teeming with tourists. In spite of all the years I'd spent there, the city had never become mine, and was now less so than ever. The hundreds of tourists sitting at cafés along Las Ramblas, the bicycles, the languages, everything was woven into a fine screen that separated me from the world. But weren't all of them alone like I was? I used to believe that encounters between people were nothing but accidental convergences. Sooner or later, everyone would continue along their own way. Even when those encounters lasted an entire lifetime, in the end, you'd go it alone on the most difficult stretch. And that idea, which was always with me, made true contact impossible. That was what underscored all my previous relationships and what ultimately suffocated them. And that life I carried around in my belly, would it also carry a stopwatch? Would the inevitable moment of separation come? I was a long way from feeling that bliss, that sudden encounter with the famous "meaning of life" that pregnancy and motherhood supposedly bring. I walked with my hands on my belly.

I got to La Goleta early. Roberto was already there. We took a couple of chairs and a basket of tangerines out onto the sidewalk. Our conversation, in the afternoon's protective air, helped stave off my anxieties. While we ate the fruit, he told me about his life in the Canary Islands, stories of sea and sand that made me forget my troubles for a moment. Beyond the light of the streetlamps, the evening took on a violet hue. We went inside. As soon as the first diners began to arrive, I realized I was incapable of producing the smile I usually welcomed them with. I felt weak. And when I saw Juan at the door, looking around for me, I thought I was going to collapse.

"Hi," he greeted me calmly.

"Did you miss your flight?"

"I found another one that leaves tomorrow."

We went out again. He wrapped his arm round my shoulders as we started to walk. Suddenly, he stopped in the middle of the sidewalk and faced me.

"I want to know if you will accept a gift."

He handed me an open ticket to Chile. I could use it whenever I wanted to. I didn't refuse it, but I didn't throw my arms round his neck or kiss him, either. I saw a look of distress sweep over his face. He looked down.

"I also want you to know that I haven't been with a woman since my wife died two years ago," he said slowly, without looking at me.

"I'm the first you've . . ."

"Yes."

He looked me straight in the eyes, a controlled expression on his face that hid, I guessed, a man who had been shipwrecked once, just like me.

"You don't know me. You don't know who I am," I mumbled.

"And you don't owe me anything. Here's the ticket. When you want to come to Chile, use it, and that's that. If you feel like it, when you get there, call me. I'd like it if you did," he added, "very much."

"Why are you doing this?"

"There's nothing wrong with someone helping you a little, is there?"

The second night we spent together, Juan told me that his wife had died of a cerebral aneurysm. He talked to me about the doubts that had made him question everything he'd ever taken to be truth, even, heaven forbid, the existence of God. He described a place of emptiness and uncertainty, a place he'd never even been able to imagine before.

My decision to return to Chile was not impulsive. Juan's gift had given me renewed energy, as well as a confidence in myself and the rest of the world that I hadn't had for a long time. For a few weeks, Ignacio kept turning up at La Goleta; then he vanished and I never saw him again. He never knew I was pregnant, as I practically didn't show until I was about four months along.

I finished my short film and took my final literature exams. In seven months I achieved more than I had in the previous several years. Lola was born in Barcelona. Edith, in spite of her slow convalescence, helped me at the beginning. The whole time, Juan and I were getting to know each other through email. He often recounted the ups and downs of his daily life in a simple, funny way. On only a few occasions did he ask about my return. When Lola was three months old and I finally received my diplomas, I decided that the time had come.

Edith took me to the airport. Before we parted, she said, "Now that you are a mother, you'll see you will start to understand yours."

It struck me as odd that she'd mention my mother. Maybe the fact that I'd never spoken about her led her to suspect that we had a troubled relationship.

My old friend Matías, with whom I'd spent my first years in Barcelona, welcomed me back to Chile with open arms. He had founded a film production company and was just starting on his first full-length film. Within a few days of arriving, I was settled into an apartment and working in his company.

Juan and I approached each other gradually. Fear of failure prevented me from making any hasty decisions. Eventually I found myself accepting his proposal that we live together and I moved in with him. A few months later, I picked up the telephone and called my mother.

"Maná, I'm in Chile and I have a daughter. Her name is Lola," were my first words.

Throughout all those years, we'd corresponded only sporadically; the few letters I wrote were terse, and I told her only about things that didn't matter to me. My mother didn't say a word, and then I heard her crying on the other end of the line.

"You'll never forgive me, will you?"

I looked around. Lola was sleeping on my bed. I realized my anger had remained intact, but now I had a reason to keep it under wraps.

"If you want, you can come meet your granddaughter," I told her.

Little by little, I began to lose that edge of impatience; I no longer wanted to be elsewhere, to reach yet another goal, because each day, with its thousands of tiny details, let me rise above myself and drove away the loneliness. I was determined to hold on to what I could see, what I knew to be real, and to ignore everything that smacked of loss and uncertainty; I was not going to get trapped in a whirlwind of my own impulses, like my mother had. The tranquility of my new life was a far cry from the passion of my past, from those vertiginous raptures that invariably blew up in my face shortly after they began, but I didn't care. And at night, when Juan wrapped his arms round me, I was sure that he, despite all his reserve, felt the same way.

My pajamas are wet with sweat. I sit up in bed. My head hurts a bit less. A car speeds past outside the window. I don't have the energy to get up and say good night to the children. I take my cellphone out of my handbag. There are six missed calls from Leo.

18⏳

The morning light is filtering in through the windows as I ride down on the escalator. The recent renovations, replete with huge sheets of plate glass and steel tubing, have made the hospital look oddly like a state-of-the-art shopping mall.

Karina is washing the cafeteria's glass wall as she does every day at this time. Seeing her, with her smile and her dimpled cheeks, always gives me a feeling of well-being. She often talks to me about the new nursing skills she's learning at night school, but this time, after saying hi, she takes a present out of the pocket of her apron and hands it to me.

"This is for you. Don't open it now."

"Why are you giving me a present?"

"You'll see!" she says excitedly as she walks away down the hallway carrying her cleaning supplies.

Whenever Alma comes to the hospital, she makes a point of saying hello to Karina. She says that Karina isn't aware of her positive effect on other people, and she's right, as she is about so many things. I remember that dream I had a few nights ago: Soledad and Alma floating away together on a ship.

When the elevator door opens on the third floor, I practically bump into Emma. She looks almost youthful today, in her black trousers and blue button-down shirt, her hair pulled back in a ponytail. Her face, however, is tense.

"Cristóbal has a fever," she says, trying to control her emotions. "What does it mean?"

"I'm not sure, but I'll find out."

On the way to Cristóbal's room, she tells me that he seems more listless and that he's been in a cold sweat. I see Emma's mother and sister in the waiting room, two thin women, quite self-satisfied, who interrupt their endless chatter only to throw disapproving glances at whatever enters their field of vision. The duty nurse is waiting for me in the hallway.

"Wait here a minute," I tell Emma, and I enter her son's room with the nurse.

Cristóbal's arms are hanging limply by his sides, and his eyes are only half open. The nurse tells me he has a fever of 37.2 degrees. Although it's not clinically significant, any detour from a steady path toward recovery raises concerns.

"A girl just gave me a gift," I say to Cristóbal. "I don't know what to think."

"Someone in my class once gave me one. You know what it was? Rabbit poop," he says, then coughs.

The slightest effort is obviously difficult for him. He shuts his eyes, then opens them, as if trying to change the channel. Cristóbal is familiar with pain: Like most children with an incurable congenital illness, he's lived with it most of his life. I'm always amazed at how stoically they deal with it, as if they simply accept it as an intrinsic part of life.

"Your classmate obviously wasn't very nice. I haven't opened mine yet. Shall we look at it together?"

"Sure, but based on its size, I don't think it's anything very interesting."

I notice his breathing is slightly labored. He should be taking

97

more breaths between words.

"OK, but first, show me your hands."

His fingers look slightly bluish. I lift the bedcovers to check his feet and I see the same thing. It's not normal, but it is within the range of possibilities. Post-operative intubation and assisted ventilation increase the risk of infection.

"I'm going to ask you to take a deep breath. Does it hurt?"

"A little."

Unlike adults, who bombard you with questions, children prefer to think about other things when they suspect danger. It's almost as if they can make reality disappear by simply not paying any attention to it.

The first time Cristóbal came to my office, he barely lifted his eyes from his Game Boy. When he did look at me briefly, his eyes showed profound disdain. It was as if he'd been through this a thousand times—somebody promising him he'd get better—and somewhere along the way he'd lost hope. This didn't mean he'd given up; he was, on the contrary, defiant and mature. It was as if his parents continued in a state of numb credulity while he'd already discovered the brutal nature of life. During our following meetings, I devoted all my efforts to breaking through his shell. It was a slow process. Cristóbal's opposition was his way of taking measure, not so much of the dangers of the operation, but of my commitment to him.

"We're going to take your temperature again, OK?"

Cristóbal lifts his other arm and points. "I want to see your present," he says.

He's restless. His difficulty breathing must be creating anxiety. While the nurse is taking his temperature, I look at his chart to find out what happened during the night. She shows me the thermometer and I see it has reached 38.1 degrees. I hand Cristóbal the little wrapped box Karina gave me.

"You open it. I can tell you're used to surprises."

He struggles to sit up. His chest is hurting more than he's willing to admit. He opens the package with his long fingers. His hair is neatly combed. Emma must have seen to that detail this morning.

"It's really cool," he exclaims, holding in his hands a tiny bottle with a wooden boat inside.

"I can't give it to you, because that would be an insult to the girl who gave it to me, but we can leave it by your bed as long as you're here in the hospital. How does that sound?"

"Good," he says, and closes his eyes.

I ask the nurse to take his blood. I stay with him for a moment after she leaves. I know Emma is waiting for me outside the door. I need to find the right words to convey my concerns without alarming her. There's no room for idle gestures. The moment you tell a mother that her child is going to recover, you change her entire perspective on life. That's why the words must be truthful as well as cautious.

Ever since I was very young I thought that the way to avoid personal setbacks was to keep my mind busy with things that were finite and practical, things that I could act on in a concrete and meaningful way. This was probably why I decided to study medicine. What I never considered, though, was the possibility that those concrete actions, the ones that were supposed to solve my existential dilemmas, would themselves lead to an endless parade of doubts and sadness. The truth is, a respiratory infection is not a very encouraging sign, not when your body is fragile and you have a newly transplanted heart, for which you're taking immunosuppressant drugs.

When I walk out of the room, Emma is questioning the nurse. I invite her to walk down the hallway with me.

"I suspect Cristóbal has developed a pulmonary infection,"

I tell her. "We'll have to do a couple of tests to make sure."

"What does it mean?" Red blotches appear on her pale face; she almost looks like she's had a sudden burst of joy.

"Emma, don't be alarmed. Nothing is certain yet. If that is what's happening, we'll find the source of the infection and treat it."

Emma places her hand over her mouth, as if to stifle a groan.

"Once we start the treatment, he should respond quickly. That's the most likely scenario."

"The most likely?" she asks with a combination of fear and defiance.

"Yes, of course. These procedures always carry a risk. But we'll X-ray his chest. If we detect any abnormality, we'll do a bronchoscopy."

I tell her what this involves. She looks at me intently without saying a word. She keeps her eyes on me as she takes her cellphone out of her pocket.

"Isaac, Cristóbal's not doing well," she says. "You'd better come."

I leave her in the hallway. The nurse on duty is making arrangements for the tests. The alarm has gone off.

By the afternoon, the diagnosis is clear. The chest X-ray showed a left basal pulmonary condensation, the sign of a possible bacterial infection. The bronchoscopy and the bacterial analysis confirmed the presence of klebsiella. We've started him on antibiotics and he's breathing easier. He is now sleeping with sedatives. We've decided not to connect him to the respirator unless it becomes absolutely necessary. If we connect him, he'll have to be continuously sedated.

You'd think that knowledge would increase with age and, along with it, the margin of uncertainty would shrink. But the more I know, the more the horizon of dilemmas expands and the more questions I have, to a point where I'm sometimes paralyzed by doubt. I want more than anything in the world to tell Emma that her son will be OK, but all I manage to see are the hundreds of unpredictable variables that at this very moment are sustaining Cristóbal's life, and that at any moment can change it forever.

19 ♐

Papa and Alma are still mad at each other, and it's all my fault. That's why when the bus dropped me off at school this morning, I couldn't go in. I turned round and walked to the plaza I usually go to when I feel like this. I've spent the whole day here. I unpacked my lunch and spread it out along the bench that's farthest away from the street. The plaza is completely deserted except for a black cat wandering around and licking its whiskers like a miniature panther. Some boys run across the street. They're probably playing hooky like me. They're laughing and jumping around, and slapping each other on the back. I don't like to be alone, but to have a friend I'd have to make a great big effort and most likely it wouldn't work anyway. I'd rather think about my next nine discoveries.

Mama killed herself; that's the first one, but how can I get to the next? Maybe putting together things I already know and that didn't seem important to me before, like, for instance, that Papa never talks about her; like, for instance, that the only thing of Mama's he's kept is that picture I took from his drawer; like, for instance, that every time anybody mentions Mama, Grandpa gulps like he's swallowed a frog; like, for instance, that we've never visited my mother's mother, who lives in Buenos Aires, not even when my grandfather there died. I asked Papa about them once and he told me that after Mama died, they decided to return to Argentina, where my grandma was born.

In the afternoon, I wait for the school bus in front of school. Nobody asks me where I've been. I'm invisible and I'm glad. When I get home, I turn on my computer.

```
ecchh u stupid peace a shit go cri 2 ur momy she luvs
u soo much go stik ur head in ur stupid books there
ur only friends u dont hav nuting els 2 do u dimwit.
```

I've seen their messages thousands of times, but they still make me feel kind of bad, like being lost. I do what I always do: I imagine horrible things happening to them. This time, I imagine a thief coming into their house at night and gouging out their eyes.

I go downstairs to get a glass of milk. Yerfa's cellphone rings— *beep, beep*—and vibrates, as if she had a live bird in her pocket. She answers it and I go back to my room. I Google my grandfather's name, Adolfo García Izquierdo. There are no results for Adolfo García Izquierdo. My grandfather never did anything to make him show up on Google. Papa has 648 results. I type in my grandmother's last name, Bulygin. There are 591 results, many of them mention a Mr. Arnold Bulygin. I click on the first one:

```
Arnold Bulygin, 1903–86. Founder of St. Ann's
School, one of the first and most important schools
for girls in Buenos Aires. Indefatigable educator.
Instructed hundreds of our most renowned women.
Those of us fortunate enough to have inherited his
great legacy are celebrating the twentieth anniver-
sary of his death with a mass in the school chapel
on November 4 at 7 p.m.
```

The announcement is signed by many people, including my grandmother, Perla Bulygin. It's very likely Arnold Bulygin is my great-grandfather. I read a few more entries—biographical data, some of his writings on education, then entries that talk about the school that he founded. I record, "*Second discovery: Mama's grandpa founded a girls' school in Buenos Aires called St. Ann's.*"

I go to Mr. Thomas Bridge's blog. He's talking into a camera. He says he won't budge until he is certain the invading journalists have disappeared. All he's wearing is a teeny-weeny bathing suit. He looks ridiculous. He says that if he stayed dressed like that where he was, at the end of the Earth, he'd be dead in forty-eight hours. He wants to show that in the same way, any interference in the lives of the Alacalufs would lead to their deaths. Mr. Thomas Bridge keeps talking. There's an address on his blog where you can contact him. I write:

```
My name is Tomás Montes. My best friend comes from
Lennox Island and we're both really worried about
the family you found. We want very much to help you
on your mission, but first we've got to solve a few
problems of our own. Nine, to be exact. Anyway,
don't hesitate to get in touch with me if you think
we can help you.
    P.S. If you send me an address, I'd love to send
you one of my drawings.
    In solidarity,
    Tomás Montes
```

I like that, "in solidarity." I press "send."

When I look out my window, I see Baby Hippopotamus Meanie in front of his house. He throws a stone every two minutes. After twelve minutes, he looks at me and shows me a snail he's holding. I open the window and say hi.

"If you want, I'll show you the rest tomorrow. I've got tons," he shouts up at me.

"I like snails, too!"

"Tomorrow, OK?"

I give him the thumbs-up, and he goes inside, waddling away just like a hippopotamus.

Overhead, a flock of birds disappears behind the thick layer of clouds. Migratory birds make me a little envious: They've got nothing that keeps them in one place, and they're always going somewhere the sun is shining.

20 〰

On my way to the studio I receive a text message on my phone. I stop at a red light to read it. It's from Leo. "*I learned to use this device for your sake. What should I do with this desire to see you?*"

I remind myself that he's a writer and knows full well the effect his words will have; he knows how to choose them and combine them to achieve the desired result. For him, words possess less truth than they do for most human beings, but I don't care. I haven't asked him for proof of his love, and I hope I'll never have to. When the lights change, I am surprised to see, between the passing cars, my mother's boyfriend, Bruno, across the street talking to a voluptuous young woman.

I've stayed late into the afternoon editing the scenes I should have finished yesterday. In the morning, Matías wanted to know what was going on. He said I looked like I'd lost weight. It's true: I've barely been eating since Miguel's wedding. He asked me if I'd seen Leo again since then and I said no. I felt a pang when I realized I'd started to lie.

I play back the scenes I've already edited. While I'm staring at the screen, other images start playing out in my mind's eye; faces and places become a backdrop to my thoughts. I think about Lola and Tommy and Juan. A tiny part of that vast world out there that belongs to me, around which everything else has until now fallen into place and taken on meaning. A life I longed for: the perfect revenge against my past, my mother. So what's this impulse that's making me turn my back on it for something that's so uncertain? Why don't I want to repress the feelings Leo provokes in me?

I sift through my memories with Juan and try to find a similar feeling. Surely it was once there, hidden among the hundreds of practical issues I had to deal with when I got back to Chile: getting to know Tommy, building trust between us, finding a place for myself in a family whose codes of behavior were so foreign to me, initiating the painstaking reconciliation with my mother. It must be buried somewhere, that thrill that makes your body tremble from head to toe. But I never thought I missed it. Our tranquil love always seemed enough for me. It wasn't so much the marriage that motivated me, but rather the fact that it allowed me to live out the idea I'd had of myself ever since I was little.

Now, though, my sense of myself and of my place in this world have become weightless, like the changing shapes on the screen in front of me. I imagine that everything is still possible, that my future remains wide open, that Lola and Tommy don't exist. I'm terrified by my ability to do this, yet somehow that's what I crave more than anything.

I feel exhausted when I leave the studio. My cellphone rings while I'm driving. It makes me jump. I answer without taking my eyes off the road. If I'd bothered to look at who was calling, I'd have let it keep ringing.

"Alma, darling, are you there?"

"Yes, Maná," I answer with a tired lilt to my voice.

"I made fish Florentine. Want to come over and eat it with me? I even got some sun-dried tomatoes."

"Maná, what's wrong?" Her invitation surprises me.

"Nothing. Only, I made it for Bruno and he just called to say he can't make it."

It's always the same story: my mother trying to use me to relieve her frustrations.

"I can't—the children and Juan are waiting for me at home. Call one of your friends. I'm sure they'd be delighted to share a meal with you by candlelight."

I'm not usually so blunt, but my feelings are coming to the surface with astonishing ease. My mother doesn't respond. I remember seeing Bruno with that girl half her age, and I feel sorry for her.

"Look, I'm sorry, but I really can't. I'll call you tomorrow, all right?"

"I got a postcard from Edith today."

"From Edith? What do you know about Edith?" I ask, the timbre of my voice rising a bit too much.

"You talked about her once."

"But how does she have your address?" I ask curtly.

"You must have given it to her."

She has slipped, and she quickly regrets it. Her voice gives her away. I'm sure I never mentioned Edith to her. They belong to completely different worlds. Edith is part of the world I built for myself. No matter how angry Maná makes me, I can't help smiling, because I'm talking to the one person in the world who'd give anything to see me in the arms of a man other than my husband. It would be the ultimate affirmation of her dogma about the farce of fidelity, about it being something human beings have invented to repress their most powerful and, therefore, most dangerous desire: to possess another person.

"No, Maná, I never gave your address to Edith."

"Well, I guess you'll have to ask her about it."

"You're hiding something from me."

"Oh, Alma, you make everything so complicated. I have to go—the food is going to burn. Call me later."

When I get home, Juan and the children are eating pizza in the kitchen. I'd forgotten that it's Yerfa's night off.

"Hi, everybody."

Juan throws me a disparaging look.

"Mama, please never come home early when Yerfa's not here. I adore the pizza that comes from the telephone," Lola says.

That "adore" belongs to my mother, and it sounds even worse in Lola's mouth than in hers.

"I'm sorry," I answer, and I lean my elbows on the kitchen table. "I had a horrible day."

Tommy kisses me on the cheek. I hug him.

"Do you all forgive me?"

Though I include them all, I mean Juan. I know how important it is for him that the house functions like clockwork, like a hospital, and I try to make sure it does.

"Should we believe her?" Juan asks, looking from one child to the other.

"How are you?" I ask as I sit down next to him.

I place my hand on his thigh. *Hold my hand*, I beg him silently. *Please. I'm going away to a place where neither you nor the kids can accompany me. Can't you feel it?* But nothing happens. I don't say those words, and he doesn't hold my hand.

"Fine," he answers, and takes a huge bite of pizza.

The children imitate him. They laugh.

"Well, I can see nobody here needs me."

I keep looking at them, hoping that one of them will contradict me, but they haven't even heard me over the roar of their laughter. I shouldn't feel offended because my husband and children are having a fabulous time without me. It should make me feel good. Juan stops and stares at me for a second.

"It's Grandpa's birthday at the end of the month and I would like each of you to make him a present," he says to the children.

Lola says she'll make the paper flowers she learned in art class. She picks up a napkin and shows us how she folds it to make it into a flower. Tommy winks at me, an imperceptible movement that I return and that washes over me like a balm. He's been watching me the whole time with his pale, whimsical face.

Ensconced on his side of the bed, Juan is reading a medical journal. There's nothing unusual in this scene: a middle-aged man with glasses on his nose and a yellowish light falling on his face, and his wife lying next to him, staring at the ceiling and waiting for him to talk to her. She doesn't know whether to apologize for her mistakes, try to reach out to him, or turn round and wait for the night to dilute his resentment.

"You are more and more like your mother every day," I hear Juan say in a stern voice.

"If you want to pick a fight, don't count on my participation."

"Don't worry—I no longer count on you for much more important things," he throws back at me with insuperable irony.

"So what's the point of saying such a nasty thing to me?" I ask him with as much coldness as I can muster.

"I'm just telling you the truth."

I get up. I don't know if he's right. I've done what I could. All I know is that his words exhaust me.

"We can talk tomorrow if you want." I look at him out of the corner of my eye. I've never had this feeling of revulsion before. "I'm going to sleep with Lola."

"As you wish."

I need air. I go down the stairs and into the hallway where Tommy's drawings are hanging. I stop in front of his labyrinth. An ethereal Theseus holds his lance over the Minotaur's body. It's a pain-free battle, as if both, after acting out their portrayal of conquest and death, will shake hands and leave the labyrinth together. A line runs through the drawing. It's Ariadne's thread, which Tommy called "the thread that leads love out."

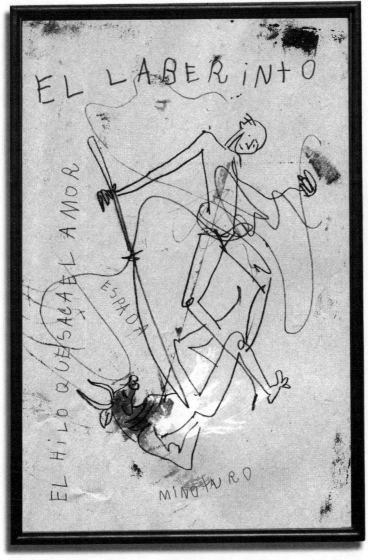

The labyrinth   Minotaur   *The thread that leads love out*   Sword

21 ↗

I like to stay under my sheets because here everything falls back into place. When I'm with Kájef, I forget that tomorrow is another day of school.

I hear someone going down the stairs. I wait and listen. I hear noises on the terrace. I go into the hallway and look out the window into the garden. Alma is behind a tree talking on her cellphone. I go back to my room. I lie down in bed and fly my red airplane over my head. I can't fly in a real airplane.

Papa always told me, "When you turn nine, I'll let you fly," and when the day came, Papa kept his word. He told me that inside an airplane was like inside a car, and that I wouldn't be afraid. Whenever I'm in a small, narrow space, my head goes into overdrive and I see horrible images. The doctor says it's a "phobia." The night before my birthday, I waited impatiently for bedtime so that the next day would come sooner, but everything went wrong. The engines had just started roaring under my seat when I felt a sharp pain in my belly and I began shaking. I closed my eyes and hummed a tune. Through my helmet I heard Papa. From far, far away he was telling me that we were already up in the air. A sharp noise stabbed me in the ears and really hurt. I wanted to shout. I dug my fingernails into the back of my hand. Papa's mouth was opening and closing, but I couldn't hear his voice. I looked down.

I thought it would reassure me to look at the ground. The cars were moving like bacteria, and we were very far away from everything I knew. I couldn't stand it anymore and I started to scream. Puffs of clouds moved slowly past my eyes. Everything was blue and gray. I kept screaming, but it was like it wasn't me screaming. I couldn't even hear myself. There were twisting roads covered with beetles, dark stretches of land, reflected sunlight. I felt a hot wetness between my legs. Without looking at me, Papa picked up a plastic bag and handed it to me. A few seconds later, I was vomiting. Papa turned a couple of times before he landed. I heard his voice: "Victor Alpha Charlie Romeo, Tobalaba flight plan, requesting clearance to land at Tobalaba. Flight ceiling 17,500 feet."

"Looks like I'll have to get you another birthday present," he said when we landed, then patted me on the head.

I'm cold; it's like someone's placed a gigantic piece of ice in my arteries to make them stop working. Alma is still in the garden. I'm positive she's talking to that man again. The one from the wedding, the one who brought her home. I make my red airplane fly again. Brrr . . . brrr. Without thinking, I throw it against the wall. The airplane falls on the ground; its wing is broken. A couple of screws roll across the floor. How could I have done that? How did I forget to count to ten? Is this how horrible things happen? Are they all written down somewhere I don't know about? If they are, maybe I could find it, and with a huge eraser erase all the moments that destroy the things I love the most.

I think Mama must have felt sad or angry for a moment, like I do now, and before she could regret what she was doing, she was dead. But what could have made her so sad that she'd forget to count to ten?

22 〰

From the terrace I can see the lit swimming pool and the lawn stretching out until it disappears in the darkness. I look for Leo's phone number on my cell and I send him a text message: "*A black cat crossed my garden.*"

A few seconds later, I receive a reply: "*Can you talk?*"

I write, "*Yes.*"

I hear his voice. "Alma, where have you been hiding?"

I can't tell him my problems. If Juan had taken my hand, Leo and I probably wouldn't be talking. At least, that's what I want to believe.

"I'm in the garden. What are you doing?"

"I'm talking to you. And you?"

We both laugh.

"Today, Matías asked me if I'd seen you and I said no."

"Why?"

"I don't know. I was ashamed."

"Because of what happened?" He sounds nervous, like I am.

"Yes."

"It was amazing. I can't stop thinking about it."

"About 'it,' or about me?"

"About everything, Alma. You, while we were making love, your eyes looking at me, your hands touching me—everything."

I remain silent.

"I want to see you. If I don't see you, I might die. I'm dead serious."

"Maybe you've been reading too much romantic literature."

"No, I'm not that desperate, but in a way you're right . . . We writers have learned to recognize the splendor of things, the sudden appearance of truth from within."

Leo and his words. If his feelings were real, modesty and fear wouldn't let him express them in that way.

"What might you be referring to?" I ask him sardonically.

"You."

"I'm impressed by your certainty."

"Will you make time for me, even a little bit?"

"I'll try."

"That's not good enough."

"That's all I can offer for now."

"Then I accept. For now."

23 ⏳

While attempting to explain the most recent treatments to Emma, I notice the light from the window falling across her profile. I feel naked when she looks at me. I know she is weighing the truth of my words, scrutinizing every expression on my face and every aspect of my body language.

I think about Alma. Not so long ago, I used to see in her eyes an image of myself I quite liked, an image that's no longer there.

Emma asks me if her son is in pain. I tell her he isn't. He's heavily sedated. She approaches him. She pats his forehead with a towel. Cristóbal breathes with difficulty through the respirator. His young features contract. The sight of him unconscious like this presses on his mother's heart, and on mine. Emma tells me that Isaac spent the night at the hospital. She wants to let me know that she isn't alone in this. When I arrived, I saw her mother and sister chattering as usual in the waiting room. Cristóbal coughs. Emma looks at him. Her face shows signs of the onslaught of emotions swirling through her.

"Did you sleep?" I ask her, to break the silence.

She shakes her head. Exhaustion has made her eyes docile. Her dark eyebrows and red lips stand out against her pale face.

"Get some rest. Cristóbal is going to need you when they take him off the respirator."

"You don't believe what you're saying, do you?"

She's right: I don't.

"In the next few hours we'll know how he's responding, but for now you really should rest . . ."

"Thank you for your concern," she says, and throws her arms round me.

Her body presses against mine. I can hear her breathing in my ear; I feel her arms tight about me. A few seconds later, she lets go, covers her face with both hands, then turns toward the window.

"It's OK, Emma," I tell her.

She keeps her back to me, hunched over, her hands still covering her face. For a second I don't know what to do. I could leave, as if nothing had happened, throw a veil over a moment that barely signifies in the midst of everything else that's going on, but I don't. I approach her, turn her round so that we are facing each other, and put my arms round her as gently as I possibly can. As I feel her body trembling, my chest relaxes, as if a valve had opened up and relieved some pressure, who knows why. Perhaps I need this hug as much as she does. When we separate, Emma smiles. It's a shy smile, still sad, but no longer embarrassed. My gesture redeemed hers, and both somehow pacified Cristóbal. We look at him and see he's breathing more easily.

In the afternoon, I do my rounds of my ICU patients. Cristóbal is still heavily sedated, breathing through the respirator. His vital signs are stable. Emma is sitting next to his bed, her eyes closed; she's probably asleep. I leave without disturbing her. She rekindles in me a kind of anxiety I'd thought I'd never feel again. It is a short-lived assault, like a hailstorm that belts my body, then vanishes.

Back in my office, I answer several emails. The afternoon advances. I force myself to go about my business and manage to maintain a healthy and necessary professional detachment, but I can't get that image of Emma hiding her face in her hands out of my head. Her intuition is right: The klebsiella has been a decisive and brutal blow. It's unlikely that Cristóbal will respond to the treatment. Although I'm still grasping at all possibilities to save him, a part of me is merely observing as his life slips away. It's the same impotence I used to feel when I would hold Soledad in my arms, trying to stop her from sinking deeper into her darkness as her mind steadily departed from reality.

The sun will soon set; there's a red hue in the western sky. My memory winds its way backward until it settles on one summer afternoon when I began to catch glimpses of the impending tragedy. Holed up in my office at home, I heard Soledad going back and forth between the garden and the house. I remember she was barefoot, wearing white trousers and a white blouse, her pruning shears in her hand. I see her small body moving about gracefully. I see her lifting her hand, waving and smiling, then placing the open shears on top of her head, like bunny ears. I wanted to believe that as long as Soledad was still capable of smiling at me like that, with such freshness and openness, it didn't matter what was going on in her head. I remember thinking that as long as appearances could be maintained, our lives could carry on as normal.

That night I awoke with a start. Soledad wasn't in bed. I went downstairs and found the French doors in the living room wide open. I went out into the garden and called to her, quietly at first, then more loudly. I took the path that led to the swimming pool and kept going to the far end of the garden. It was a perfectly clear night. I spotted something dark next to the hedge. It was Soledad, curled up on the branches she had cut that afternoon. I went up to her and saw that her face was covered with drops of dew, the moisture that gathers in shady corners. I started wiping her face.

When she came to, she stared at me. Her lips were twisted, and she looked both puzzled and disoriented. She began to tremble. When she realized what she had done, she looked at me, her eyes dim, and asked me to forgive her. Her words hurt more than if she'd got up and returned to the house without talking to me, more than if she had yelled at me for having woken her from such a sweet sleep. The trees swayed languidly. My eyes had grown used to the darkness, and the garden had an impassive beauty that at that moment I found unbearable.

24 ↗

When I get home from school, I go to Mr. Thomas Bridge's blog. He's still stopping the invaders from landing on the island. He's posted articles that have appeared in newspapers and magazines all over the world. The experts are analyzing the situation; a Canadian mystic claims that the Alacaluf family are part of our human heritage and that by studying their way of life we will learn more about ourselves. Mr. Bridge is standing next to an English ethnologist. They both insist that any intervention would destroy their six-thousand-year-old way of life forever. They send a message to the Chilean authorities and the United Nations, asking them to clear all ships and helicopters from the area. He shows the video he shot of the family that morning. The two children and the adults are sitting on the beach looking at the sea. Mr. Thomas Bridge says that they haven't gone fishing for three days. The presence of the ships terrifies and upsets them. He says they will die of hunger if things continue like this. I'll write again to Mr. Bridge when I get back, but now I have to get my backpack ready for my trip.

Today, I'm going to Uncle Rodrigo and Aunt Corina's house. She was Mama's best friend. "I'll never have another friend like Soledad," she always says, looking very tragic.

I remember that Alma gave me Baby Hippopotamus Meanie's

phone number. All I have to do is dial it. The hardest part is summoning up the courage. I pace back and forth. Yerfa asks me if I'm training for a marathon.

"Hi. This is Tomás, your neighbor."

"Hi. Want to come see my snails?"

"No, I want to ask you a favor. If somebody asks for me, can you tell them I'm with you?"

"Why?"

"It's a secret."

"OK, I'll say you're in the bathroom," he agrees.

"Thanks."

"That's what friends are for," he declares.

I just discovered something that's got nothing to do with Mama, but I think it's important. I record, "*Discovery, addendum: We share lies with friends.*"

I tell Yerfa I'm going to spend the afternoon with my neighbor. She's surprised, but also happy, because she worries about me being alone all the time.

Aunt Corina's house isn't far away. Once, I went there with Yerfa. We took a bus and got off at the stop in front of the shopping mall. I remember the way perfectly and all I do is retrace our steps.

When I'm finally on the sidewalk in front of Aunt Corina's house, I can't believe what I've accomplished. Too bad Lola, or my classmates, or Papa can't see me now. I ring the doorbell, but nobody answers. I wait a minute, then ring again. Aunt Corina never leaves her house; that's what Yerfa says. She also says she never has anything to do, and that's why she's always in a bad mood. I ring again. I sit on the curb and wait. A boy rides by on a bicycle, looks at me, then keeps going. It would have been exciting if he'd ridden into a telephone pole. A few minutes later, I hear some whispering. I stand up and walk along the fence surrounding the house. I see two boys hidden in the bushes, crouching down, and they don't look very friendly at all.

"What are you doing here, you little brat?" one of them snarls at me.

His face is all sweaty, and he's pulling up his trousers. I look through a hole in the fence and see the swimming pool and Aunt Corina floating on a plastic mattress. She's wearing a bikini that shows most of her tits, which, according to Yerfa, aren't actually hers. I can't imagine who she might have stolen them from.

"I know what you're doing." I pretend I'm in a movie so I'm not scared.

"Oh, you do, huh? What might that be?"

"You're masturbating."

"So what?"

"So nothing. And now I'm going inside to see Aunt Corina because I have to talk to her."

A delicious bubble rises up my throat as I say this. The gap in the fence is too narrow for them, but it's big enough for me. I squeeze through and into Aunt Corina's huge, sunny backyard.

When I appear on the other side, she stretches out her neck and lifts her head, like geese do when they're looking for food. I turn round and discover that one of the boys has stuck his head through the hole. Aunt Corina smiles and waves, as if me arriving in her garden through a hole in the fence is the most natural thing in the world.

"Hi, Aunt Corina." I sit down on the edge of the pool and turn on my recorder.

"*Hello, darling.*"

"*I came in that way because nobody answered the door.*"

"*No problem. Anita never hears anything. She's a bit deaf.*" Aunt Corina closes her eyes and stretches out her arms.

"*I brought you a present.*"

123

I take a drawing I made for her out of my backpack. It's of a
man whose body is made of stars.

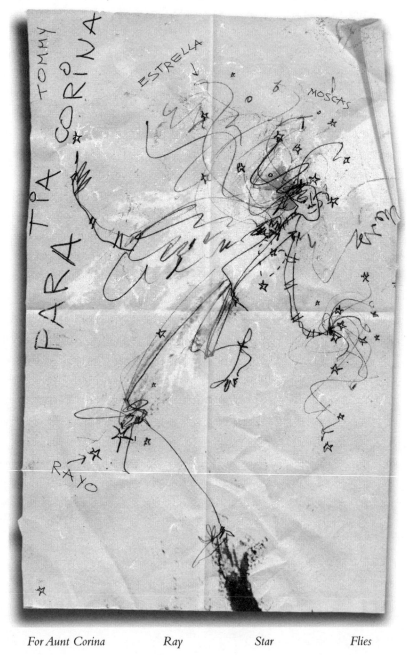

For Aunt Corina   Ray   Star   Flies

I show it to her from the edge of the pool. She looks at it, thanks me, and tells me it's beautiful. I can tell from her smile that she really likes it. I explain that all living beings are made out of stars. She thinks I'm just joking.

"*It's true. Almost all the heavy elements our bodies are made of, like iron, calcium, and carbon, were formed in the heat of the explosion of a star,*" I explain.

Aunt Corina says she had no idea and that she thinks it's wonderful. When we finish talking about stars, I say, "*I want you to tell me about Mama.*"

"*Oh, Soledad. I'll never have another friend like her.*"

"*I already know that, Auntie, but I want to know more.*"

"*Tomás, my dear, will you fill this up for me?*" she asks, handing me a glass. "*The bottle is under my towel. That's a good boy.*"

It's a little bottle with a silver top. It has a really strong smell.

"*Fill it up halfway.*"

I do what she says and I give her the glass. When her mattress gets close to the edge, I see one of her nipples, dark and pointy. Aunt Corina takes a big gulp, then says, "*Ahh.*"

"*Auntie, I want you to talk about my mama,*" I repeat.

It's a good long time before she says anything. First, she smiles; then she looks real serious; then she takes another sip from her glass; then she coughs. While I wait, the garden is making a strange noise. I'd say that silence, when it's been waiting a long time for somebody to break it, starts to crackle.

"*I don't know what your mother saw in me. She was much more intelligent than I am. She'd stop by and pick me up in her car and we'd go places. Not the kinds of places other women like us went. We'd go hang out around the university where she studied art history. Soledad was very sophisticated. We'd sit in a café called Las Terrazas and we'd drink coffee and smoke, and drink coffee and smoke. That's all we'd do, but it made us very happy.*"

She closes her eyes and takes another sip. The sign on her forehead is blank. It probably says what she feels. I watch her dry her eyes. I take off my tennis shoes and put my feet in the water.

"*Those sonsabitches*," she suddenly says.

"*Who, Auntie?*"

I wait. I move my feet around in the water. I look at the bottom of the pool and imagine it is the mouth of the planet and any minute now it's going to swallow up Aunt Corina.

"*Who?*" I repeat a moment later, but she doesn't answer.

I think about the bullies at school and their emails. The sun is going down. The creatures that live in the garden are in their hiding places, waiting for me to leave. I don't want to leave Aunt Corina at their mercy. I think she's fallen asleep, like Grandpa always does.

"*You should get out of the pool—you might catch cold. You want me to call Anita?*"

"*No, no, I'm OK here. Goodbye, my darling*," she says without opening her eyes, waving her hand in the air like a movie star.

"*Bye, Auntie*," I say, and leave the way I came in.

While I'm sitting on the bus, I take the photo of Mama out of my backpack. I look at it carefully and discover a mark on the left side of her face. I try to find *my* mama in the picture of this woman, but I can't. Just like I made up the way she died, I probably made up what she was like, too, because a child can't live without his mother, and if he doesn't have one, he'll invent her. The one I invented hated sports and riding in elevators and airplanes. She liked to spy on people from the window, learn about how ostriches live, use a high-precision watch to calculate the time it takes for a speck of dust to fall to the ground—things like that.

I press my face against the window and take a deep breath. A few stupid tears fall down my cheeks. I wipe one away and another one comes. When I look outside, everything looks sad: the workmen waiting at the bus-stops with their lunch bags, Aunt Corina floating over the mouth of the Earth, Alma talking on her cellphone to a man, the Alacaluf family all alone in the universe, Mr. Thomas Bridge . . . The mark on Mama's face has spread to my body and then covered the street and the whole world. By the time I get to my stop, the bus is almost empty.

Lola and I eat dinner with Yerfa in the kitchen and watch a show on TV. Papa and Alma will be back late. Yerfa's cellphone rings in her pocket. She answers it and goes into her room. Lola says she saw B.H.M. playing on the street with some snails and I wasn't with him.

"Where were you, you bugger?" she asks.

"Where did you learn such an ugly word?"

"Don't change the subject."

Lola looks at me, waiting for me to answer, but I remain silent, my eyes glued to the television screen.

"So?"

I'd like to tell her I went to Aunt Corina's house alone, that she talked to me like I was a grown-up, and that I saw her cry.

"I'm going to tell Papa you went out without permission."

"Tell him what the hell you like, you bugger. I couldn't care less," I counterattack without looking at her.

Faced with my indifference, Lola starts playing with her mashed potatoes. I look at her out of the corner of my eye. She stabs the pieces of meat with her fork and throws them in the trash can one by one. She looks at me defiantly.

"Now we're even."

"I don't have anything to hide." Even I'm impressed by how cool I am.

"I've got other dirt on you, bugger, so you'd better keep very quiet."

I'd rather not find out what her other dirt is, so I throw my food in the trash, too. I'm not hungry. When Yerfa comes back to the kitchen, we are both watching TV like two little angels. Yerfa is in a hurry to put us to bed; her cellphone hasn't stopped beeping in her pocket.

When I get to my room, I open my email. I'm waiting for Mr. Thomas Bridge's reply. I find another one, same as always.

```
stupid lil jerk peepee asshol go get fukt but u cant
cause your 2 stupid hahaha go strait 2 hell.
```

I imagine a hurricane swirling down from Mars and across the soccer field at school. Their arms and legs get sliced off and are hurled through the air; then they get burned to a crisp by solar flares that fall on what's left of their bodies and they die.

I open Mr. Bridge's blog. He's talking to the camera. He says the family has disappeared into the forest on the islet and hasn't come out. They're running away from the helicopters flying overhead. Mr. Bridge says that they won't survive in the forest. He tells how the Alacalufs were exterminated by the English missionaries. They not only brought diseases the indigenous people had no defenses against, they also tried to make them adapt to their customs. They gave them clothes and tools, like knives and harpoons, and that's how they destroyed their way of life. They no longer needed to go out to sea for hours at a time to get their food, because they could get enough fish for several days with their harpoons. Little by little they abandoned all the activities that gave meaning to their days, they became sedentary, and they started to die off. The existence of this family is inexplicable.

I turn off the computer and get into bed. The darkness collapses on my head and the phosphorescent stars Alma stuck on my ceiling appear. Every time I think about Alma, which is a lot, I remember her coming home with that man. That's why now I try to think about her as little as possible. It's time to leave for the bottom of my bed, where Kájef is waiting for me. The waves are tossing his boat from side to side. Right in the middle of the boat, on a bed of wet sand, is a fire of burning embers. He's clutching his oars. The storm is getting stronger; the boat rises up on a huge wave, then falls, then rises onto the next one, but Kájef doesn't give up. I hear his voice in the distance. He tells me that he's going into the forest to look for the Alacalufs and lead them to another island where nobody will find them.

"Tommy," I hear Lola's voice outside the door, "open up."

"Why?"

"Please."

"What'll you give me?"

"Whatever you want. Yerfa's gone. I went to her room and I've looked for her everywhere."

I open the door. Her teddy-bear pajamas and the stuffed seal she always carries show her for what she really is: an insignificant little girl. The perfect opportunity for revenge has finally come.

"Come in."

Here I am, throwing overboard the best opportunity I've had in a long time to get back at Lola. I'm a total idiot. She sits down on the edge of my bed with her seal. I lie down and turn off my lamp. Lola rocks back and forth.

"Who's the woman in the picture?" she asks in the darkness.

Damn! I forgot to hide Mama's picture. Lola must have seen it before I turned off the light. I don't answer.

"She's beautiful," she says. "She's got a bruise on her face. What happened to her?"

How could I be so stupid? What I thought was just a smudge was really a bruise.

"It's your mama, right?" I don't answer. "I'm cold."

129

"You can get in my bed, if you want," I say.

"You sure you don't mind?"

"I do mind, but you can do it anyway."

She stays where she is without moving.

"Why did Yerfa leave us alone? Maybe it's because of her boyfriend."

"Probably."

"I miss Mama."

"Me too," I admit.

When I think that Alma might be with that man, I feel like screaming.

"They go out a lot, don't they?"

"A lot."

We've never agreed on so many things in one conversation. It seems like she notices that, too, because she decides to get into my bed. She curls up with her seal on her side. Luckily, my bed is pretty wide.

"Yeah, that's my mama. She committed suicide."

When I say those words out loud, I realize how difficult they are to pronounce, as if it is something that wasn't made to be named.

"What does that mean?"

"It means she killed herself, that she decided to leave me alone, that she didn't care what happened to me. That's what it means."

We lie there quietly, both of us curled up on our own side of the bed. Suddenly, I feel something in my arms. It's Lola's seal, and Lola's the one who put it there. It worries me when I realize that my opinion of Lola is going to need some adjustments in the morning.

25 〰

After our encounter at the studio, we've met nowhere except in the apartment Leo rented next to a plaza. I come here every afternoon after work. When he opens the door, he opens his world and stops it for me.

"Hello, my love," he says, and wraps his arms round me.

My love. Infinitely overused words, but I begin to like them all the same, if only because they make everything feel unreal. It doesn't matter if on the other side of the door they cease to be true.

"I wish I knew how to cook so I could prepare a great feast for you, but I'm useless," he confesses without letting go of me. I can feel his breath against my temple.

I take his hand and lead him to the only armchair in the living room. It's a large, uncluttered space. The picture window in front of us looks out onto the plaza, which is full of chestnut trees. From this height we can see their crowns. I put my hand under his shirt and feel his breathing through the movement of his torso.

"I have the same thought, that one day I'll arrive with bags full of ingredients to cook for you, but then I figure it'll be like one of those romantic Hollywood movies and I lose interest." Leo laughs in my ear. The cool afternoon air wafts through the half-open window. "I prefer the food that comes through the telephone. That's what Lola calls it."

Her name carries with it a blast of reality that stuns me. That's how it happens. The sounds of certain words break the dams and sorrow pours in through the cracks. Leo places his index finger on my lips and hugs me. His touch is not at all strange or unfamiliar, but it is exciting. My anxiety vanishes.

After making love, we watch the sky turn from red to gray. We wrap ourselves in a blanket. The city spreads out before us, echoing a constant rumble. It's the time of day everybody is returning home, the time I usually get up and leave.

"I told them I wouldn't be home tonight," I suddenly say, before I have any regrets.

I don't explain anything. I don't share with Leo the lies that have become part of my everyday life.

"This apartment is like a glass house," I say.

"You're right," he agrees. "When I first saw it, I loved it straightaway, this spectacular view and the feeling of being suspended in the air."

Night approaches. The buildings' brightly lit windows float in the dark blue of the evening; Leo points to the golden rectangles and shows me how the inhabitants move back and forth in them like flames.

"Look at me," I tell him.

I want to find that sparkle in his eyes, the one that would shine only for the woman he loves, but I can't. The tiny black snail inside his pupils is hiding in its shell. I laugh.

"What are you laughing about?" he asks as he stretches his arms above his head.

"Once, I heard a friend say that for men, sex could be reduced to a hole and a stick."

"I'd say your friend is slightly limited. For a man, sex is infinite cavities and a stick. A nice pair of legs also helps."

"Leo!" I exclaim, and I place the sole of my foot on his sex.

I gently press down and move back and forth. I feel him returning to life.

I wake up screaming. Beyond the picture window, the lights of the
office buildings are still shining bright, as sharp as the nightmare
from which I want so badly to escape.

"What's wrong?" Leo asks me, alarmed.

The tears well up in my eyes.

"Come here." He pulls me toward him.

"I had a horrible dream."

"Tell it to me. Do you want me to turn on the light?"

"No. It's OK like this." I rest my head on his shoulder. "You
sure you want to hear?"

"Of course."

"I'm at a school that's under construction. It's big and empty.
I'm looking for Lola. I roam through empty hallways shouting her
name. There are metal boxes scattered all over the floor. I hear
mumblings. I open one of the boxes and inside I find a little tiny
woman, asleep and naked. She's talking in her sleep. Her body is
covered with flour. A woman wearing a blue suit appears in the
hallway. She's carrying a plastic bag in her hand. 'Do you know
Lola Montes?' I ask. 'Of course. She left with her mother,' she
answers. 'But *I* am her mother!'" My voice is shaking; I stop.

"You poor thing," Leo says, and kisses me all over my face, as if
I were a little girl.

In the morning, when I open my eyes, Leo is talking on the phone,
pacing back and forth outside on the terrace. He's wearing black
trousers and a white shirt. The green of the plaza is intense under
the morning light. He's moving his hands and smiling, like he

133

smiles at me, and his voice rises and falls. He doesn't look over at the bed where I'm lying watching him. I feel like an intruder. I'm overwhelmed with loneliness. It's that wall I erect every single day, behind which only Leo and I exist. Right now he's on the other side, over there where he's animated, talking on the phone, where conversations are held and agreements made, where new relationships are formed and end. He stops, scratches his head, then starts to laugh. I guess the experience of pleasure goes hand in hand with the awareness that it's temporary; in any case, I can't stand the idea that Leo exists beyond these four walls, that his life, after our encounters, carries on without me. A lover's jealousy, the same story lived and retold thousands of times. Leo returns.

"Good morning, my love." He sits on the edge of the bed and leans over me. "It's a joy to see you in the morning with your hair all messed up."

He gently grabs one of my breasts. I like the way he claims my body; he makes me feel that it's here to be touched, and that he can't resist doing so.

"I have a surprise for you," he announces.

A few minutes later, he brings in a breakfast tray.

"Just like in a Hollywood movie," he says.

Coffee, orange juice, toast, and fruit, watching the city lazily from afar, just like in the movies.

26 ↗

I can't sleep. Instead of tossing and turning in bed, I copy my recordings onto the computer and edit them the way Alma showed me. When I listen to the ones from the wedding, I discover that Mama was in a hospital called Aguas Claras. I create a file called "Ten Discoveries About Mama". Then, since I still can't fall asleep, I go to Mr. Bridge's blog. The family is still hiding in the forest. Some journalists have landed on the island. It's highly unlikely that the family will return to the beach. Mr. Bridge says that they haven't come out to fish for six days and he fears for their lives. I send him another email:

```
Dear Mr. Thomas Bridge,
    Please do something. You are the only person who
can help them.
    Tomás
```

When I get home from school, I look for the address of Aguas Claras in the telephone book and then find the street on MapQuest. It's not very far away and I'm sure I can make it there on my bicycle. I haven't used it very much. I only ride with Papa, and I always want to keep riding more. I call B.H.M. again. This time, he beats me to it.

135

"You've got another problem needs solving?" he asks, acting like a spy.

"Precisely, B.H.M.," I say without thinking. Now I'm really in trouble.

"Why do you call me 'B.H.M.'?"

I can't tell him about Baby Hippopotamus Meanie. Then I remember a book of Papa's in his library, something about the hollow man.

"It stands for 'Best Hollow Man'."

"What's that?"

"Don't you know? It's a man who has a hole right above his heart that makes him invincible."

"Am I one of them?"

"Of course you are!"

"OK. I'll cover for you. No problem. Just let me know when you get back."

"Understood."

I've packed my backpack with the map I printed with directions to Aguas Claras, a sweater for the afternoon, a bottle of orange juice, my voice recorder, and the picture of Mama. While I'm doing these things, I'm also watching myself from the outside. That kid who's about to leave on an adventure doesn't seem so despicable after all. Kájef says that for something to be an adventure, it doesn't necessarily have to be a battle against terrorists or aliens, or anything like that; all you have to do is be on a quest, even if you don't really know what you're looking for.

Before I leave, I check my email again. I'm expecting a reply from Mr. Thomas Bridge. I can't believe it! There it is:

Dear colleague,
Thank you so much for your support. I am confident that things will turn out fine in the end. As soon as

I get home, I will send you my address, as I would
love to see that picture you promised me.

   Yours sincerely,

   Thomas

   P.S. We have the same name—I'm sure that's a good
sign.

It's definitely a good omen to receive his reply right before I
embark on my adventure. I go through the kitchen and tell Yerfa
I'll be next door. She's talking on her cellphone and nods to me
that it's OK. I wave goodbye and leave. It's 4:32 p.m.

When I ride my bicycle, the wind blows against my face and arms
like a million feathers. *Don't run, don't jump, don't get excited, don't
move.* I go down a deserted street. The pavement's smooth surface
offers no resistance, like water. *Take your watch, check your heart rate,
don't go too far away.* I go full speed downhill. *You can't do that—be
careful!* I'm free, I tell myself. Even though I've heard the word
"freedom" many times, I don't really know what it means. I know
that normal children think they're invincible, so could this be how
they feel?

   Now that I'm far away from my neighborhood, the houses are
smaller, the front yards less well cared for, and there are fewer trees
along the sidewalk. My heart starts beating very quickly. I get off
my bike, take some deep breaths, and imagine I'm in the water,
which always calms down that old man's heart of mine. When it
returns to a normal rate, I get back on the bicycle. A while later, I
have to stop again. I can't pedal anymore. I start to walk.

   At 6:18 p.m. I finally arrive at Aguas Claras Hospital. A three-
story building stands behind an empty parking lot. The blinds are
pulled down over all the windows. I look inside through a crack

137

in the front door. There's a strong burnt smell. Everything is dark; nothing inside is alive. I go round to the back of the building and discover a park. The trees look tired, so do the paths, which are overgrown with weeds. I sit down on a bench under a big tree and take the picture of Mama out of my backpack. When I look at it again, I discover something incredible: She's sitting here, under this same ash tree. This ash tree isn't just any tree; it's nothing less than the world ash tree from Norse mythology Maná told me about. It grows in the center of the cosmos and produces a sap so sweet the bees can turn it into honey. The problem is that underneath it there lives a dragon that feeds on cadavers and eats the tree's roots, trying to destroy it. I put the photograph down on the bench, with Mama's face looking toward the leaves, and I take out my MP3 voice recorder.

"*Third discovery: Like the ash tree, Mama had a dragon wrapped round her roots and no matter how hard she struggled to defeat it, the dragon ended up winning.*"

I don't know where all this is taking me. I don't think I've got very far. Suddenly, everything looks really difficult. In front of the building there's a swimming pool in ruins and a tree with blue flowers. Every once in a while the birds fly up and start screeching. The park is filled with shadows. It's 7:15 p.m. and I should have been home a long time ago.

On my way back to the street, I come across a little shrine. It's weird that I didn't see it before. It's like a miniature white house, very well cared for, with a wooden cross and two plastic vases with yellow flowers. I go up to look at it. I can't believe it! Finally, I've made a real discovery: The little house has Mama's name on it— SOLEDAD BASTIDAS BULYGIN.

I throw my bike down and kneel on the sidewalk to look inside. A shrine like that is used to mark the place where somebody died a violent death. People think their souls stay there; that's why they bring flowers. I close my eyes and try to breathe calmly. Then I look again at the shrine. SOLEDAD BASTIDAS BULYGIN. I poke my head inside. There's a Virgin with a blue dress and blond hair, like Lola's Barbie dolls. She's holding a comet in her hand. Behind the Virgin, hanging from the ceiling, is a big star with six points made out of a dull metal.

"Good evening," somebody says behind me. I look up and find myself face to face with an old man with the eyes of a mosquito.

I stand up. The old man puts down a book he was carrying under his arm, wipes his hand on his trousers, and shakes mine.

"Good evening. I'm Tomás Montes, and Soledad Bastidas is my mother," I blurt out.

"Good evening. I'm Roberto Milowsky. I live across the street." He points to a two-story building. "I'm the one who brings flowers for your mother."

"Did you know her?"

"Just a little. My wife knew her better. She worked as a volunteer at Aguas Claras. Elena was very fond of her. That's why we always bring flowers. So, you are her son. You look very much like her," he observes, the whole time looking at me extremely carefully, as if I am somebody really special.

"Do you know why there's a star in there?"

"It's a Star of David, because your mother was Jewish, like we are."

"How do you know?"

"Because that's just the way it is. When you're Jewish, there's nothing you can do about it," Mr. Milowsky says, smiling.

"So that means I'm Jewish, too?"

"Yes, indeed."

The sun is going down fast. I ask him if I can come back one day and talk to his wife. Mr. Milowsky answers that this would be a little difficult because she is dead.

"So why did you say, 'We always bring her flowers'?"

"Because she lives in me and there are certain things we do together, like for example bringing flowers to your mother."

"Were you the one who hung the Star of David in there?"

"Yes, that was me."

"Mr. Milowsky, would you like me to give you a back scratch?"

"That would be very nice of you."

I climb on a rock and start to scratch him.

"Mr. Milowsky, can I ask you one last question?"

"Go right ahead."

"Did Mama die here?"

Mr. Milowsky nods, yes.

"How did she die? Do you know?"

Mr. Milowsky looks at me without saying a word.

"You're not going to tell me, are you?"

He shakes his head, no.

"It's time for me to go," I say.

"Did you come alone?"

"My house isn't very far away."

"Good. Whenever you want, you can come help me with the flowers for your mother, now that you know where I live."

I say goodbye, get on my bicycle, and pedal down the street.

When I first discovered that my penis was different from my cousins', I asked Papa what that was.

"It's called a glans," he answered.

I said, "It looks like a mushroom, and of all my cousins I'm the only one who has it."

I remember Papa put down the book he was reading and made a face like I was disturbing him. At that time, I still hadn't discovered that adults wear signs on their foreheads, and I thought he would scold me for pulling down my trousers in his office, but what he told me was, "Your mother and I decided to circumcise you for reasons of hygiene. Just so you know, in the United States, they circumcise most boys when they are born." Then, of course, he had to explain to me what the word "circumcise" meant. The kids at school told me that they only do that to Jews. They made fun of me. I explained to them about the kids in the United States, but they didn't believe me. They kept saying I was Jewish, and for a long time instead of calling me by my name, they called me "Kike."

I stop on a corner and record, "*Fourth discovery: According to Mr. Milowsky, Mama was Jewish and so am I. Fifth discovery: Mama died in the street, in front of Aguas Claras.*"

I've always thought that those shrines must be very sad, constantly making you remember someone's death, but Mama's shrine, with her Barbie, her comet, and her Star of David, seems like it's saying, "Come, look at me. Things aren't half bad for me here inside."

The way back is longer. The map doesn't work in the opposite direction. I try to find the points of reference I memorized, but my head is full of ideas that make me confused. Soon it will be dark. I know I have to ride toward the cordillera. We live in the foothills. Going uphill is much more difficult when you're already tired, but I don't have time to measure my heart rate. At one point, I have to stop; I just can't breathe anymore. I throw down the bicycle, bend over, and rest my hands on my knees, staring at the asphalt without seeing it. My heart clenches and I feel pain. I want to hold it in my hand and help it beat like it should. I take a sip of orange juice. It's warm and bitter. It's 9:05 p.m. I keep walking. There are no downhill parts, it's straight up, and none of the streets looks familiar. I have to make such an enormous effort that I feel like just giving up, sitting down on the curb, and waiting for whatever is going to happen to happen. The buildings made of glass and steel are already lit up. Everything seems so far away: my room, my

Hold-Everything Box, Kájef. My ribs ache. I rub my eyes again and again, until they hurt. It's 10:03 p.m. when I finally recognize the neon corner with the gas station. A white moon, like a horrible soccer ball, rises from behind the mountain. What's waiting for me at home is worse than the street. My only hope is that Papa and Alma aren't there. It's a probability that isn't all that remote, if I think about it.

Yerfa opens the door and throws herself on me, hugging me tight. "Tommy! Tommy!"

I push her away. I don't like to be touched like that, or for anyone to cry in my neck. Not even Yerfa.

"Do you have any idea how worried I was about you? Do you?"

"Sorry. I didn't mean it."

Lola appears from the hallway in her pajamas carrying her seal. She smiles at me. Yerfa keeps shouting. I smile back at Lola.

"And Papa?"

"Luckily, he hasn't arrived. Alma hasn't, either. If they were here, you would be in big trouble, and so would I. They would have thrown me out, and it would have been your fault."

"OK," I say. "So we won't say anything."

"Nothing about anything," she says, and moves her hand back and forth like she's wiping a mirror.

27⧗

To evade: to take refuge in escape or avoidance. *To elude*: to avoid adroitly, especially an anticipated difficulty. To run away. To escape.

That's what I do when I start up the engines, press down on the accelerator, and a few minutes later lift the nose of the airplane off the ground. The art of flying disguises the even more complex and subtle art of escape. This escape was, of course, premeditated. Before leaving for the hospital this morning, I threw my flight jacket and the other things I always take along on short trips into the trunk of my car. And here I am, soaring above the coastline, looking for the exact word for the color of that strip of sand, or the exact distance between a freight ship and the shore. Subtleties of evasion. About thirty miles away, a host of clouds approaches from the sea. Or I could say that I'm still in shock, that this is how I hope to pull myself together, gain some perspective on what's just happened. That would also be true.

Cristóbal is dead. I can still see Emma, her hands clutching the metal bars of his bed, her eyes glued to the monitor, waiting for me to say something. It was as if I was standing on the outside watching the scene, like so many other moments of my life, always convinced that reason is the only possible way out.

"He's dead, isn't he?" she asked without taking her eyes off the monitor.

Tragedy is always a possibility when you straddle this razor edge between life and death as I do in my work. The very first day you decide to enter an operating room and saw into a human being's thorax, you begin to construct a whole mechanism of defenses. You have to be extremely meticulous about placing yourself beyond the realm of guilt, suffering, and, along the way, emotions.

Where is God in all this? Ever since I was a child I've believed that if I kept Him in my heart, everything would turn out all right. I've tried to act prudently, scrupulously, and with kindness, but it doesn't seem to matter. Cristóbal is dead. Soledad is dead. And I'm so far away. I try to pray, but the words sound like gibberish and they're shrouded in darkness and they disgust me. God cannot possibly both be omniscient and destroy people like them. This contradiction has been chipping away at my faith for a long time.

Protected by thick armor, I feel like I've been trudging along a frozen surface for ages, and those cracks in the ice that appeared here and there, and that I've been avoiding so skillfully, are nothing but life itself.

Certain images keep surging up from that depth and shaking me to the core. It would happen suddenly. Soledad would simply stop whatever she was doing—looking for a number in her address book, tidying her desk, changing Tommy's clothes—and just fix her glassy stare at some spot on the wall, as if she had been taken over by an unrelenting force inside her. Her eyes were blank, dark, and impenetrable.

This kind of episode became more and more frequent until one Monday morning I got a call from the landlord of the space Soledad had rented for the gallery. She hadn't paid the rent in three months. I dropped by that afternoon to see what was going on. I had been there with Soledad when she'd first started the project. The access was blocked, but I could see through the windows into the large empty space; it was exactly as it had been that first time I saw it. All those meetings Soledad had been going to in the mornings, with the architect, the contractor, all her consultants, and nothing had come of any of it. Or maybe—it was the first time I'd even considered this possibility—none of it had ever taken place.

I decided to follow her. I had to find out where she went every day with our son, whom she was meeting, what she was hiding. The following morning, I parked the car at the corner and waited for her. At around ten, I saw her drive past. I followed her into the neighborhood she grew up in. She stopped in front of the plaza where she used to play as a child and took Tommy out of the car. She sat down on a bench and spent a long time just staring at the ground in front of her, not moving, her knees pressed together with her hands between them. The whole time Tommy was playing at her feet. At one point, he climbed onto the bench and snuggled up to her, and there he remained. It was a cold morning and from my car I could see the clouds from their breath floating in the air. I was afraid Tommy would get hypothermic. I didn't understand how, knowing how fragile he was, she could expose him to the cold like that. I felt an urge to grab my child and get him away from that woman who no longer even resembled the one I'd fallen in love with, but I had to know everything, to the bitter end.

After about an hour, Soledad got into her car and started driving east. She drove recklessly, as if that long period of stillness had suddenly exploded in her head. She parked in front of the gallery space, took Tommy out of his car seat, and covered his face with kisses to wake him up. Here was the Soledad I knew. She moved a couple of boards that were nailed loosely over the door, bent down, and entered. Once inside, she put the boards back in place. I waited a while, then got out of my car and peered in through one of the windows. Soledad was sitting on the floor, her body slumped over; Tommy was curled up on her lap. I banged violently on the window, almost breaking it, but Soledad didn't budge. She was squeezing her eyes shut, as if she were trying to block out the clamor of a bombing raid. I entered the same way she had. I called her name. Tommy started crying. Soledad clutched him to her breast so he couldn't escape. I pulled my son out of her arms. Tommy screeched. Soledad began to scream, kicking and punching me. I grabbed her wrists, but she kept screaming, her mouth wide open and her eyes blank.

I brought them home. Sitting next to me in the car, bent over, Soledad looked like a broken puppet. Suddenly, she started trembling. I wondered if I'd ever have anything to say to her again.

For the next few weeks, Tommy stayed at my father's house, as much to protect him as to help Soledad break the dynamic she had created between them. The psychiatrist explained to me that the pressure of the last few years had built up to the point where it had shattered the very foundations of her sense of self, her identity. At the beginning, Soledad spent her days watching television, her face painfully expressionless. Little by little—and with the help of medication—she started to return to her old self, to our world, to her life. That's why we let our guard down, why Yerfa, who had strict orders not to let her go out alone with Tommy, didn't stop her one day when she said she was "going for a ride".

She drove the car into the side of an underpass. It was three in the afternoon and there was almost no traffic. The only way she could have hit that wall was deliberately. Tommy wasn't in his car seat. We found his coloring pencils on the ground. He must have leaned over to pick them up at the exact moment Soledad rammed the car into the concrete wall. That's what saved his life. She ended up in hospital with several broken bones and cuts all over her face. When she recovered from her injuries, we committed her to a psychiatric hospital. I've never forgiven her for taking Tommy with her.

My airplane shudders. It feels like I'm flying over the choppy surface of the ocean. I've brought with me the ship inside the glass bottle. I hold it up to the light. There are details I never noticed before, like an anchor hanging from its bow. The roar of the engines reverberates in my ears. I squeeze the bottle so hard it breaks. I lift my hand and drops of blood fall on my trousers. I recognize this rush: I've broken something irreparable. I remember Alma's words the day of Miguel's wedding: "Your greatest joy is opening the door to the operating room and seeing those faces looking at you as if you were God, isn't it?" She's right. But what she doesn't know is that those grateful faces help me forget what an angry man I am, how I am full of guilt and pettiness. A pettiness I'm afraid will spill out over everyone else.

When Emma asked me if her son was dead, I pulled her toward me. "You can cry," I said. "I never could."

While Soledad was in the hospital, slipping further away from us, I was building up a thick armor and keeping myself going with one fixed idea: I would not allow myself to succumb to sadness. I would transform all of it into strength and rage. This was my last, and only, certainty. But Emma didn't cry. She stood there, her face buried in my chest. That's how Cristóbal's father found us. He started shouting. Emma pulled away from me and held him by the shoulders. I picked the ship up from Cristóbal's table and left the room.

I suddenly have a view of something I've never seen before. As the sun is just about to drop into the sea, the moon appears between the mountain peaks in front of me: white and immense. At another time, such a sight would have made me think of

147

God's grandeur, but not now. My whole life I've been hoping to experience grace and revelation, but He remains absent, over and over again.

28 〰

Instead of remaining hidden away in a dark and lonely place, my childhood house of water has now become transparent and is floating above the city. Another stolen night. I observe Leo while he sleeps. When his features are at rest, he looks younger, more sincere. The lines on his forehead vanish, as does the shrewd look in his eyes, his energetic movements, and his skepticism. In spite of his apprehensive view of the world, in spite of his history of addiction, Leo exudes an air of satisfaction, as if he's spent his life collecting pleasures. Sometimes I think this is what most powerfully attracts me to him. He opens his eyes and blinks a few times before I come into focus. He smiles. The light shines on his handsome, angular features. Under the sheet, he pulls me toward him.

"Can I ask you something?" I say.

"Depends."

"When I first met you, you'd just come out of rehab; then, two weeks later, you were at it again. Why?"

"What are you talking about?"

"Remember when we met?"

I'm leaning my head on his shoulder. Leo nods.

"You left the party early, and you were determined to stay sober. When we went up to La Pirámide, you did coke. What happened in between?"

"Why do you want to know now?" His muscles tense. "That happened so long ago, Alma. It wasn't the first time I'd relapsed, or the last."

"I want to hear about it. Please."

Leo changes position and I accommodate my body to his.

"My memories of that period are so muddled. It was a miracle you found me sober at that party."

"At La Pirámide, you told me you had another woman and that's why you didn't want to get involved with me," I continue, and bring his hand to my cheek.

"It's amazing how you remember those details. A woman . . . It must have been that yoga or meditation teacher I was with for a while. Yes, that was it. She had this incredible hair, like yours, and her bracelets jingled when she moved her arm."

"Was she pretty?"

"You are infinitely prettier."

"I'm not fishing for compliments."

"I'm just saying . . . She was quite a bit older than me. I think I asked her out the first day I met her. I was shameless back then."

"You still are," I say.

The moon shines between the dark edges of the buildings in the background. The sky shivers and a light dusting of white powder settles on the crowns of the trees.

"Did she know you'd just got out of rehab?"

"Why are you so interested in this?"

"Just curious."

"She had no idea. I never mentioned it to her. I think it was with her that I started drinking and smoking pot again. It didn't last long. One day, she threw me out of her house and I never saw her again."

"That woman was my mother."

"What?" Leo sits up and looks me straight in the eyes.

I speak calmly, like someone telling a dream dreamed long ago. I watch the moon, so awake and wide-eyed, hovering outside our window.

"I saw you that morning. You were sleeping, naked. I stood there looking at both of you for a while, at you and my mother."

"I can't believe it . . ." He squeezes me tightly in his arms. "I can't believe it." He pauses for a minute, as if trying to remember, then mutters, "That woman was your mother."

"Did it bother you that she threw you out of her house? Did it hurt you that she erased you from her life, just like that?"

I know how perverse my question is, and that's why I ask it. Because this whole thing is perverse, but necessary.

Leo remains quiet for a moment, then says, "I'm sorry, Alma, really I am."

"But you had no idea. In fact, she didn't know we knew each other, either. Even now, she doesn't know."

"Alma . . . it's still awful. I'm so sorry." He hugs me, now even more intensely.

"For what?"

"For not having seen you, for having been an alcoholic, drug-addicted bastard, and for not having seen you."

"For having fucked my mother?"

"For having fucked your mother," he repeats seriously, and I start laughing. "Why are you laughing?"

"I got you to talk seriously, I managed to get a peek at what's underneath your ironic veneer. I got you to feel something."

"But I always feel you."

"Not as much as right now," I assert.

"Not as much as right now," he admits.

29 ♐

A huge moon hangs over the house of Baby Hippopotamus
Meanie and observes me menacingly. The ceiling of my room is
a hole that shadows can squeeze through like rats. I turn on the
light. I think about the A-minus I got in English and the B-plus
I got in Spanish and the A-plus I got in drawing last week.
Unfortunately, I also remember the C-minus I got in math. I
pretend they appointed me king of a country called Tommyland,
but F.O.T.N. —Fear of the Night—is bigger and stronger than all
my inventions. Bigger than me. I get up and walk into the hallway.
My body is aching from the bike ride. It won't do me any good
to go into Papa's bedroom. Alma's not there—she's working
all night—and Papa says that I'm too big now for F.O.T.N. I go
down to the first floor and knock on Yerfa's door. She answers
wearing a long, white nightgown with only her feet showing.
Without saying a word we crawl into her bed. Yerfa's belly is soft
and warm, so are her breasts. I look out the window. There's the
moon again.

"The moon followed me all the way here," I inform Yerfa. "In
fact, it follows us everywhere."

She answers with a grunt. I can hear her breathe. Her belly
moves up and down, up and down. When all is said and done, the
full moon isn't that bad. Nights without stars or a moon are even

worse, because darkness comes down from way up high and brings its demons along with it. I fall asleep thinking about this.

Yerfa turns and pushes me out of bed. I'm on the ground with one of her shoes poking into my ribs. The sun is rising. The first blue lights of dawn have defeated the moon. I go back to my room and turn on my computer. I don't understand why they never give up.

```
hehehehehehe u r a stupid eejit and wer gonna
beet the shit out a u unles u giv us 10 bucks.
goddit???????????????????????
```

I feel as angry as ever, but this time I don't have the energy to imagine something horrible happening to them. Sometimes I wonder if I should tell Papa, but he'll just think these things only happen to really stupid and really weak kids.

Luckily, now I have Mr. Bridge. Before visiting him, I copy the recordings of my latest discoveries onto my computer. When I open his blog, it's dawn at the ends of the Earth, just like it is here. The camera is focused on the island of the Alacaluf family. Mr. Thomas Bridge's hoarse voice interrupts the silence. "Good morning," he says, and his red face appears on the screen. He rubs his eyes and smiles at me. You could say we're friends now. I smile back at him. It's too bad he can't see me.

Suddenly, he says, "Huh! Uh-oh! They're finally leaving the forest!"

Now they're all in a canoe. The mother is rowing. They haven't gone far when the canoe stops. I can't make out what they're doing. It looks like they're in a hurry to do something. Mr. Thomas Bridge is wondering the same thing as me. Suddenly, it all becomes clear. I can't believe what I'm seeing. Mr. Bridge can't, either, and he starts shouting in English, "What the fuck! What the fuck!"

First, it's the boy. I see his little silhouette, like mine, climbing onto the edge of the canoe with a stone tied to his ankle and throwing himself into the sea. In less than five seconds the sea gets calm again, as if nothing had happened. It looks like the girl is hugging her grandmother. She lets go and moves to the edge of the canoe. She stops for a moment and then, like her brother, disappears under the water. Her father goes next and, a few minutes later, her mother. The grandmother waits until the water grows calm; she puts out the small fire on the bottom of the canoe with her feet, then jumps in. They've disappeared. The sea, indifferent, has swallowed them up, and now it pretends to be asleep.

Mr. Bridge stands there in silence. He turns off the camera and everything disappears.

"Mr. Thomas Bridge!" I shout at my computer screen. It's black and empty like water. "Mr. Bridge! Mr. Bridge!" I shout again as loud as I can. I stretch out my hand to touch him, but it's no use; Mr. Bridge has sunk into the screen like the Alacalufs into the sea, like Mama in her street.

30⧗

The rabbi is singing the Psalms in Hebrew while each of the men throws three shovelfuls of dirt onto Cristóbal's little coffin. A wrought-iron arch, with a simple Star of David hanging from it, stands at the head of his grave. Emma faces the men and watches. Cristóbal's father has not lost his feverish, clouded expression. A white canopy gives shade to the group of friends and relatives bidding Cristóbal farewell. Some have their eyes closed and are mumbling, very close together, forming an impenetrable wall. An old man with white hair like a lion's mane has begun to pray.

This is the cemetery where Soledad should be buried.

Tommy was two years old when an Argentinean cousin got in touch with her and told her that her grandparents were Jewish. Apparently, her grandfather had arrived in Buenos Aires from the Ukraine and converted to Catholicism so he could found a school for girls, and after that all the children in the family were raised as Catholics. Finding out about her Jewish heritage was a major upheaval for Soledad. It affected her in some intangible way that she could never explain to me, and it became a source of endless questions and exhaustive research. I was just setting up my surgical practice, so it was hard for me to keep track of where she was going with it.

One night, just months before her first alarming symptoms

appeared, we were lying in bed about to fall asleep, and she said, "I had Tommy circumcised today."

I blew my top. I shouted at her that she had no right, that she should have consulted me before doing it.

"I want Tommy to be Jewish, like me," she responded calmly, like someone who had rehearsed their words a thousand times.

"But . . . he is anyway," I argued.

"I want him to always know his origins, to carry it on his body, so that what happened to me won't happen to him."

"But you'll always be around to remind him," I shot back in anger.

Soledad sensed my scorn. My words, in a way, confirmed her worst fears.

"Not if I die," she said with deep sadness.

I hugged her and apologized for my outburst. I told her I wasn't upset that she had circumcised Tommy, but that I would have liked for us to do it together.

"I can't be alone," she said. "I need someone in our family circle to be part of this with me."

Even when I understood how significant this was for her, I was angry that she'd marked my child with an indelible sign. It was the same anger I felt later, when she left me alone with Tommy. I resented her utter lack of awareness of others, her morbid intensity, which ended up killing her.

All of this to explain why I hid the truth from Tommy, about his mother's death and the fraction of Jewish blood he had. And I didn't bury her in this cemetery. That was my revenge for what she'd done to us. Resentment has a vitality and a clarity that grief lacks; that's why I held on to it for so long. But right now I am overwhelmed by a sadness so deep that I feel like crying. Instead of thinking, I should just believe; that's what I tell myself over and over again, but it's no use. God has never before seemed so inhumane. Maybe His greatness resides in the fact that nothing truly human reaches Him, which is why we're condemned to live in pain and sin.

Emma throws a flower on her son's coffin, now covered with dirt. Our eyes meet. She lowers her eyelids, then lifts them, as if waving her hand goodbye. It's time to go home. I want to see Alma, Tommy, Lola. I feel like I've been gone way too long.

31 ↗

I think Papa often keeps quiet because saying something simple to other people sometimes ends up being terribly complicated. At least, that's why I prefer not to talk.

Today at school we read the poems of a poet named Vicente Huidobro.

I've discovered that words can be used to express and understand things that otherwise would be impossible. In one of his poems, Vicente Huidobro says he never stops thinking about the dead, the ones he saw fall. That they've stayed so strongly imprinted on his memory that they keep falling over and over again in front of him. When the language teacher read us that poem, my heart skipped a beat. I never imagined there could be a place, deep down inside our bodies, where we were all the same. Because otherwise, how would it be possible for Mr. Huidobro, who died sixty years ago, to talk about what's going on inside me?

But the most important thing I discovered is that he used words to construct stars, chapels, kaleidoscopes, arrows . . . That's why I've finally decided to do something. I will construct my own Letterbox, where I'll keep all those messages, and all their words will be trapped forever.

TOMMY'S LETTERBOX

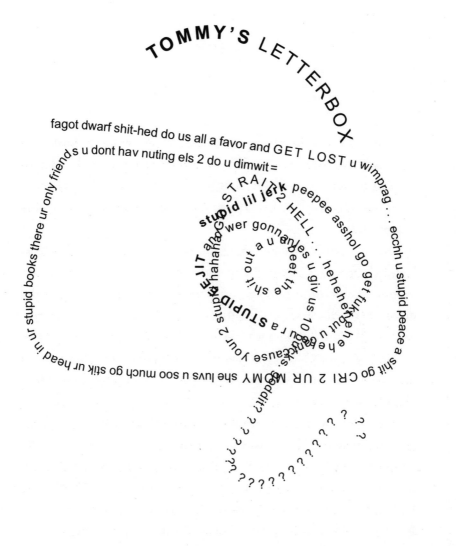

32 〰

I sit on the arm of the sofa, then slip down onto the pillows next to Leo. I watch him reviewing an article he wrote and needs to send in to a newspaper. He wrinkles his brow, then crosses out a few lines. He stretches his arm round my shoulders and pulls me toward him.

"I don't know what I'm going to do when I get back to Bogota," he says. Only one part of his face is smiling.

He tells me I tame his demons and help him connect to the place where the stories come from. I make a face of disbelief and we start to laugh. We both know he's written several novels—without anybody's help—that have brought him acclaim and a decent livelihood. I pull away from him and hug my knees. Leo picks up his papers.

Now that he has mentioned the future, I can't stop it from casting a shadow. A little while ago, when we were naked in bed, he spoke to me about his life, a free but also perversely solitary existence. I wanted to embrace that wide world of his, overflowing with opportunities, but as I watched the intensity in his face, which is never completely happy, I glimpsed the emptiness behind the self-confident way he told his story.

"Do you know that poem by Brodsky, where he speaks of Telemachus?"

"I don't think so."

"It says that when you've been wandering around for a long time, all islands begin to resemble each other." He has a mischievous twinkle in his eye.

Is he trying to tell me that the time has come for him to settle down? I'm not going to solve Leo's riddles. I refuse to make what I do, or don't do, with my life subordinate to what he decides to do with his.

Behind the tall, lighted high-rises, the dark blue of the sky begins to take on an orange hue. Everything is still. Anxiety strikes. Once again, I'm terrified of my ability to break off so easily from the world I share with Lola, Tommy, and Juan.

The fact is that Juan and I can still enjoy each other; all we need is a couple of drinks. The difference with Leo lies in all those details that seem so insubstantial, like how he scratches his head, the timbre of this voice, the weight of his body on mine, the way he possesses me, the explosion of pleasure he gives me.

After a while, passion dies and we begin to live according to agreements, goals, loyalties, and emotions that are just as valid, or maybe more so, than the passion they replace. Until a few weeks ago, I thought that understanding that was a sign of maturity, but now it looks like an elegant but empty box. Maybe Leo's nothing but an obsession, a mirage conjured up by my longing for a different life, a new beginning. In the midst of this great big muddle, the only thing I'm sure of is that I'm incapable of living in a wasteland, alienated from my feelings and the warmth of an intimate, beloved body.

"Alma?" Leo interrupts my thoughts. "You know what I'd like to do?"

"What?"

His eyes are shining with resolve and sincerity.

"I'd like us to go to the movies together. They're showing a Coen brothers movie right nearby. It starts at eight thirty."

He looks at me expectantly, then jams both his hands into his trouser pockets, leaving his thumbs outside; I guess that gesture is supposed to infuse me with enthusiasm.

"You know I can't do that."

It's not the first time Leo has tried to get me out of this apartment, this glass house.

"Why is it you think we'll run into somebody you know, no matter where we go?" he suddenly asks.

"I've told you a thousand times, this city is too small." I get up and walk over to the window, my cheeks burning with rage. Leo doesn't seem to notice.

"You think if we go to the movies on Tuesday evening, we're going to run into somebody? That's really what you think?" he asks in the same lighthearted tone.

I'm determined not to let anger take over. If I start quarreling with Leo the way I do with Juan, this whole thing will lose the little meaning it has.

"I know a lot of people. Anyway, the other day you told me that Maugham says passion needs to be somehow hampered for it to flourish."

"Don't be so clever—he wasn't talking about not being able to go to a movie together. Anyway, what can they accuse you of? Going out with an old friend?"

I'm trying to avoid a confrontation, but Leo keeps provoking me. Maybe he wants to end this before it becomes unbearable for both of us.

"That certainly won't be how they see it," I reply.

"So they'll say you have a lover. So what? Seventy percent of the married women in this country have or once had a lover." He swings round and splays out his hands like a magician.

"I'm not a statistic, Leo, and your numbers are a joke. What, you think they conduct yearly surveys?"

"I don't need official numbers. I know that's the way it is."

"Probably because you've had a go with more than one yourself."

"Don't be such a masochist, Alma. What's the point?" He cracks a half-smile and takes hold of my arm with a weary gesture.

"None of this is the point," I say sharply, and push him away.

I'm using all my strength to control myself: I refuse to let Leo see me cry. I let my gaze skip across the wall and get lost in the treetops.

"I know, Alma. It's just that sometimes it makes me sad that I can't share the things I love with you, like a good movie, or a meal . . . Forgive me. I'm just frustrated." He seems to be in the clutches of so many conflicting feelings. He stretches out his hand and touches my waist, then immediately and, with gentle pressure, he slips his hand under my blouse.

"I'm sorry, really I am. The last thing I want is for us to get into stupid arguments."

"Me too."

Leo wraps his arms round me, and I don't push him away. My joints lose consistency. I am made of a fragile substance that needs to be cared for so it won't disintegrate. He feels me surrender. He kisses me. When we pull apart, we stare at the lights shining outside the glass house.

"It's time for me to go," I say suddenly. "I promised Lola I'd help her with her English homework."

I pick up my purse and my coat. Before leaving, I tell him that I have a meeting at Tommy's school tomorrow afternoon and I won't be able to come.

"That's fine."

"Are you giving me permission?"

"No. I'm telling myself that it's fine that you go, that nothing bad is going to happen to me if I don't see you."

I look away before he does and say, "Nothing bad is going to happen to you, Leo, I guarantee."

33 ✗

During recess, a sixth-grade boy with a pointy head and eyes set far apart like a sheep's asked me about my stag beetle. I opened the little box and let him touch it. Its surface is smooth and shiny, and the boy kept saying it was plastic. I closed the box and promised myself I'd never open it again.

A few minutes before the bell rang, I saw the science teacher in the hall. I often talk to him about the science programs I watch on TV. This time I asked him, "Mr. Berley, is it true that if a little piece of sun the size of the head of a pin falls on the Earth, it can burn all the people within a two-hundred-and-fifty-mile radius to ashes?"

Mr. Berley answered that instead of thinking up atrocities, I should think up things that would be good for humanity. I explained that when I find out about something, I can't pretend it doesn't exist and that this is called "raising my consciousness." He looked at me with his eyes the color of sunflowers and said I was quite philosophical. I liked him saying that. Since he's an old man, I offered to give him a back scratch, but he thanked me and said, "Let's leave it for another day."

I put my box with the beetle in my backpack and walk to the library. Today is Friday. Three hours of P.E., time to do some research on Google. I pass a couple of classmates in the hallway.

They look at me as if they're about to say something, but they just laugh and keep walking. Their stare penetrates my body and stays wiggling around inside me like a bunch of worms.

When I get to the library, I type, "Arnold Bulygin Jewish." I find a letter in a newspaper with the following title "The Truth About Arnold Bulygin."

When I read in the newspapers that it was the twentieth anniversary of the death of Arnold Bulygin, I thought that enough time had passed for the truth to be told. I knew him when I was a little girl, in the Once neighborhood of Buenos Aires, where we both used to live. My parents had a shop where we made Shabbat candles, and every Friday Arnold would come to buy them for his family, and he would often engage in long conversations with my brother, Miguel. Arnold was a very serious young man who dreamed of becoming a great educator. My brother and I both looked up to him.

One day, his family sold their house in Once and they disappeared. Years later, we heard about the prestigious girls' school the Bulygin family had founded in Belgrano, one of the most elegant neighborhoods in Buenos Aires. But what really surprised us was that the school was called St. Ann's. We didn't understand what had happened. We Jews could emigrate to the ends of the earth, go from being lawyers to chandlers, from Ukrainians to Argentineans. Nothing was definitive, except that we would always continue to be Jews. Arnold Bulygin—that handsome and enterprising young man—married an American Jew and founded a select Catholic school. They say he was happy. I hope so. If he had founded a Jewish school, he wouldn't have become so rich, and he never would have been able to be part of high society as he was and as his descendants are today.

My brother ran into Arnold a few years ago, soon before he died, and he asked him if he remembered the time they spent together in the Once neighborhood. They were both old men. Arnold looked at him, confused, and told him he was mistaken, that he had never lived in that neighborhood. This is the story of Arnold Bulygin. That's what truth does; it rises up from the depths and alters the orderly surface of things. I hope one of his descendants, who has perhaps lost track of his roots, will read this and understand some aspect of his own character, and things that had been incomprehensible will finally make sense.

Sarah Ravskosky

I have the feeling Sarah Ravskosky is talking to me. I am a descendant of Arnold Bulygin; there are lots of things I don't know about and lots more that I can't understand. I record what she said about truth so I can think about it later. "*Discovery, addendum: Truth rises up from the depths and alters the orderly surface of things. Sixth discovery: Mama's grandfather, my great-grandfather, hid the fact that he was Jewish so he could be accepted in society.*"

"What did you say?" Miss Patricia, the librarian, asks me.

"I'm sorry. Sometimes I talk to myself without realizing it."

"Don't worry—it happens to everybody."

Something huge and ugly lights up in my head. I have to get home quickly. The rest of the day in class is a blank. Not exactly, because I fill a page in my math notebook with the following sentence:

Mama and I are Jewish

In the end, it doesn't seem so strange. Something new and powerful unites me with Mama.

When I get home, I lock myself in my room. A while later, I find what I was looking for. It's a conversation I recorded a while ago, when Alma and Papa were still talking. After listening to it, I record, "*Discovery, addendum: This is what Alma told Papa—when she met Grandpa the first time, he asked her if she was Jewish. She said she wasn't and Grandpa was very pleased.*"

My classmates told me that Jews get their penises cut when they're born, to mark them. They also told me that Jews are selfish and all of them are shopkeepers. Since I'm circumcised, they call me "kike," and when they ask me for money in their emails, I have no choice, I've got to give it to them. I record, "*Seventh discovery: I think my grandpa, like my classmates, doesn't like Jews.*"

I copy my recordings from the last few days onto my computer and go over to B.H.M.'s house. We call a taxi and then he talks to Yerfa. He explains that we want to watch the new episode of *Avatar* on TV and that I'm going to stay with him till late. When the taxi shows up in front of the house, we give each other high-fives like the cool kids. I have the feeling he's as happy to slap hands with someone as I am.

When Mr. Milowsky opens the door to his house, I ask him, "Mr. Milowsky, would you like me to scratch your back?"

"I would be delighted," he says with a friendly smile.

"I also brought you a present. It's a kaleido-scope. I made it."

"Now that's even better."

I show it to him.

Mr. Milowsky looks through the hole and probably sees a halo of light, because the kaleidoscopes I make aren't for real. He also takes a good long look at the drawing; he turns it round, looks at it every which way, as if it was an object that fell from outer space. He says it looks interesting, and he puts in on a shelf next to his books. He has a lot of pictures and books in his house. The books don't just fill the shelves that cover all the walls; they're also piled up on the ground in towers that look like they're about to fall over. The only furniture he has is a dining-room table, an armchair, and a standing lamp, which is turned on. The windows are little and let in just a tiny bit of light.

As if he were reading my thoughts, Mr. Milowsky says, "I know, I've got too many books, and that's why there's barely any furniture, to make room for them."

"Have you read them all?"

"Almost all. I've got a few left to go, but my vision is getting worse."

There are also many photos of his wife. She's got big ears and a smile that makes you want to keep on looking at her. I'm not going to ask him if he loved her, because it's so obvious.

"You've arrived just in time," Mr. Milowsky says.

"For what?"

"It's seven twenty—time to light the Shabbat candles. Eighteen minutes exactly before sunset. A woman is supposed to do it, but there are no women left in this house, and lighting them makes me feel close to Elena. I'm sure God doesn't mind."

Mr. Milowsky lights two candles, stretches his arms out wide, makes three circles round the candles with his hands, and says,

בָּרוּךְ אַתָּה יְיָ אֱלֹהֵינוּ מֶלֶךְ הָעוֹלָם
אֲשֶׁר קִדְּשָׁנוּ בְּמִצְוֹתָיו וְצִוָּנוּ
לְהַדְלִיק נֵר שֶׁל שַׁבָּת: (אָמֵן)

"What I said was, 'Blessed are you, Lord, our God, sovereign of the universe, who has sanctified us with His commandments and commanded us to light the lights of Shabbat.' *Shabbat Shalom*, Tomás Montes."

"*Shabbat Shalom*, Mr. Milowsky," I repeat.

"Very well done," Mr. Milowsky says, then hugs me and gives me a kiss on the cheek. A little bit of sadness is slipping out of me.

"How did you like it?"

I nod because it's hard for me to talk with the sadness dripping out my nose.

"Your mother loved to light Shabbat candles."

"What else did she love?"

"According to Elena, she loved to swim in the swimming pool. She'd dive down to the bottom and swim from one end to the other without taking a breath."

"I like to do that, too," I whisper.

I hear a siren far away. I imagine they're going to get someone who's about to die or someone who's going to donate their heart. I haven't turned on my recorder, and I don't want to. Recording this moment would take me far away from it, and I want to dive into it, like water.

"Mr. Milowsky," I get the courage to say a few minutes later.

"What is it?"

"Did my mama kill herself because she was Jewish?"

"What makes you think that? Anyway, how do you know your mother committed suicide?"

"I heard someone say so."

"Someone you trust?"

"I don't know."

"So maybe you're not so sure about what you heard."

"I know you aren't going to tell me that my mother committed suicide, and I understand, because it's really hard to say something like that to a twelve-year-old kid, so I suggest you just tell me if it upset Mama that she was Jewish."

"For a twelve-year-old, you are very perspicacious."

"What does 'perspicacious' mean?"

"Smart."

"So?"

"I didn't know your mother well enough to say. I know she talked at length with Elena about the history of the Jewish people, about our customs and rituals. I'm sure your mother wasn't upset about being Jewish, quite the opposite. What I do think is that her interest came late. I mean, once she was already a grown woman."

I think about the family of Alacalufs who escaped from the world into the depth of the sea. We both get quiet. Me, because suddenly I feel really tired; Mr. Milowsky, I don't know why. The sign on his forehead is written in the language of Shabbat. The noise from outside sneaks in through the little windows: a radio playing, someone hammering, a dog barking. The sounds float around the living room and bring me closer to Mr. Milowsky and everything around me.

"Tomás," Mr. Milowsky says. I lift my eyes and look at him. "You still haven't scratched my back."

On my way home, I wonder again what could have made Mama so unhappy that she forgot to count to ten, and I think that I'll never know for absolute sure, because, at least for me, it's the things that are invisible that hurt most of all. When I get home, I record, "*Eighth discovery: My and my mama's element is water.*"

For the first time since I started this search, I've discovered something that, instead of hurting me, tickles my heart.

34 〰

"Would you like to go get a bite to eat?" I ask Juan, looking in at the door of his office.

"You should have told me you were coming home early. Yerfa already made me a sandwich," he answers without moving his eyes from the computer screen.

He looks at me for a second, then back at the light that's reflecting off his face. The room is sunk in evening's peaceful half-light. The shadows stretch across the predominately beige and brown room.

"Are you going to be long?"

"I just need to answer a few emails. I'll be right up."

I approach him, run my hand across his neck, and kiss him on the forehead. I've always admired his composure, but now I'd like to be able to strip off the shrouds his thoughts are wrapped in, leave him exposed and naked.

"I'll go so you can finish."

After putting the kids to bed, telling them stories, and staying with Lola until she falls asleep, I lie down in bed. Juan is still in his office. The light from the streetlamp filters into the bedroom through the leaves of the trees while I wait for him.

Maybe Juan is waiting for me to fall asleep; maybe he can no longer stand the constraints between us, and our lack of intimacy.

Every effort I make to break through to him must just add to his disdain for me. The silence sticks to my body. I wrap the blankets around me and close my eyes. In the darkness, Leo's image comes to me with unusual strength. He called me the morning after our quarrel and I didn't answer the phone. It's been five days and I still haven't heard from him. Our relationship is made of a fickle substance. Exhaustion gets the upper hand. I sink into sleep as if someone were pulling me down by the feet into the depths.

The sound of the door opening awakens me.

"Is that you?" I don't know how much time has passed.

"I'm sorry—it took longer than I expected to answer those emails. Go back to sleep," Juan says, as he goes into the bathroom.

When he lies down on the other side of the bed, I embrace him, climb on top of him, and begin to move.

"What are you doing?" he asks me with half a smile.

"Nothing." I keep moving until I feel his erection under my belly.

He rises up and pins me down on my back, making love to me at first cautiously, then with more fury. I can feel his eagerness, his desire. I get a glimpse of something perverse and twisted under our shells. Juan is looking for something in me that has nothing to do with me, and of course he can't find it. When he finishes, he collapses on his back next to me. He reaches over and turns off the lamp. His being zips up tight again until no part of it, not even the tip, is left showing.

PART TWO

Time, Water, and War

35 ↗

Papa promised me we'd visit Mama's grave before going back to Santiago. Next week is the anniversary of her death, and every year around this time we go to Los Peumos Cemetery, where she's buried.

Alma usually invents games to play on the way, but this time she stares out the window the whole time. Lola, lucky her, has fallen asleep.

"How's Cristóbal Waisbluth?" Alma asks, as she takes a tissue out of the glove compartment to blow her nose.

"Fine," Papa says, and presses down on the gas so hard the tires screech on the road.

I don't understand why Alma talks to him about things that put him in a bad mood. Lola wakes up and vomits on Grandpa's present. Papa stops the car and we all get out.

"Damn!" Papa curses, then runs both his hands through his hair.

Lola looks like she's in shock. Alma helps her change her clothes, then wipes off the back seat with today's newspaper.

After the first course, Lola and my younger cousins go out to the garden. Lola's status is always the same: She's "a little girl," which means she doesn't have any responsibilities. I, on the other hand, don't have a definite role. I'm either "a big boy" or "just a little boy," depending on the circumstances. This time I have to sit at the table with my older cousins until the bitter end, listening to the same conversations my aunts and uncles and grandpa have every time we get together. They talk nonstop; that's how they batten down the hatches against the black silence. I have my recorder on. My cousin Rodrigo kicks me under the table. Now comes the time for complaining about life in a country like this that is so provincial. When the coffee arrives, they begin listing all the cities around the world they've visited and all the ways Santiago can never measure up, which makes them feel a little more miserable than before they began these imaginary trips. Miguel and Julia got back a few days ago from their honeymoon, and they are raving about Paris.

"*Nothing beats Parque Arauco, right here in Santiago,*" Aunt Corina interrupts. Her cheeks are red and swollen like two balloons about to pop. I remember her tits floating in the pool.

"*You've got to be kidding,*" Uncle Rodrigo answers with a smile that doesn't smile.

"*What, doesn't anybody in this family have a sense of humor?*" Aunt Corina shouts.

Uncle Esteban—still chewing—moves his ostrich head up and down. My cousin kicks me again. I look out the window. I see the aviary. Grandpa's biggest bird is a peacock and his smallest is a bee hummingbird. Grandpa usually feeds his birds in the morning. Nobody tells him that there's birdseed all over the lapels of his jacket; it reminds me of the story about the emperor who has no clothes. Every time I try to tell him, someone interrupts me. All I can do is watch the seeds falling onto his plate one by one. The cake arrives and we all sing "Happy Birthday" in English. My cousin kicks me again. Third time. This time I look up at the chandelier with its six golden arms holding up the Napoleonic eagle.

According to Grandpa, it's the same chandelier the emperor had in his office. When my cousin kicks me again, I think that the only way to stop him from continuing to hurt my shins is to get the attention of the adults.

"*Grandpa,*" I say. Everybody turns to look at me. "*I want to wish you a happy birthday.*" Papa and Grandpa look at me approvingly. I've never spoken at the table before. "*I also want to tell you that I have a friend named Sarah. She's Jewish.*"

"*Tommy,*" Papa says in a not very friendly voice.

"*She was born in Buenos Aires and she has a marvelous accent,*" I continue, pronouncing the double "l" in "*maravilloso*" like a "j," the way Argentineans do. "*Her family makes Shabbat candles. Grandpa, do you know what 'Shabbat' is?*"

"*I bet you can tell us what it is,*" Alma says to me.

"*I think now's not the time,*" Grandpa says, and moves his bony fingers, which look all papery.

"*Why, because it's about Jews?*"

Everybody sits quietly and my words keep bouncing around the dining-room walls. I look at Papa for approval, but all I see is disgust. If I didn't know him, I'd think he'd swallowed something that tastes really nasty. He rubs one of his elbows and presses his lips together. Aunt Corina makes a pout like she's about to start crying. I'd like to tell him that both Mama and I are Jewish, but then I'd have to explain everything from the beginning.

"*You are really pushing it, little boy. Watch your step very carefully. Do you hear me?*" Grandpa shouts. He touches his nose with one finger, then looks at Papa as he moves his head from side to side. Nobody says a word. "*Bad-mannered children like you shouldn't interrupt grown-ups.*"

"*I'm sorry,*" I say, but nobody seems to hear me because they're already talking about something else.

Once Grandpa stands up, the rest of us can, too. Before Papa can get to me, I jump out of my chair and run outside. Lola and my cousins have disappeared. I walk to the aviary. The Chinese pheasants are standing right in front of the door to the cage, one next to the other, absolutely still. It looks like they're waiting for someone to open the door to let them out for a walk. And that's just what I do. I open the door very wide and the two Chinese pheasants walk out cautiously, their white necks very stiff. They go a few meters, then stop and look back, without blinking. The golden pheasant comes up to the door, hesitates, then crosses the threshold. A couple of little birds with red breasts fly out. The peacock comes out waving his long, greenish tail. A tiny bird flies against the netting, unable to find its way out. Suddenly, a whole flock takes flight over my head and in a few seconds the cage is empty.

36 〰

Through the living-room window I can see the ocean and its swathe of azure streaked with darker blue.

"It's just that she lives in a different world; she doesn't understand anything that's going on."

María Jesús, Juan's only sister, is talking, as usual spouting banalities in that serious, decorous tone as if she were discussing something transcendent. She reminds me of my mother. While she's talking, her eyes frequently dart over to her boyfriend, sitting in a corner. For the first time in two years she's brought someone to the family home. I've never heard her speak openly about the depression she went through when her husband left her for her best friend. If someone happens to mention something about it, they always do so in a way that seems equivocal, and I can never work out if their tone is paternalistic, ironic, or simply the result of some kind of cowardice. Each time she looks at him, María Jesús's eyes light up and she looks ecstatic, like I do when I look at Leo. I lift my glass of cognac and silently toast her. It's been six days since I've heard from him. It's painful to think about him. What stops me now is not the fear of losing what I have, but rather the conviction that no matter what happens, in the end, I'll have to face reality and all its misery. Taking Tolstoy's words one step further, you could say that all happiness is not only the same, but also imaginary, and that unhappiness, on the other hand, is always unique and quite real.

"It's an eighteen-day treatment. A friend of Paula's lost fifteen pounds. The masseur is from Thailand."

"Are you talking about Paula Vicuña? She's had some awful problems with her youngest son," interrupted one of my sisters-in-law, who always focuses on others' misfortunes.

Leo. One more passion destined to be lived out until it consumes itself. Nothing new under the sun. So many novels and stories written about the same thing: this inability to focus on anything besides the object of one's desire. No matter what I'm thinking about, certain images keep popping up, and when they do, I tremble.

"She paid more than five thousand dollars, but I swear it was worth every penny. You should see how she looks."

Sitting behind a large vase of white lilies, Juan is chatting with his brothers. They're talking about Wimbledon. The sea breeze that wafts in through the open window muffles their words before they reach me—rhythmic, meaningless syllables that heighten my sense of unreality.

My cellphone rings. I take it out of my pocket and look at the screen. It's Leo. I answer without saying a word. I hold the phone to my ear and leave the room, walking out into the garden.

"Are you there?" Leo asks.

The sunlight flooding the lawn is blinding.

"Yes, I'm here, at my father-in-law's house, in the garden, a few feet away from where we ran into each other," I answer when I reach the grove of trees.

I sit down on the grass in the shade of a Peumo tree. Everything is damp and aromatic. The perfectly groomed lawn and the fountains are desperately staid.

"I'm sorry," I hear him say. "I should never have pressured you like that."

"But you're right. This whole thing is ridiculous. We can't even step foot in the street together. I'm scared to death and even though I know it's irrational, I can't help it." I speak quickly. "And also . . ."

"Also what?"

"I can't deal with this, Leo. It's not what I want."

"I've missed you, Alma. I want to see you."

"You weren't listening."

"You haven't missed me like I've missed you. That's why you're talking like that."

I look for the traces of irony in his voice that are so obvious on his face.

"You have no way of knowing that."

"You're right. So you have to agree to what I'm going to propose."

"What are you plotting now?"

"I want us to go away where we can spend a few days together. You can say you need to check some locations with Matías. He told me you were working on something like that."

"You seem to have all the bases covered."

"So, what do you say?"

"I don't know."

I look over at the aviary and see that it's empty.

"Next week, I leave for Bogota. I can't delay my return any longer, and I need to see you."

I feel a trembling in my neck and shoulders.

"It's a goodbye trip, then?"

"If you want to put it like that. Do you see the sea from there?"

I am stunned by his agility at diverting the conversation. I feel like I'm riding on a high-speed train and I can either keep looking out one of the windows or say, "Now!" and jump.

37 ♐

"Yes, I can. Does the place you want to take me to have a sea? . . . No, I haven't said yes. I'm just asking . . . I want to see you, too."

Alma stands up and takes a few steps toward me. I've been listening to her conversation for a while. I'm crouching, hidden behind a tree. She looks at me without talking. I know she's rewinding her words; she doesn't have to go very far back to realize that she's already said too much.

"I've got to go," she says, and puts the cellphone in her trouser pocket. *"You shouldn't listen in on adult conversations, Tommy,"* she shouts at me. *"It's just not OK, and you know it!"*

"It's not my fault you didn't see me. I wasn't hiding. I was right here."

"What were you doing there?" Her voice is calmer now, but I know she's controlling her urge to strangle me.

"Nothing."

"You have your recorder?" Her eyes try to dig into my head, so I look down and start making drawings in the grass with the heel of my shoe.

"As always."

She doesn't ask me if I recorded her conversation. She sits down next to me. I look at her out of the corner of my eye and I see she's scratching her head. I can see the sea through the branches of the trees. We both pretend to be staring at it.

I don't know how much time passes. I don't care. The sooner we go, the better.

Alma gathers up her hair, then rubs her hand along the grass over and over again, as if she's lost something. Then suddenly she says, "*I love you very much, Tommy.*"

She knows her words will be recorded forever.

"*Yeah, Papa says the same thing, that he loves me a lot,*" I add with that mocking tone he sometimes uses when he's angry.

"*You are the person he loves most in the world.*"

"*That's the biggest lie in the world, bigger than the tallest mountain, bigger than the biggest telescope in the world.*"

"*You mean the A.L.M.A. telescope.*" Her face is white now. "*But you're wrong, Tommy, totally wrong. I swear.*"

"*You don't have to swear. I don't believe you anyway,*" I say, and run off.

"*Tommy, Tommy, don't go, please!*" I hear her shouting.

I look behind me as I run toward the house. Alma is standing in the middle of the little hill. I stop to read her hands.

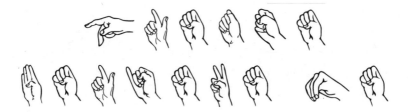

PLEASE BELIEVE ME

I take out my recorder and say, "*That woman is a different Alma and I don't know her.*"

I run another stretch and stop again. My heart is beating very hard. I look up at the tops of the trees and I see one of Grandpa's birds with a red breast. Any minute now somebody is going to

186

realize that the aviary is empty. My cousins are playing on the terrace. I can hear the sound of a flute. The windows of the house shoot out yellow rays. It looks like they are in flames.

38⧗

I look up and, for a second, I think I see one of the rare birds my father brought back from Indonesia. I wonder where Tommy is. He vanished the moment we got up from the table. This time he really crossed the line; I'm going to have to be much stricter with him. Where on earth did he find this Jewish friend? Why did he confront his grandpa like that?

I watch Alma's somewhat clumsy movements as she walks into the garden. She's such a different kind of woman—in all ways—from my brothers' wives, with their sparkling jewelry and those giggles that never become full-fledged laughter because they're afraid it wouldn't be appropriate, giggles that vanish instantly at the mere hint of a disapproving glance.

When I met Alma, I remember thinking that nothing in my life had that kind of originality, that free way of looking at the world. With her by my side, I imagined that I could live closer to some kind of romantic ideal I had always thought impossible. I'm not sure I achieved that, but I do know that one day I found myself married to a woman I loved, I was the father of two children, and my family life, along with my work, completely absorbed me.

"Old Man Zañartu is furious," my brother Rodrigo says.

"He let himself be hoodwinked like a real ass; it was obvious those guys never planned to pay him," Esteban explains.

Papa admonishes them. He doesn't think it right to swear and talk about business in front of women. Baltazar, our old servant, serves another round of liqueurs.

When Alma asked me about Cristóbal on the way here, I lied to her. I wouldn't have been able to stand one of her looks of compassion. I know she's waiting for the chance to prove my fallibility, and she would be right. I can't elude death, nor can I protect the people I care most about.

A group of children run into the living room. Lola's among them, with that mischievous look on her face. I don't see Tommy.

"Grandpa, we have a present for you," one of the children announces, "a play we prepared just for you."

"Wonderful!" Papa exclaims.

He waves his cane proudly in the air and we all file out behind him. This scene brings back the memory of the four of us brothers walking behind my father's firm steps, expectant and fearful of what would happen if we didn't obey him.

The rest of the children are waiting for us on the terrace. They have made several trees out of cardboard and placed them round a shorter one that's been painted yellow and decorated with lights. The children holding the trees look very serious. Lola, behind one of them, makes funny faces at me. One boy plays a flute off-key. Rodriguito steps forward.

"We chose the story about the President of the United States because we know Grandpa really, really likes that country," he announces. He takes some sheets of paper out of his pocket and begins to read. "'George Washington's father was a very rich man, and he brought a cherry tree from Japan, a tree whose flowers and fruits were admired all over the world,'" Rodriguito reads.

Another of my nephews, wearing shorts and a straw hat, walks in and out between the cardboard trees with another boy who has a mustache painted on his face.

"'He planted his one and only cherry tree in front of his window, where he could see it when it bloomed.'"

As I listen, I see Soledad's room at Aguas Claras, in shadows; I search for a solid memory there to grasp hold of, but everything is unfamiliar. Her empty eyes, her empty smile, her empty gestures. We'd grown up together, but in the end had I ever really known her? After her death, the only way to avoid the vicious circle of questions with no answers was to step outside it. I refused to allow Soledad to become an obsession, a sterile regret, but no matter how hard I tried, the memories pursued me until they caught up with me. Soledad kept cropping up in the most unexpected places. I'd see her hurrying down the street, through the window of a restaurant; it was always her and her long, dark hair and the sensation that there was something left undone.

"'As a birthday present, George's father gave him his first ax. Happily, the little boy went outside to try it out.'"

The boy with the shorts starts pretending to cut the trees down with his ax. The children fall, one by one. The moment Alma sits down next to me, Lola is felled. She looks at us from the ground with a heartbroken expression. Alma signs something to Lola, then gathers her hair up into a bun. Her whole body, her being, is emitting some kind of intense energy.

"'Without realizing it, George Washington chopped down his father's beloved cherry tree,'" Rodriguito continues reading.

The yellow tree falls down and the girl holding it bumps into Lola, who is already on the ground.

"Do you remember my tree?" Alma whispers to me. I look at her without answering. "Don't you remember?" she repeats, as if imploring me.

Alma takes my hand. I know exactly what she is talking about—the night she was a tree in a school play and discovered that her mother had a lover—but I don't want to share her memories with her, and I don't want her to invade mine. If she thinks that one small gesture can make up for her recent distance and absence, she's wrong.

I hear myself say, "No, I don't remember," and am surprised. My voice sounds as cold as ice. Alma pulls her hand away and takes hold of her elbows, staring straight in front of her without blinking.

"Have you seen Tommy?" I ask her.

She shakes her head and squeezes her eyes shut.

39 ♐

" 'When he saw that his cherry tree had been chopped down, his father called together all the people who worked on the farm to find out who had done it. While they were all standing there in front of him, shaking in their boots, little George stepped forward and confessed that he was the one who cut it down.' "

It's kind of weird that while they were rehearsing that stupid play, I was doing a deed that wasn't all that different from little George Washington. They have no idea what it's like to do that. Papa and Alma are together, sitting in the front row. I watch them from my hiding place behind the wall that protects the terrace from the wind.

" 'At first, his father got very angry and threatened to punish him, but then he realized that George had been courageous to confess his mistake and he decided to forgive him. For him, the most important thing was to bravely tell the truth.' "

Sarah Ravskosky, in her letter, said that no matter what we do, the truth will always rise to the surface, but the problem is that everybody thinks that their truth is the only truth and that it's the most brilliant truth, and that all the other truths just go in circles round theirs.

If I say that I opened the cage because it made me sad that Grandpa's birds had never flown freely, they'll think I'm lying.

Grandpa will say it is Papa's fault for not being able to control me, and that will be his truth. Alma will think I did it out of spite after listening in on her conversation, and that will be her truth. Papa will think that I do these things and say nonsense at the table because I don't have friends, because I'm always bored and need to call attention to myself, and that will be his truth.

A flock of birds flies low to the ground across the terrace. Everybody looks at them. Another group flies above them, then keeps flying round in circles. They are Grandpa's birds. They seem disoriented. They don't want to leave; they don't want the freedom I gave them. Maybe they have their truth, too.

Grandpa raises his cane-sword into the air, and one of my cousins shouts, "Those are the birds from the aviary!"

I look over at the park and see that the peacock and the pheasants don't want to escape, either. They are walking calmly along the grass, not going anywhere very fast, as if they were still in their cage. Everybody gets up and runs to the aviary. Grandpa is at the front. Behind some bushes, I see Black, one of Grandpa's dogs, with a pheasant in his mouth. When he hears all the fuss, he runs off. One of my aunts screams as if she were the one being killed. Grandpa shouts orders in an incomprehensible language. I leave my hiding place and walk over to the spot where everybody has gathered, in front of the open door of the aviary. Aunt Corina is carrying her shoes in her hand. Alma is the first to see me. She looks at me with her eyes wide open. I wish so badly she was the other Alma so I could hold her hand.

Grandpa enters the empty cage and exclaims, "*This is a disgrace!*"
Papa comes up to me. "*So here you are. Where were you?*"
"*Somebody call Baltazar. I need the birdseed!*" Grandpa shouts, flapping his arms and racing here and there.

One group runs to the house to get Baltazar, while the rest enter the aviary with Grandpa. My cousin Jaime leaves the group and comes toward me. He stares at me and makes a face. I can hardly breathe. He must have seen me open the cage. Would he be able to speak out in front of all these grown-ups and snitch on me? Who is more courageous? Who jumps first? I look at him in silence. Jaime's smile is glued to his face. "You're a goner, you insignificant bug," his eyes say to me.

I take five steps. I am standing in front of Grandpa.

"*Grandpa, I'm the one who opened the cage.*"

Grandpa looks at me the same way he looks at people he doesn't know when they talk to him.

"*Don't speak nonsense, little boy.*" With so many grandchildren, sometimes he forgets our names.

"*It's the truth. I opened the cage.*"

"*How dare you? Are you crazy? This boy is completely crazy!*" he shouts. "*As crazy as his mother!*"

All the grown-ups remain silent.

Grandpa keeps talking. "*Juan, this is your fault. You never raised him to be a decent person. You treat him like he is an imbecile, and where has that got you? This.*" He points with his cane, first at my chest and then at the drops of blood on the ground left there by the dead pheasant. "*You don't have enough strength of character to deal with what life has doled out to you. It's a disgrace. Now leave. Everybody leave—the party's over.*"

Papa, instead of answering back, keeps quiet. The grown-ups, and the children behind them, begin to leave the cage. Some go over to Grandpa to say goodbye, but he rejects them with a flick of his hand, never taking his eyes off the inside of the empty cage. Alma tries to hold my hand, but I don't let her.

I leave and walk to the parking lot. Papa's car is open. I enter and curl up into a little ball. I have that pain in my chest, the one that makes me think someone is shoving a soccer ball in between my ribs. What good does it do to tell the truth? That story about little

George Washington is a farce. I think I've finally understood: People lie because the truth always destroys everything, like the hurricanes in the United States.

I record, "*Ninth discovery: Grandpa is right. Papa is a weak man and I am crazy, like Mama. That's why I can't count to ten before hurting other people.*"

On the way home, Papa focuses all his attention on the road and doesn't talk to us. From time to time he presses his foot down harder on the accelerator. I ride with my window open and let the wind hit me in the face. Papa accelerates aggressively to overtake a truck. Alma asks him to calm down; she says we'll all end up in the cemetery. Papa, without slowing down, shouts at her not to be so hysterical, that nothing is going to happen to us. For a moment I think I should tell him that I need to be alive tomorrow to take my English test, but I hold my tongue.

"Juan, please," Alma begs.

Papa keeps accelerating. Alma does the same as me. She opens the window. I see her face through her hair, which is being blown by the wind, and I realize that she's crying. Once again, it's my fault that Papa and Alma are fighting. If I could do anything to make it so that Alma doesn't leave us, I'll do it right now. Anything at all. Papa is one half of the two people closest to me in the world and that makes me not be able to hate him like I want to. I take the drawing I did for Grandpa from my jacket pocket and throw it out the window.

Grandpa   Hi   I love you   Ship   Cage

Far away, the ocean is big and blue. I imagine that it always keeps Mama company with all its sounds. There's a ship on the horizon. I climb up a ladder I find on the prow and escape.

40 ~

I'm watching the esplanade rush past my eyes. Without letting go of the steering wheel, Leo reaches his right arm across the back of the seat and takes hold of my shoulder.

"Are you OK?" he asks.

His air of satisfaction makes me feel a strange and contradictory mix of emotions. Although I share his delight, I can't help but see how flimsy his feelings are.

"Yes, I'm fine."

I take off my shoes. I see his computer bag and at least a dozen books on the back seat of my car.

"You packed as if we were going to spend a month at the beach," I say.

Leo wrinkles up his nose and lets out an infectious laugh. "Maybe it's because I want to stay with you," he says.

As we leave the smoggy city and approach the coast, the light turns grayish, with yellow splashes of sunshine. A small airplane buzzes overhead and it makes me think of Juan. Leo turns on the CD player. Jazz rhythms fill the car.

In a few days, everything will have disappeared: Leo, all the feelings he provokes in me, our passion, the cabin on the beach waiting for us. After he leaves, I'll be able to recover my sanity and focus on salvaging what is mine. I try to make sure these thoughts prevail over the others, the ones that tell me that when Leo returns to Bogota, I'm going to feel an enormous emptiness. Sometimes this works, especially when I remember happy moments with Juan, when I see Lola and Tommy, when I imagine concrete events like our next vacation—which we've already planned—at a beach in the Caribbean. Leo guesses my thoughts; I can tell by the way he bites his lip, then sighs.

"We're going to have an incredible time, Alma. You'll see. The place is gorgeous. I discovered it by accident a couple of years ago when I went with some friends who were buying a house there," he says.

He looks at me with eyes that seem to be turned more inward than out. I let my gaze linger over his harmonious physique, large hands, strong but slender limbs, slightly crooked nose, and smooth, broad forehead. I place my hand on his naked thigh, slip it under his shorts, then pull it back. Contact with his skin excites and energizes me. I'm not even going to try to resist the spell his physical presence casts over me, nor am I going to probe too far into the deeper truth about his feelings for me. I know I'll never find satisfying answers to any of those questions, but answers are precisely the hook I need, the only hook that anyone considering the possibility of abandoning their life would need. Some minimal certainty, no matter how precarious.

"What question should you never ask a lover?" I ask him.

"Let's see, something like 'What are you willing to give up for me?'" he guesses.

"Exactly!"

"Do you want to ask me that?" A crack has opened up inside him, through which I can glimpse a hesitant and fearful Leo.

"Do *you* want to ask *me*?"

"No, I don't." He recovers his normal expression, ironic and impenetrable.

"I don't, either," I answer quickly.

Leo slows down. A few yards ahead, he pulls over to the side of the road, stops the car, and opens the door. I can't figure out what he's up to.

"Get out," he orders me.

I obey. We are standing facing each other; his hands are on my shoulders. The passing cars whip up the wind, shooting strong blasts at us. My hair blows up between us and over our faces, but I can still see the miniscule spirals staring at me out of the depths of his pupils. We wrap our arms round each other. This is not a promise, I tell myself. It's only one person infiltrating another's dream.

"I want us to live together," he whispers in my ear.

At first, his words surprise me; then I feel a rush of emotion. It's what I've been wanting, what I've been waiting for: a gesture that will carry me over to his shore.

"Repeat what you just said."

"I want us to live together. I want to watch you live your life, do your thing. I want to share my life with you."

"Where?" I ask. I don't know exactly why, perhaps to slip back into the real world, to lend some solidity to a life that's unimaginable for me.

"I don't know. Wherever you want. Here, in Bogota, in Paris, in Barcelona; I couldn't care less," he says, shrugging his shoulders.

"When we quarreled the other day, I thought I'd never see you again."

"Me too."

"So what happened?"

"Those ten days without seeing you became unbearable, Alma." He looks at me the way you look at someone you know very, very well.

"Aren't you afraid that we'll turn a corner and find that all of this has been a horrible mistake?"

"No. I know it isn't."

He looks strangely calm.

"How can you be so sure?"

"Because I love you."

"But you don't have those words in your lexicon," I tell him.

"They're words that no amount of cynicism can destroy, which is lucky because they express exactly what I feel for you."

"What about your freedom?"

"No reason to give that up," he says, then gives me that cheeky smile. I pull away from him.

"You're joking, right?"

"Of course I am. About that. But about everything else I'm dead serious."

He takes me in his arms. I feel slightly dizzy and sense his excitement as well as how uncomfortable a moment like this, so devoid of irony, makes him.

"Did you hear me?" he asks.

"Yes, I heard you."

"So what do you say?"

Smiling, I hug him and hide my face in his shoulder. Despite the wind, I don't feel cold.

"I thought we were saying goodbye," I mumble.

41 ↗

Alma left two days ago. She told Papa she was going away for work, but I know she's at the beach with the man who brought her home in the taxi. Lola is staying with Maná, and Papa is hardly ever home. Since Grandpa's birthday we haven't spoken. He's still angry, and with good reason. Out of forty-five birds, only twenty have returned.

The minute I get home from school I lock myself in my room. Yerfa thinks I'm sick and brings me food. I'm not hungry. I eat only what's absolutely necessary, and I throw the rest down the toilet. When I hear Yerfa going down the stairs, I stick my head under my blankets and go to meet Kájef. We ride through the rough surf in his canoe and stop in the middle of the ocean. The dark sky has a strange glow, as if it were being lit up by a gigantic spotlight. Kájef stands and stretches out his arms. I smile. He looks big and strong, and if he wasn't my friend, I'd think he was a god.

"You can do it, too," he tells me.

I stand up next to him and glide with my arms spread wide open; I hold my breath, but I'm not afraid. The wind strokes me and whispers in my ear. Suddenly, the canoe shakes. I hold on to the sides, but our boat turns over and we both fall in. Kájef disappears under the sea. I'm floating. I feel like I've lived this before. But when? *When?* I curl up into a tiny ball and the memory gets thicker. I hear a loud noise, then a voice talking to me. I try to hold on to it with my hands, but it's going away. I squeeze my fists, but I can't. The thread of my memory breaks; the memory sinks into the dark waters in the depths of the ocean, along with Kájef. I panic. My teeth are chattering. I want to shout, but I know it's useless. I throw off the blanket and jump out of bed. It's dark outside.

Papa knocks on my door when he gets home from the hospital. He scolds me for locking it. Before I open it, I turn on my recorder and hide it behind some books. We sit on my bed. He sits with his legs spread a little apart and his elbows resting on his knees, and I'm next to him with my knees pressed together and my hands on top of them. We both look out the window. He is quiet and I wait. He looks tired. Suddenly, he starts talking.

"*Look, Tommy, I know it's difficult to not be able to do all the things other kids do. It's difficult to be different . . . Maybe I shouldn't say this, but I think you are a big boy now and you should know. It hasn't been easy for me, either. And you know why? Because I love you very much, and everything that happens to you affects me as if it were happening to me. Do you understand?*"

I nod.

"*So when you do something foolish, like letting Grandpa's birds out of their cage, it affects me doubly, because I feel responsible for you. Before doing something like that, please try to think about your papa. Think about the harm you do me, and then maybe you won't feel like doing it anymore. Do you think you can do that?*"

I nod again and change positions because my legs start to hurt from pressing them together so tightly.

"*Yerfa told me that you still have your imaginary friend. Tommy, I've told you a thousand times that it's not good for you. There's nothing wrong with using your imagination, but not when the things you imagine become more important than reality. I know it's fun to make up your own games, live in your own world, but reality is what nourishes you; it's where you can relate to others ... Can you imagine what would happen if we all lived in our own imaginary worlds?"*

I bet Papa wouldn't like to know that for a long time I followed the kids in my class around like a shadow. I didn't care if they didn't talk to me, because I wouldn't have known what to say anyway. Then the messages started. In first grade they admitted they'd only let me follow them because they felt sorry for me. Then I stopped trying. I didn't need them anymore.

Papa doesn't raise his voice. He speaks calmly, enunciating each syllable. He knows how to control himself. I've learned how, too. Papa is embarrassed by me; he's ashamed of my body, that I don't play soccer, that I'm afraid of closed spaces, that I do things he thinks are stupid, but he should understand that what I do is who I am, and *that* is something I can't change. I'm not pretending to be a philosopher, like Mr. Berley said; it's just the way things are. And that is always with me, everywhere I am, and for me to get rid of it, I'd have to take myself out of me.

Before leaving, he pats my head and says, *"Agreed, champion?"*

"Agreed."

I've never told him that I hate that word "champion." Champion of what? It's like he's talking to some other child, like he doesn't see me.

I have to go to sleep, but the memory of Kájef's body disappearing into the ocean keeps returning. I take the picture of Mama out of my Hold-Everything Box. Her face is divided in two: on one side, the bruise, and on the other, a light. It must be the reflection of the piece of paper she's holding in her hand. It seems like the good things and the bad things are in her face both at the same time. After looking at it for a long while, I discover something I've never seen before. What Mama is holding in her hands is a drawing by a child, and I'm the only one who could have drawn it. Now I can see it so clearly! On the side of her face that's lit up is me. My heart starts to beat wildly. I close my eyes. The image of Mama that's always seemed so unfamiliar finds its way through the passageways inside me, until it reaches a hidden chamber, and that's where the real memories are. That space is warm and doesn't have any images. I don't need any proof. It's Mama's hugs. I sink down into her, like I sink in the pool. Her warmth surrounds me and carries me away.

Outside, the night is still. I take a big, deep breath of air and try to calm down my heart. I look again at the glow on Mama's face and I hear a murmur running up and down my body. Suddenly, everything makes sense in my head.

I record, "*Tenth discovery: Mama knew that that was what made me be who I am, and it was that that she loved about me. There was nobody else in the whole world who Mama loved as much as me, there's nobody in the world who loves me like she loved me, and there's nothing in the whole universe I love more than my mama.*"

I go back to bed. I hold on tight to my pillow and sink into sleep. I go slowly down the elevator to the bottom of the sea. There's total silence, but I'm not afraid. It's almost dawn when Yerfa knocks on my door to wake me up. I upload my latest recordings onto my computer, then pack my backpack. I need to take a change of clothes. And money. I've saved enough in the last few months. Also a jacket and a wool hat to cover my ears. I pack my MP3 player and voice recorder, a Swiss Army knife Papa gave me for my birthday, and the photo of Mama.

42 〰

I wake early and curl up tight against Leo's body. Lying like that, his face buried in the sheets, he reminds me of a boy halfway to manhood. Yesterday afternoon, after greeting Leo with exaggerated enthusiasm, the landlady asked him about Inés. Leo must have made her a sign, which I missed, that dissuaded her from insisting. I hadn't even considered the possibility that I wasn't the first woman Leo has brought to this cabin, and having my face rubbed in it was quite a blow. The minute we entered our room, I told him I wanted to move the bed, then the table, the armchair, and even the oval mirror. The emotions I'd felt after his proposal turned to anger, and then disappointment. How could I have possibly considered, just moments before, living with a man who's never made a commitment to anybody but himself, and, even worse, who's proud of it? Then immediately I understood that neither Leo nor I had found solid ground, that our feelings for each other were precarious. They must be if a question from a stranger can hurl me into such a downward spiral, into such destructive conjectures. When we'd finished rearranging the furniture, we lay down on the bed and made love.

The bed is now next to the door, and the air that filters in through the gap underneath makes my nose cold. I get up carefully, trying not to wake Leo. I pull a sweater on over my pajamas and slip on my tennis shoes. I promised Lola I'd call her before she left for school. She's at my mother's house. Even though they enjoy spending time together, I don't usually leave her there. My mother's lack of common sense sometimes reaches worrisome proportions. But this time I simply couldn't leave both children with Juan. Or maybe it was a defining act, a way of beginning to separate the waters.

It's cold outside. The silvery ocean, blanketed in a layer of fog, spreads out in front of me. On the deserted beach there's a white sign with red lettering: NO SWIMMING ALLOWED.

The wind pierces my clothes. I get into my car and dial Maná's number. Lola answers; she must have been waiting next to the phone.

"Mama, where are you?"

"At a cold, cold beach."

"Maná says she'll pick me up at school and take me to a farm where there are animals."

Leo pokes his head out the door, a blanket over his shoulders. He looks toward the beach, trying to find me. He holds his elbows and jumps around. I knock on the windshield so he'll see me.

"That sounds fantastic, but don't forget to do your homework," I tell Lola.

I feel tenderness when I look at Leo, so defenseless against the cold and maybe against the idea that I'm having a moment of regret.

He walks a few feet toward the beach. Even like that, with the blanket over his shoulders, I like the way he walks, the way he pauses, indolent yet energetic, between each step.

"You're such a pain, Mama. Can't you ever just relax a little?"

"It's just that I'm a mother, Lola, and that never goes away. I love you, darling. Be good."

"Yes, Mama," Lola agrees, and then breaks out laughing, because

206

we both know that her deferential "Yes, Mama" means exactly the opposite.

Leo turns round and sees me. He gestures to me to come to him. I jump out of the car. His morning smile enchants me. I give him a hug and suggest we go inside to eat the delicious breakfast I'm planning to prepare for us.

43 ♐

I watch everything pass by through the window of the bus: mountains, fields, wood huts, bare trees, leafy trees, billboards advertising paradise, traffic signs, two kids on bicycles, six cows, one dog, poles and more poles. I start counting them, but they go by too quickly and I get dizzy. I look at the sky and think it's a very long gray ribbon, but since there's nothing to count in the sky, I begin to be afraid and feel like going back home. Then I remember why I'm here.

I lean back in my seat and listen on my MP3 player to the rock opera *Tommy*, which Alma gave me. At the sound of the first chords, I already feel better. We drive through a sleepy town. I think about the people in their houses, whom I'll never meet. I sing along softly.

It was easy to get to the station. When the bus dropped me off in front of the school, I waited for it to disappear, turned round, and walked to the stop in front of the plaza. A few days before, I'd seen a bus standing there that was going to the station. When I got there, the first thing I did was go into the restroom, take off my uniform, put it in my backpack, and pull on a pair of jeans. That way, nobody will realize I've escaped from school.

But now that I'm in Los Peumos, I'm lost. This is a part of town I've never been to. I suspect I'm in Los Altos, where Baltazar's family lives. Some of the passengers get off quickly; others wait next to the bus for their bags, saying hi to the people who've come to pick them up. A group of children hug a woman with white hair and a long, gray cape. Her face is full of wrinkles, which crinkle up when she smiles, like an accordion. The children's voices echo off the sidewalk. I stand there, without moving, my backpack on the ground. The passengers walk away, one by one, their heads burrowing down into their coats, like turtles. The woman with the accordion smile is still standing in front of the bus. Suddenly, she looks at me and smiles. Her wrinkles smile with her. Her gaze is so deep and so unexpected it makes me embarrassed. She cocks her head and lifts her eyebrows. She seems to be saying to me, "So, are you coming?" I throw the backpack over my shoulders and start walking downhill, toward the sea.

44 ♒

Leo is writing on his computer. I feel like I'm hearing the tread of his thoughts in his gentle keystrokes. I look at his books and papers—piled up on the only table in the cabin—and I let myself be carried away by the illusion of permanence they evoke. I also brought something to read, a book of stories by Alice Munro, whose work I always keep within arm's reach. A light drizzle doesn't quite hide the line of light along the horizon. The long fingers of the wind make the window vibrate. I observe the drops falling, shimmering in the elusive glow of the sun. Leo looks up; our eyes meet. I sense that our thoughts are converging, and the eagerness in his eyes confirms it. We smile, and I turn back to my book. I like to defer desire, knowing that a single gesture would be enough to carry us away. I like to watch Leo from a distance, but still close enough to be able to stretch out my hand and touch him. I could destroy my world for something this simple. One word would be enough and everything would come to an end. I now understand why I left Lola at my mother's house.

I think of Pauline—the heroine in one of Alice Munro's stories—when she receives a call from her young, troubled lover from a motel near where she's on vacation with her family. She's talking to him while holding her little girl in her arms, and the other child, a little older, is circling round the telephone whining for a piece of chocolate. The same story told a thousand different ways.

Even so, some part of me believes that my story is unique, while another part knows that passion always has that deceptive quality: Each instance seems somehow exceptional.

A bird flies into the window. We are both startled; then we see it get up and fly away.

Without doing so consciously, by leaving Lola with Maná, I broke the bonds that tied me to the house where I built a life with Juan. Our life. I close my eyes and imagine, like Pauline a few hours after her lover's call, that nothing in that house and that world belongs to me; the only thing I have is my desire; to my surprise, I don't even feel like shouting. On the contrary, I feel at peace, as if finally a truce has been called on the battlefield. I have jumped off the train, and my bruises are minimal, considering. Leo's proximity softens the impact. It even makes me believe that my future life—near him or far away—will actually be different and better. Leo awoke passion and there's no going back, because yearning for it would make my life with Juan unbearable. It's not only his aloofness. It's that I wanted so badly to distance myself from my mother's chaos that I deliberately set about making an institution of our love, without realizing that by doing so, I was destroying love's inherent spontaneity.

The heat from the wood-burning stove melts away my fear. Leo turns to look at me. He must be alarmed by the look on my face. He gets up and caresses my cheek. I don't move. I try to smile as I tell myself that with Leo by my side, everything will be OK.

"Do you feel like talking?"

I shake my head. I can't explain to him the comings and goings of my thoughts without at least hinting at a response to his proposal.

"Don't worry—I know this is much more difficult for you than

211

it is for me. I have nothing to leave," he says, smiling calmly. "Anyway, it's time to drink some hot tea. We didn't come here to have a bad time, right?" He holds my chin and forces me to look at him.

He picks up the kettle we'd left on the wood-burning stove and brews two cups of tea. The first sip warms my throat. Inside the cabin, the shadows stretch out like dark gauze. We sit in silence.

45 ↗

After wandering around for a long time, here I am on the hill where the cemetery faces the sea. The wind is blowing really hard, and there are lots of clouds in the sky. The first graves I come to have low white fences around them. They also have dried flowers and little pinwheels. These are the children's graves. I'm walking down the paths lined with graves when suddenly, from far away, I see Mama's tree. I start walking faster. Of all our family's graves, Mama's is the one closest to the trail that goes down to the sea. When I see it, my heart starts beating really hard, as if someone were hitting my chest from the inside. I did it!

"Happy anniversary, Mama," I say out loud.

I sit down on the stone planter box along the edge of her grave and look up through the thick branches of the tree. I pick a blue vase up from a corner where somebody threw it, wash it out at the faucet, and fill it with water. Since I didn't bring any flowers, I go from one grave to another stealing flowers here and there, so that nobody will notice.

I hear voices coming from another part of the cemetery. A fat woman wearing pink trousers is walking quickly toward me along one of the paths. A bored-looking boy is following a few feet behind. I scrunch up behind a white gravestone so they won't see me. I don't know why I'm hiding. I'm just a boy visiting his mother's grave. When I think about that, I come out of my hiding place and keep walking, holding my head up high.

I put the flowers down on the smooth surface of Mama's grave and place them in the blue vase one by one. When I finish, I take the photograph out of my backpack and lean it against the vase, facing the sea. I can't see the horizon through the fog, only the choppy shimmering of the waves crashing against the rocks.

It's time to dig into the loot I pinched this morning from the kitchen. I took a chocolate milk and some yogurt from the refrigerator, and a bag of cereal and one of potato chips from the cupboard. I decide to eat the potato chips and the yogurt. The wind gets colder. I put on my wool hat and my jacket.

When I'm full, I lie down on the grass to one side of the grave. The sea reflects the gray color of the sky, and moves like the skin of a restless animal. Mama, in her photograph, is looking at me.

"I don't know if you realize this, but I got here all by myself. I think I grew a few inches on the way, because I feel taller. I wanted to ask you a few favours, but this time they're a little bigger than the usual. Please don't let Alma leave with that man; also, take care of Lola, even though she's always bugging me, and make B.H.M. be the friend I've been hoping for."

The waves crash, spilling foam all over the rocks. At one moment, I think I see a great big white whale. This is how time passes: slowly. Gradually I sink into a world with no bottom where there are no potato chips, no yogurts, no fat ladies with pink trousers, no mean people sending me emails, no hurricanes destroying cities, no people who throw themselves into the ocean out of despair, where there is no death. A flock of birds trace lines in the sky, then fly out to sea until they vanish. I wonder why they make those shapes. Maybe they are secret messages for wise men. I pick up my backpack and put it over my shoulders. I use a rock to prop Mama's photo up against the gravestone, making sure her eyes are looking out to sea.

I climb down the steep and rocky path that leads to the rocks below. As I walk, the pebbles roll downhill. If I don't watch out, I could also fall down the hill, so I go very slowly, being careful where I place my foot each time. I take a deep breath and that mouthful of pure air goes straight into my lungs. When I stop, I watch the birds flying across the sky carrying their messages. I tune my ears to their piercing, far-away squalls. I hear children shouting. Up on the cliff, not far from where Mama is, I see the woman with the accordion face. The children are running around her. She raises her hand. I can't see her smile, but I know it's there, with her hundreds of wrinkles that are also smiling for me. I'd like for Mama, if she were alive, to be like her.

I keep climbing downhill, my eyes always glued to the path. When I reach the breakers, I'm exhausted. The woman and children have disappeared. I climb onto a rock and rest. The sea is very rough; the waves are getting higher, stronger. I take off my backpack and go forward a few feet along a black, smooth boulder that rises above the water, like a great big hanging terrace. I keep looking at the sky, until the sun starts to go down between the swirls of the dark clouds. I lift up my arms like Kájef taught me and close my eyes. I see the woman's smile; I see the light side of Mama's face; I see myself, big and smiling in her sparkling eyes; I see a ship in the middle of the sea; I see what will never return; I see hundreds of birds taking off in flight; I see the impact, the twisted iron over my head, Mama's bleeding face; I hear a shout; I see my heart beating faintly under my ribs; I see Kájef at the bottom of the sea, his body floating, like a fish. All of that is inside me; all of that is me.

46⌛

It's Yerfa on the telephone. The school bus should have brought Tommy home an hour ago.

"I called the driver and he said that Tommy wasn't at the bus-stop when the children got out of class," Yerfa adds.

"How could that be? He got on the bus this morning."

"That's what I told him, but he said he waited for him for a long time and finally gave up and left."

I call the school. They connect me with the dean's office. A few minutes later, the dean informs me that he checked the attendance record and it shows that Tommy was absent today. I tell him that's impossible. Tommy left for school this morning, like every other day.

"His teacher's already gone, but I'll try to get in touch with her and let you know," he says.

I call Yerfa back and ask her to look through the list of his class-mates. Tommy must have gone to one of their houses, maybe to work on a project, and he forgot to tell us.

In the meantime, I see a patient. When I'm finished, I call the school. The dean left his cell number with the caretaker to give me. I call him. He tells me that he spoke with the teacher; Tommy didn't show up in class today.

"Are you telling me you lost him on the road between his

house and school? Because I can guarantee he left this morning on the school bus, on 'his' bus," I say with sarcastic emphasis. "This is extremely serious. Are you aware of that? Very serious."

"Of course, yes, I understand. I'll call the principal immediately. In the meantime, please feel free to call the teacher. She might be able to give you more information about Tommy. You never know, maybe he played hooky."

"I can't quite imagine Tommy doing that," I say. I feel like giving him a piece of my mind, but I remain calm; it won't do any good to lose my temper with him.

He gives me the teacher's phone number. It's seven in the evening. If Tommy didn't go to school in the morning, he's been gone for eleven hours. That's a long time for a twelve-year-old boy. I call Maná. Lola's staying with her. I ask her if she's heard from Tommy.

"Last night after talking to you, Lola called him and they spoke for a few minutes."

"She didn't tell you anything?"

"No, but I didn't ask her. Why?"

"No, nothing."

"Are you sure?"

"Yes, yes, don't worry," I lie, not wanting to alarm her. "I have to go now. A patient is waiting for me. Give Lola a kiss and tell her that I'll definitely call her tomorrow."

I dial Alma's number. She doesn't answer. I begin to feel an anxiety I can barely tolerate. I call my cousin Pedro Ortúzar on his cellphone. We are not very close, but he knows the Interior Minister well. A call from him and the search effort will go into full swing. His voicemail comes on. I ask him to call me urgently. As I pronounce the word "urgently," I feel like I'm suffocating.

I tell Carola, my secretary, to call all the hospitals in Santiago. I wait and try to think clearly. A while later, she tells me that she's called everywhere and there's no sign of Tommy. There are still a few hospitals on the outskirts of Santiago she's not yet tried. I call Pedro's office in Parliament. His secretary tells me he is in session. I ask her to please try to get him to the phone, that it's very serious. I wait, my elbows leaning on the desk. I hear voices in the hallway. Everything happening outside my door seems unimportant. The phone rings. It's Pedro. I explain what's going on and Pedro is alarmed; he has a boy the same age as Tommy.

"I'm going to call the general of the carabineros. I think that's the best thing."

"Thank you, Pedro."

He tells me a lieutenant will come to my house to collect more information.

"Don't worry—I'll call you back as soon as I know anything. Try to relax. We'll find him, you'll see."

I try to say something, but I have a lump in my throat and I can't get a word out. *You'll see . . . You'll see . . .* His voice echoes inside me. Before leaving, I ask Carola not to mention anything to anybody at the hospital. It's probably just some mistake. When I say that, I want it to be true.

On the way home, I call Alma's number again. She doesn't answer. Maybe, wherever she is, there's no signal. If Tommy didn't go to class of his own free will, like the dean said, he must have had a reason. But what? Maybe he's been having problems with his friends. But then, who are his friends? Do I know any of them?

The day is ending, the shadows of its final hours spreading and becoming night. I can't help being jumpy. Where is my son? What if somebody kidnapped him for money? I park the car on the street in case I have to go out again. I look at the garden. The sight of it calms me. Hedges, interspersed with flowers, line the path that leads to the front door. Tommy must be somewhere I haven't thought of yet.

Yerfa is waiting for me at the door. Her eyes are red. We sit down at the kitchen table. I ask if she noticed anything unusual about Tommy. She tells me he's had very little appetite and has seemed down, that a few weeks ago he went out on his bicycle and came back after dark. She didn't realize it because Tommy had told her he would be at the neighbor's. I refrain from asking her why she didn't tell me before. It's not the right moment to admonish her.

"He didn't say where he'd been?" I speak slowly.

It's unlikely Tommy could get very far. The few times we've ridden together, his cardiovascular capacity has been extremely limited.

"He didn't want to tell me."

I shut myself up in my office. The silence makes Tommy's absence painfully real. I call Cristián, the boy who lives next door. I ask him if he's seen Tommy, if he told him anything at all. He says he hasn't seen him for a couple of days. Yerfa knocks on my door.

"It's the carabineros," she announces, sounding alarmed, as if we were criminals they've come to arrest. I ask her to show them in.

Two men in uniform, their hats in their hands, enter the room. One of them, clearly the higher-ranking one, holds out his hand and introduces himself as Lieutenant Sergio Ríos. He has dark hair, bowed legs, an aquiline nose, and an almost arrogant demeanor. The other one, by contrast, is squat and a bit pudgy around the waist, and looks like a family man. I offer them a seat. The lieutenant asks; I answer; the junior officer writes. Behind the lieutenant's curt, exacting manners I get an inkling of the world he comes from, a world of conflict, bluster, and physical violence. Every now and then the subordinate looks up from his pad, and though his expression remains impassive, he seems to be apologizing for his superior's rudeness.

"We're going to need a picture of your son," the lieutenant says. "We'll also need to see his room."

The whole time he has been referring to him as "your son", never once as Tommy. In the hallway, I stop in front of one of his drawings: *The Minotaur's Labyrinth*. Tommy has done dozens of drawings of the story of Theseus, but this is the one Alma likes best, because he called Ariadne's thread "the thread that leads love out".

"My son did this," I show them, knowing they couldn't give a damn.

The lieutenant clears his throat, and we continue down the hallway. We enter Tommy's room. I turn on the light. The men walk around, looking at everything. The presence of these two strangers in my son's room gives me a sense of inescapable doom. They open his closet, poke around in his drawers, his notebooks, and pick up his toys. They almost seem scornful, and their curiosity doesn't feel genuine.

"Is anything missing?" the subordinate asks.

I look around.

"Nothing."

He wants to know how he was dressed.

"In his school uniform. The last time we saw him, this morning, he was on his way to school."

"I need a detailed description of the uniform."

"I can give you a photograph of him we took this year at a school event."

Before going downstairs, I enter my bedroom and get the picture of Tommy I keep by my bedside.

Before leaving, Lieutenant Ríos explains, "We were sent here from the top. All our units will receive this photo and no effort will be spared to find your son. Good night."

The subordinate says goodbye with a handshake and a resigned smile. Neither of the men offers me one word of reassurance. Their experience must have taught them to avoid such niceties.

I call my cousin Pedro back. I tell him the carabineros have come and gone.

"Look, man, try to relax, OK? He'll probably show up any minute now. Just in case, they're checking all the hospitals again. Just in case. The major I spoke to told me these things are happening a lot. Kids have some problem or other and go off, but they soon come back. It's a way of getting attention."

I thank him and hang up. I wanted to keep talking: His voice is reassuring and gives me the illusion that I'm not alone in this. I call Alma. I hear her phone ringing in my ear. I wish she were here.

I really should tell my father or one of my brothers, but, apart from worrying along with me, there's not much any of them can do to help. Anyway, I wouldn't know what to tell them. That Tommy ran away? Where could he have gone when he's never gone out of the house alone? That some psychopath kidnapped him and he's in a basement where he'll spend the next twenty years of his life if we don't find him? I get up from my desk, taking quick, shallow breaths. Outside, the breeze is rustling the leafy branches of the oak tree. I sit down again and look at the list Yerfa gave me. It's eight forty-five. It's still early enough to call some of his classmates, but first I call his teacher. I ask her if Tommy has been having any problems at school.

"Well, apart from his absences, he's seemed OK, normal, always a bit withdrawn, as you know, but no more than usual."

"What absences?" I ask.

"He's missed a lot of school lately, but he's always brought absence letters signed by his mother."

Maybe Tommy has had a cold, as he often does, and Alma hasn't wanted to worry me. I usually leave the house before he gets up. I ask his teacher if he hangs out with anybody in particular. She tells me he doesn't have any friends. Her words don't surprise me, but they do make me sad. She asks me to keep her informed.

Yerfa is waiting for me in the hall. I ask her about Tommy's absences. She tells me he hasn't missed a day of school in months. I tell her what the teacher said. Yerfa insists that Tommy has been going to school regularly. I notice how nervous she is, how afraid she is of being blamed, but I know she's telling the truth.

"Try to get some sleep, Yerfa. We'll see what happens tomorrow."

I call Alma as I climb the stairs. I keep trying, again and again. Just dialing her number makes me feel closer to her.

I turn off the lights. My steps echo through the empty hallway, where I'm used to seeing Lola and Tommy coming and going. When I close my bedroom door, silence descends, implacable, a silence that sucks in everything around me, everything I believed to be immutable.

It's nine thirty at night. I sit down on the bed. On my night-stand, my telephone is shrouded in muteness, as if it knows how anxious it makes me just to look at it in the semi-darkness. This lack of action is killing me. If someone had kidnapped Tommy, and wanted ransom, they'd have been in touch already. I pick up the remote control and turn on the television. I watch the news. I can't bear the voices, or the world that erupts from the screen. I mute the sound. The images move silently across the cold surface of the glass. A blind man walks through city streets with a police dog. I make an effort to think about something concrete, but my brain isn't functioning very well. I get up and look out the window. In my garden, with its carefully designed lighting, spring is exploding. I hate it. I hate its exuberance and the illusion of happiness it creates.

I can't sleep. I'm having difficulty breathing. I toss and turn in bed. Images race wildly through my mind, tear into my brain, and leave me trembling. I wipe my sweaty palms, then my forehead. I feel like I'm sinking into a tar pit.

I remember finding Tommy, for the hundredth time, hiding and recording our conversations. I scolded him, grabbed him by the ear, and sent him to his room. I heard him crying behind the door, but I resisted the temptation to comfort him. The next day, feeling calmer, I went to his room. Tommy was lying on his bed, making his red airplane fly over his head. The sound of children's joyous summer voices filtered in from the neighbor's garden. I would have liked Tommy to be out there, with them, and I assumed that's what he wanted, too. I asked him why he taped other people's conversations. He looked at me suspiciously without answering. I waited. A few minutes later, he told me that he did it to find the invisible order of things.

"I don't only tape other people," he said. "I also tape my own voice, ideas and things. When I say them out loud, I know they exist."

His words impressed me, but I didn't relent. I had to get Tommy to stop eavesdropping on adult conversations. If I had shown I was proud of his perceptiveness, his acuteness of observation, he would have thought I approved. I repeated my usual speech about respecting other people's privacy, but this time I didn't have the courage to look him in the eye. I kept talking, pacing around the room with my hands clasped behind my back. Later, I realized I could have been more understanding. That's why I tried so hard to be honest with him yesterday, by showing him my vulnerability, by telling him that his behavior caused me pain. I imagined showing him my feelings would be more effective than any ethical or intellectual argument. And I thought we'd come to some understanding and achieved a degree of closeness. Maybe I made a mistake, but where?

If Alma were here, she'd help me understand. Alma. It's been a long time since I've needed her like this. It feels like I've been on a trip with her, but we haven't been together. It's as if we've been gradually deserting each other, leaving each other more and more alone at each stop along the way. This long night makes a mockery of all my efforts to pretend that everything's fine, that Alma hasn't drifted away, that Tommy hasn't run away from home, that we are a happy family. I've tried to overcome my pain and all I've done is hurt other people. Then I turn to Soledad, wherever she is, and ask her to help him come home.

I wake up confused, in a sweat. I'm sharply aware of a big hole inside me, as if a thief has entered my body and stolen something essential. A nonexistent telephone rings in my ear. My clothes are wet, my muscles tense. For a second I feel relieved to discover that I'm in my bed, but an instant later Tommy's presence, his absence, assaults me. I jump up and rush to his room. I'm so befuddled I think I might find him there asleep. I lie down on his bed.

Obviously, I could have done things differently. We all could have, but it's a question of survival, not blame. I was sinking along with Soledad, and the only way I could avoid it was to hide away. And that's what I've been doing all these years; like one of those war survivors you read about who remains in their underground shelter long after peace has been declared. I've let time, Alma, and life itself go right by me. I remember when Alma tried to hold my hand during the children's play; it was as if she were offering me the chance to come out into the open, to ask about her continual absences, to tell her that I missed her. The chance to keep her by my side.

I take in Tommy's obsessive orderliness, his toys lined up on the shelves, his airplanes, his galactic soldiers, his miniature motorcycles, his pencils all sharpened and neatly arranged on the desk, his computer. Tommy spends hours in front of that thing. I turn it on. The screen lights up, but I need a password to get in. I try his name, his date of birth, I try to remember the name of his imaginary friend . . . Kofa . . . Kafa; I try different spellings, but it's no use. I can't get in.

The telephone rings. I run to my bedroom to answer, on the way falling and banging my elbow. It's my cousin Pedro. He asks me if I've heard from Tommy. His voice sounds worried. He tells me he's spoken with the general and they still don't have any leads. At least he's not dead, I think.

"Did you sleep?" His tone is gentler, more personal.

"A little."

"Juan, shouldn't you call your father?"

"How do you know I haven't?"

"I guessed. Tommy is most likely somewhere safe and sound, but the family should still be informed."

"You're right."

Seconds after I hang up, my phone rings again. I see Alma's name on the screen. I hear her voice.

"Juan, I've got twenty-two missed calls from you. I left the phone in the car last night and didn't realize till right now." The intonation in her voice is both smooth and childlike. "Is something wrong?"

"Yes." Now that I finally have her closer, I find it difficult to speak. My skin is turned inside out, all the nerve endings exposed.

"What's happened?" she asks impatiently.

The timbre of her voice rushes toward me from far away. I close my eyes and absorb the warmth it fills me with.

"Talk to me, Juan—you're frightening me."

"Tommy has disappeared."

It feels like somebody else is saying those words that have been endlessly echoing in my ears for hours.

"But how could he have disappeared?" she asks, her voice rising.

I explain, step by step, what's happened since Yerfa called me at the hospital. I try to speak calmly, but I know my voice sounds desperate. Every so often she interrupts me and asks for a particular detail. Then, for several moments, she is quiet. It seems like she's not there, and I imagine her covering the telephone so I don't hear her crying. Slowly, the weight in my chest begins to lift. As I tick off each event for Alma, they become more real and at the same time less decisive. I know that Tommy's disappearance is as devastating for her as it is for me, and that nobody else feels about him as we do. This certainty unites me to her like never before.

"I'm leaving right now. I'll be there in a few hours."

"I'm waiting for you," I say, my voice cracking.

I feel relieved, as if someone had been choking me and has finally let go.

Seconds after hanging up, I call her back. I ask her about Tommy's absences from school. Any information could be valuable.

"But, Juan, I haven't signed any absence letter for at least five months."

"So he forged them."

"He must have."

"This changes things," I say.

"Just wait for me. We'll see together."

"Alma, I know that recently I've been doing everything wrong . . ."

"Don't say anything right now . . . Anyway, it's been both of us."

"We have a lot to talk about."

"We'll see each other soon."

"I love you." Alma has hung up before hearing my last words. I promise myself I'll repeat them to her when I have her in my arms.

47 ∿

Leo is lounging in bed, the blanket covering him up to his nose. I hold my cellphone in my hand and look at him from the doorway.

"What's going on?" He blinks hard, trying to open his eyes.

"Tommy has disappeared. Looks like he ran away. I have to go, Leo."

"What are you talking about?"

"I have to leave," I repeat, turning away to avoid his enquiring eyes. A feeling of dread has lodged in my stomach.

"But how could that be? I thought you were a happy family," he says in that mocking and petulant tone of his I've heard dozens of times but never directed at me.

The solicitous lover shoots me with one of his darts, a piercing attack I don't know how to protect myself from. I turn and take my bag out of the closet.

"I'm sorry," I hear him say behind me. "Sometimes I don't know what I'm saying." He gets up, wraps his arms round my shoulders, and pulls me toward him. "It's just that I wanted us to stay in bed till late," he explains, and gives me a kiss. "When did it happen?"

"Yesterday. He didn't come home from school. Juan has been calling me since last night. I left my cellphone in the car yesterday morning, when I was talking to Lola. I don't know how I did that.

I never forget it. When I woke up, it was the first thing I thought of, that I didn't have my cell. And there were his calls. Poor Juan."

When I say this, I realize that the last few weeks I'd forgotten the possibility that he could move me.

"I have to leave right now," I say, as I wriggle out of his arms.

I start getting dressed. Leo puts on a pair of jeans and a T-shirt, and sits down on the bed. He watches me. I go into the bathroom and leave the door ajar. While I brush my teeth, I look at his reflection in the mirror. He's resting his elbows on his knees, his eyes staring out the cabin's only window. I catch a trace of uneasiness in the curve of his lips.

"You want me to go with you?"

"I don't know. It's up to you."

"No, Alma, it's up to you."

I walk to the door.

"I really don't know," I say, and I think I'm being honest.

One part of me wants Leo not to hesitate or even ask, to simply stay by my side with an iron resolve, no matter what, even against my own better judgment, his need to be with me stronger than any circumstance; but the other part of me wants to drive the hundred miles thinking about Tommy, mulling over my own responsibility in this whole business, alone.

"I don't think I can be any use to you once you get home, unless you want me to drive so you can relax," he suggests, looking up at me.

His eyes dig into me.

"You don't need to, Leo—you're right. Once we're there, there's nothing you can do. It doesn't make sense for you to ruin your days here."

Leo looks away and rubs his chin. Since that first day on the highway, neither of us has mentioned his proposal. I suppose he's been waiting for me to give him an answer. I'd been thinking we'd talk today.

"You'll be able to do some writing," I add.

"Yes, of course."

I see him lie down on the bed. His gray T-shirt is outlined against the white sheets. Everything around me seems to have been emptied out.

When I'm ready to leave, Leo picks up my bag. I take him by the arm and we walk together to the truck, like old friends. The morning is sunny and clear. A few light clouds pass slowly over our heads. The breeze is so gentle and the atmosphere so serene that my troubles seem as if they're from a different world. Leo hugs me. I can feel his restraint. I think about Tommy and a shudder runs through my body.

48⏳

After showering and eating breakfast, I shut myself up in my office. I call the hospital and tell Carola to cancel all my appointments for the day. I dial Papa's number. I tell him what's going on. He's still furious about his birds, but I can hear the upset underneath his gruffness. He asks me details about the search that I haven't even thought of. He'll let my brothers know, he says. When I hang up, silence descends again. I pace back and forth. I wait. One by one my brothers call. They're all very concerned.

I go back to Tommy's room. I sit on his bed, right where we sat when we talked two nights ago. What happened between then and now? I'm scared and I know I can't do anything to make it better. I remember all the times I came into his room and found him staring out this same window.

Once again, I turn on his computer. I keep trying with first and last names, important dates, some of his games, his drawings, I type in, "Minotaur," then, "Theseus," "Ariadne," "thread," "Alma," "Soledad." I've found his password. I'm in. Why didn't I think of that sooner? I open his documents folder. I find one file that's called "Tommy's Letterbox." It's full of separate sentences. I read them and discover they are a litany of curses and insults. Jesus! The way they're written seems like they were sent by email, probably from some of his classmates. I wonder how long Tommy has been dealing with this. This must be the reason he ran away. I keep searching. I find a folder with the MP3 icon. There are several files, but one catches my attention: "Ten Discoveries About Mama." I open it. I hear my own voice:

"*Carmen, what a pleasure to see you! Please don't get up.*"

"*It's been a long time, Juan.*"

"*Five, six years?*"

"*At least.*"

It's from Miguel's wedding. There's a pause. Tommy must have edited his recordings.

"*Anyway, it's a good thing Juan got remarried; Soledad's illness was so tragic and sudden.*"

"*Illness? Ah, the lies we swallow.*"

"*What are you talking about?*"

"*Oh dear, I shouldn't have said anything. Sorry. Please, let's change the subject.*"

"*You can't leave us hanging now.*"

"*Soledad didn't die of an illness. She committed suicide.*"

"*Didn't she have an aneurysm?*"

"*That's what they told everyone to avoid a scandal, but Soledad committed suicide. I know it for a fact. It's one of the best-kept secrets of the Montes family.*"

Everything is becoming clear and getting even more confused at the same time. I close my eyes. Tommy has been living with this knowledge, this anguish all these weeks. I shake my head quickly from side to side and take a couple of deep breaths. Here, in the silence of his room, the only thing I want to do is hug my son. The recording continues.

"*You've changed so much, Alma. You look beautiful, really.*"

A man's voice, which doesn't sound familiar.

"*This is Tommy.*"

"*Hi, Tommy. I'm Leo, an old friend of your mother's.*"

231

Another "best-kept secret," I say to myself.

Now it's Tommy speaking. "*I think that when Papa is staring off into space and seems like he isn't listening to anybody, he's thinking about Mama.*"

I press my fingers against my eyelids. I feel dizzy. In the meantime, Tommy keeps talking. "*One: hang yourself. Two: eat rat poison. Three: shoot yourself in the head, the mouth, or the heart. Four: throw yourself in front of a moving car.*"

That's how Soledad killed herself. I can picture her skull split open by the impact, her fists clenched. I stand up and pace around the room, trying to chase away this image. The night before, I'd promised to come get her in the afternoon and bring her home. We would eat together "like in the good old days," and then I'd take her back to Aguas Claras. We'd tried this several times before, but each time, just minutes before leaving, Soledad would stop. I had compassion for her inability to get better, her lack of reliability, her vulnerability, but it also exasperated me. I didn't want to have to tell Tommy, yet again, that his mama was still sick and couldn't leave the hospital, that she sent him all her love, that she'd be home soon. The same words, the same disappointed expression on his little face. So I forgot. I forgot that Soledad was waiting for me.

She left through the main door with her bag over her shoulder. She crossed the street at the exact moment a truck was passing by at full speed. There were several witnesses, and not a single person failed to confirm that Soledad had thrown herself under its wheels deliberately. A few days later, the doctor admitted that during a therapy session that morning Soledad had given him a kind of veiled warning, that my not showing up when I said I would had had no bearing on what she'd done. I wanted to believe his words, but it was like clutching at straws; it gave me no relief from the pain that followed. I tried to train myself, make myself stronger, hoping to learn something along the way. How else could I give any meaning to her death?

Nine years have passed, and whatever I might have learned is useless to me. Where's the strength I thought I'd built up? I am as crippled now as I was then. Maybe we never learn from our pain; maybe we just get through it, over and over again, and always alone. But I should have been there for Tommy's pain. I feel an overwhelming urge to burst out of here running at full speed, to break something, to scream . . .

I hear his modulated and slightly hoarse voice pronouncing each word carefully. *"Five: sink to the bottom of the pool and breathe until your lungs fill with water. Six: jump off a building or a very tall tree. Seven: cover your nose and mouth until you suffocate. Eight: stop eating and drinking. Nine: slit your wrists. Ten: fall asleep in the snow. Eleven: stick your head in an oven and turn on the gas."*

Tommy continues. His voice, so alive, makes his absence that much more painful. *"Second discovery: Mama's grandpa founded a girls' school in Buenos Aires called St. Ann's."*

I don't understand how he found that out, but he did.

"Discovery, addendum: We share lies with friends."

I have no idea how he figured that out, but once again he has hit upon another truth.

"I don't know what your mother saw in me. She was much more intelligent than I am. She'd stop by and pick me up in her car and we'd go places. Not the kinds of places other women like us went. We'd go hang out around the university where she studied art history. Soledad was very sophisticated. We'd sit in a café called Las Terrazas and we'd drink coffee and smoke, and drink coffee and smoke. That's all we'd do, but it made us very happy."

That's Corina's voice. I can picture them going out, all spruced up.

"Those sonsabitches."

"Who, Auntie?"

I know who we are: all of us, all of us who live complacently under our shields of civility and decency, surrounded by the hypocrisy that protects us from evil.

"*Third discovery: Like the ash tree, Mama had a dragon wrapped round her roots and no matter how hard she struggled to defeat it, the dragon ended up winning.*

"*Fourth discovery: According to Mr. Milowsky, Mama was Jewish and so am I.*"

Who on earth is Mr. Milowsky? Where has Tommy been all this time when I thought he was in his room, cut off from everything?

"*Fifth discovery: Mama died in the street, in front of Aguas Claras.*"

For a split second before I realize what a horrible image this was for Tommy to have in his head, I feel proud of my boy, of how far he has come.

"*Discovery, addendum: Truth rises up from the depths and alters the orderly surface of things.*"

Jesus. I'm frightened of his discoveries, his lucidity, the ideas he gets in his head, the deep and complex feelings that I've never even suspected.

"*Sixth discovery: Mama's grandfather, my great-grandfather, hid the fact that he was Jewish so he could be accepted in society.*

"*Discovery, addendum: This is what Alma told Papa—when she met Grandpa the first time, he asked her if she was Jewish. She said she wasn't and Grandpa was very pleased.*"

Maybe that was the opportunity to drag the truth out of the depths where it was buried.

"*Seventh discovery: I think my grandpa, like my classmates, doesn't like Jews.*

"*Eighth discovery: My and my mama's element is water.*

"*Grandpa, I want to wish you a happy birthday. I also want to tell you that I have a friend named Sarah. She's Jewish.*"

"*Tommy.*"

"*She was born in Buenos Aires and she has a marvelous accent. Her family makes Shabbat candles. Grandpa, do you know what 'Shabbat' is?*"

"*I bet you can tell us what it is.*"

"*I think now's not the time.*"

"*Why, because it's about Jews?*"

"*You are really pushing it, little boy. Watch your step very carefully. Do you hear me?*"

"*Yes, I'm here, at my father-in-law's house, in the garden, a few feet away from where we ran into each other . . .*" Now it's Alma talking. "*But you're right. This whole thing is ridiculous. We can't even step foot in the street together. I'm scared to death and even though I know it's irrational, I can't help it. And also . . . I can't deal with this, Leo. It's not what I want . . . You weren't listening . . . You have no way of knowing that . . . What are you plotting now? . . . You seem to have all the bases covered . . . I don't know . . . It's a goodbye trip, then? . . . Yes, I can. Does the place you want to take me have a sea? . . . No, I haven't said yes, I'm just asking . . . I want to see you, too. I've got to go . . . You shouldn't listen in on adult conversations, Tommy. It's just not OK, and you know it!*"

"*It's not my fault you didn't see me. I wasn't hiding. I was right here.*"

"*What were you doing there?*"

"*Nothing.*"

"*I love you very much, Tommy.*"

"*That woman is a different Alma and I don't know her.*"

I don't know her, either. My eyes are stinging. Suddenly, everything around me—Tommy's desk, his airplanes, the garden, the refreshing sound of the sprinklers, even myself—seems confused and meaningless.

"*Grandpa, I'm the one who opened the cage.*"

"*Don't speak nonsense, little boy.*"

"*It's the truth. I opened the cage.*"

"*How dare you? Are you crazy? This boy is completely crazy! As crazy as his mother! Juan, this is your fault. You never raised him to be a decent person. You treat him like he is an imbecile, and where has that got you? This. You don't have enough strength of character to deal with what life has doled out to you. It's a disgrace. Now leave. Everybody leave—the party's over.*"

"*Ninth discovery: Grandpa is right. Papa is a weak man and I am crazy, like Mama. That's why I can't count to ten before hurting other people.*"

It's true: I am a weak man, incapable of preventing my son from having such feelings, a man without the courage to stand up to his own father, unable to prevent the world he has constructed so carefully from collapsing around him.

"*Yerfa told me that you still have your imaginary friend. Tommy, I've told you a thousand times that it's not good for you. There's nothing wrong with using your imagination, but not when the things you imagine become more important than reality. I know it's fun to make up your own games, live in your own world, but reality is what nourishes you; it's where you can relate to others . . . Can you imagine what would happen if we all lived in our own imaginary worlds?*"

What "reality" am I talking about? His world now feels infinitely more real than my own.

"*Tenth discovery: Mama knew that that was what made me be who I am, and it was that that she loved about me. There was nobody else in the whole world who Mama loved as much as me, there's nobody in the world who loves me like she loved me, and there's nothing in the whole universe I love more than my mama.*"

"I also love that in you, Tommy," I say out loud, "and there is nobody in the world I love as much as you. Believe me. If only you could hear me."

49 ∿

I drive with both hands on the steering wheel and without taking my eyes off the road in front of me. I am thinking about Tommy, about his quiet games, his sprawling gait, his questions, the twenty-two missed calls from Juan.

I've reached Santiago. The sky is solid gray. I join the freeway and go underground. It's five past eleven. Where did Tommy spend the night? What if he had an accident? I feel a stab of pain, almost unbearable. Tommy must have noticed my distance, how withdrawn I've been. I wonder how much of my conversation with Leo he managed to hear, though I could tell by how he acted that he understood. What were they like, the moments I've spent with him in the last few days; can I recall his facial expressions, his words?

If only I had him in front of me right now, I'd sweep him up, hold him in my arms, tell him how horrifyingly close we were to losing each other, tell him that no matter what happened between his father and me, we still had each other, everything we shared— editing his recordings, learning sign language, telling each other our secrets. I would tell him that I love him and that my love is much, much bigger than that telescope that has my name, but Tommy's not here, and I can't tell him all that, and I wish so badly I could.

The freeway emerges into the light of day. I look up at the sky;

seagulls follow the path of the river toward the mountains, which are peeking out from behind the fog. I had decided to shed my old skin like a snake, and if now I am hesitating, it's because I suspect that after squeezing through sharp rocks to peel it off me, I'll still be covered in sores and wounds. I hear a horn. I'm so buried in my thoughts I didn't start moving when the lights changed. I step on the gas.

Though it's not difficult for me to imagine a life with Leo, I'm struck by the suspicion that I'd be running away from something I would soon find again. The crisis I'm facing goes back a long way, to issues I've tried to hide or push aside to avoid confronting them. I've been wanting to escape, and there's nothing wrong with that, but I guess that perhaps that would only lead me further into my fantasies, my detachment, my silence. It's strange that until a few hours ago I couldn't see any of this, but now I can picture my present life so clearly. Tommy, Juan, Lola: I see their faces, so amazingly real, down to the last detail, and the spaces I've tried to leave blank in my imagination begin to fill up with powerful, vibrant emotion.

I press on the gas again. Soon I find myself in front of my house. I open the door. I feel like I left here a century ago, so many twists and turns in the last few days, the last few hours. I hear no sounds at all where I stand under the amber light of the entryway.

I rewind the movie, I go back in time, groping for the feelings that united me with Juan, and I discover that they're still there, trampled but alive. My first memory of him appears clearly, the cool and calm man who saved Edith's life. In spite of his reserve, Juan transmitted a strength and confidence that filled the space of our panic and brought us all comfort. I remember him looking at my belly, three months pregnant, the way he adjusted his embrace, in consideration of and to welcome this being that was between us.

I walk toward his office. The flowers in the vases are old and their rancid smell wafts down the hallway. I open the door. Juan, sitting in his swivel chair in front of the window, is holding the telephone up to his ear. When he hears me enter, he turns toward me. I want to hug him, but the look on his face stops me short. I don't understand. Even so, I walk up to him. He stands up and gestures for me to wait. He turns his back on me and keeps talking. The air is heavy and sickly sweet. The sunlight ripples over the spines of the books on the shelves.

"Thank you. I'll let you know," he concludes, and hangs up. "I was just going out."

He observes me, clearly uncomfortable. And then a grimace of anxiety.

"Have you heard anything?" I ask.

"No, nothing yet. I'm on my way to my father's."

"We'll go together."

"No, you don't need to. I'd rather you stay here."

"I'm going with you, Juan."

"I want to be alone." He sounds irritated.

"Why?"

"What do you mean, why? I've spent the entire night racking my brains, thinking that something terrible has happened to *my* son, and I am perfectly capable of continuing in the same vein."

He moves with grim intent, runs the back of his hand hurriedly over his mouth. His eyes shine feverishly, as if he were ill. Aggression is his way of defending himself against feelings he doesn't know how to control. He's done this so many times in the past, and each time it's pushed me farther away from him, but not today. This time I can see his heart as if it were hanging off his chest.

"I'm sorry. I want to go with you . . . Forgive me," I say. I hear the falseness in my own voice as the words come out.

239

"What should I forgive you for?" He stops his pacing. He looks me straight in the eyes, his face probing and threatening. His eyelids are red.

"For not being here when you needed me, for leaving my cell-phone in the car, for taking so long . . ."

Juan lets out a dismal laugh, then says, "Forget it." He dismisses me with a flick of his hand, a gesture I recognize from his father. Then he turns round and goes out into the hallway.

I follow him. Juan climbs the stairs, enters our bedroom, and closes the door behind him. I go into the kitchen to say hello to Yerfa. I have a cup of coffee while I wait for him. Yerfa is mumbling a continuous prayer. I take the cup in both hands and bring it to my chest. I think about Tommy's loneliness, his disappointment. I never thought I could hurt someone I love so much.

I finish my coffee, say goodbye to Yerfa, and go outside to wait for Juan. When he appears, I approach him. I have the urge to caress his face, ease his pain even a tiny bit, but before I can make a move, that same face, both bitter and detached, stops me in my tracks. We stand there, facing each other, not moving. I gather my strength, reach out my hand, and touch his cheek. Juan squints at me as if he were looking through a bright light into a strange room. I feel a sudden flash of fear. It all happens so quickly I can't even react.

Juan grabs my wrist and squeezes it hard. It hurts. For a second I think things aren't that bad; at least there's engagement. Then he lets go and, without moving his eyes, which are brimming with rage, he spits out at me, "Don't touch me. Do you hear? Don't ever touch me again."

"What have I done to you?" I ask, turning my eyes away. My voice sounds dull.

Juan doesn't answer.

I repeat, louder this time, "What have I done to you?"

I can still feel the ferocious pressure of his hands.

"You don't need to keep lying to me. I know everything." His words sound dark and ominous.

"What do you know?" I dare to ask.

Juan doesn't answer. My head starts racing, searching, tying up loose ends, digging around in my memory until I come up with the recording Tommy made at Los Peumos. Juan must have listened to it. He doesn't say a word, he doesn't look at me, he's all sealed up, and I don't blame him. How could I?

"Don't bother, Alma, not now," he says, walking toward his car. "I don't have time for it. I have to find Tommy."

I follow him. I get in and sit down next to him. I squeeze my eyes shut. I can't even cry.

"Don't leave me out of this. I need to see Tommy. I need to know where he is, how he is," I blurt out, propelled by a feeling that is beginning to crush my chest.

"What for?" he says, bringing his hand to his forehead.

"He is my son, too."

"Please, no, Alma. Really, don't continue," he says. "I don't want to talk to you. I don't want to be near you. Your presence repels me. The only thing I need right now is to concentrate all my energies on finding Tommy." He lets out a sound of exasperation.

"I understand. Just let me go with you. Please, I beg you."

He sits in silence without turning on the engine. He is gripping the steering wheel with both hands, his eyes glued to the empty street.

Finally, he sighs, and without looking up, he speaks. "Even if none of this were happening, with Tommy I mean, I wouldn't ask you. I don't want to know. I hope my meaning is clear. I'm not that kind of man." His voice is devoid of all texture, flat. He addresses me as he would a stranger.

"What kind of man are you?"

"That's a question that from now on has absolutely nothing to do with you," he says tersely.

The fact that Juan won't tell me to my face what both of us know, that I am responsible for his son's disappearance, instead of giving me some relief, makes me so anguished I can hardly breathe. How much I would love to tell him everything. Only now do I understand how meaningful confession is. During the silence that follows, I can almost hear something disintegrating in one corner of the car. I glance at Juan's sharp profile and see that his love is dead.

"Please just get out. You are not part of this, not anymore," he says.

I open the door and get out. Juan turns on the engine and in a few seconds his car has disappeared from sight.

50⧗

I'm not going to my father's house; in fact, I'm not going anywhere. I'm just driving around aimlessly. I'm incapable of sitting
still, or of talking to any human being, unless my cellphone rings
and it's somebody telling me that Tommy is OK. Everything is
losing its consistency and meaning. Bark with no sap. The world,
the people, all empty. My cellphone is ringing. I look at the screen.
It's a blocked number. My pulse quickens.

"Is this Mr. Juan Montes?"

"Yes," I confirm.

"Good afternoon. This is Lieutenant Ríos. I was at your house
yesterday afternoon."

"Good afternoon."

"If you'll forgive me, Mr. Montes, I'll get straight to the point.
They found the body of a boy on the coast, about a mile from Los
Peumos. According to the sergeant in charge of the region, the
child couldn't be more than eight years old, which makes it
unlikely to be your son."

"My son is the size of an eight-year-old," I whisper, my voice
barely squeezing out of my throat.

"He's not wearing a school uniform. Your son was wearing a
uniform," Ríos continues.

"How is he dressed?" I ask, my voice wispy and thin.

243

"In jeans and a red fleece. He's not wearing shoes. The water must have carried them off. We sent the photograph you gave us by Internet, but the child's face is disfigured by the fall and we haven't been able to confirm his identity."

"His grandfather's house is in Los Peumos . . . and his mother's grave," I mumble.

The officer, not listening to me, keeps talking. "According to what I've been told, the local children go to that area when they play hooky. It's a dangerous spot, and this would not be the first time an accident has occurred. We suspect it's a local child, but school hasn't been dismissed yet, so nobody has reported a disappearance. A few months ago, a girl's body was in the morgue until the evening without anyone claiming it. That's what the sergeant in charge told me. I'm telling you this so you understand that we're not at all certain this is your son. His name is Tomás, right? Anyway, I'd like to ask you to go there, just in case."

"Where is it?" I ask.

"They're bringing the body to the San Benito de Los Peumos Hospital as we speak."

"How did they find him?" I keep questioning him.

"Mr. Montes, not so fast—he probably isn't your son."

"Probably not," I say without any conviction. As we talk, I start to drive toward the airport.

"When you arrive at the hospital, ask for Sergeant Rojas. He will be expecting you."

"I'll be there in forty minutes," I say, and hang up.

I drive as fast as I can through the crowded streets of Santiago. I pass a Mazda and then a Fiat, race through a yellow light the second it changes to red, pass a delivery truck and a school bus. As I keep going, I watch the movements of that strange and distant city.

★

I open the throttle, start up the engines, taxi to the runway, receive permission to take off, pull back on the control wheel, lift the nose of my plane, and seconds later I'm flying. Over the trees and the rooftops, the glint of the sky rises toward the yellow peaks. I pass through a front of low clouds, then emerge into a stretch of light. To the south, a few clouds edged with gray float by. I plow through the sky at a constant speed. The engine makes a monotonous sound that smashes time, renders it powerless. The altitude acts as a local anesthetic.

And then a child appears in the passenger seat. I tell myself he is a figment of my imagination, of course, but everything about him is so very real: His sleepy yet penetrating gaze coming to rest on me, his hands with those delicate fingers, his pale skin, his feet dangling from the seat that is too high for him, and that gesture, so peculiarly his, of scratching his head to give himself courage when he is about to speak. But Tommy is not going to talk to me, because Tommy is the boy they found at Los Peumos. I have the urge to nosedive into the sea. Nobody is going to tell me that suffering and death are an innate part of life; nobody is going to convince me that without them existence is incomplete. Tommy is dead. He's dead . . . and that makes absolutely no sense.

51 〰

While she makes coffee, Maná observes me with one of those horrible wise-woman expressions on her face. On the way here, I called her to tell her about Tommy. I can't tell her about the rest of it. It would be like turning my weapons over to the enemy. She doesn't ask me why I'm here, why I'm not with Juan, looking for Tommy. I sit at her kitchen table waiting until it's time to pick Lola up from school. I want to hold my daughter. I have on my lap the bag she brought to Maná's house. Her pajamas with apples on them peek out through the half-open zipper. I have the urge to pull them out and bury my nose in them, but I control myself.

The table is covered with little boxes of the beads Maná is using to decorate a figure with a human torso, the head of a chicken, and two snakes for legs. I peer into every corner of the room, look at her wooden cabinets filled with baskets and pottery. I try to conjure up their stories, but it's useless; I can't get Tommy out of my head. Maná sits down next to me. She pours two cups of tea, then spreads an embroidered cloth over her lap.

"This is Abraxas, a deity who unites the divine and the demonic. You know why I'm embroidering it?"

I shake my head.

"So I don't forget a basic principle: That in order to achieve a minimum of peace, I must embrace the darkness inside me. That was one of Jung's major themes," she explains. She stops when she realizes I am barely listening to her.

Tommy once mentioned to me that Maná reminded him of the good witches. I asked him what he was talking about and he told me that they were the ones who could do good as well as evil, which made them doubly powerful. Maná picks up a few beads and threads them onto the needle. Her movements are slow and mindful. The morning clouds begin to dissipate and a few spots of blue peek out here and there. Every once in a while, Maná looks up from her work and watches me. I take in her gray hair, the wrinkles around her eyes, which, instead of marring her good looks, endow her face with an aura of serenity. It's almost as though she's given them permission to settle on her face. I hadn't realized it before, but Maná lacks that shadow of resignation that women like her, with furrows and drooping skin, usually project. We hear an engine in the distance. The rest is silence, the tranquility of her kitchen and her world.

And then it happens. The house of water implodes. I no longer have anywhere to hide. I break out in tears, my body heaving convulsively. I fold in two and bury my head in my hands. I sob, leaning over my legs, as if expelling poison from my body. My mother wraps her arms round me and brings me close to her chest. I hear her heart pressing against my ear. I don't know how long I remain like that, whimpering in her arms, before I manage to peel myself away from her wet blouse. I lift my head and run my hands over my face.

"I've ruined everything," I say in a whisper.

"That's impossible. Look how hard I tried to ruin everything and here you are."

"But I did it. I did everything I could to be different from you. I swore I'd never hurt anyone the way you hurt me."

Maná crosses her hands, squeezes them together, and brings them to her lips.

"I've been deliberately constructing the whole edifice. I thought I'd achieved it. I thought I'd done it." I move my hand in a gesture of despair, and my voice goes silent.

Maná takes a deep breath. I have never confronted her like this. When I left her sphere of influence, I also gave up the idea that she was in any way responsible for my life. "Alma, sometimes . . ." she whispers, but leaves the sentence unfinished. She looks out the window without breathing, then exhales in a sigh that fills the entire space. "Sometimes, no matter how hard we try, life passes right over us. Our actions and our feelings don't completely belong to us. They're also determined by what others give us and take away from us, what they don't tell us, what they do tell us, by our history, so many things . . ."

"If I could believe your words, I might not feel this horrible guilt, but the pain, how to relieve the pain?"

"There's a space, a tiny space that belongs to us, and that's where our essence resides. It's what makes us what we are, what allows us to change the course of our journey. Like the flame of a candle. Sometimes the most imperceptible movement is enough to blow it out, or make it burn forever." Her voice takes on a cautious and prophetic tone that grates on my nerves.

"Too bad," I say, "because mine are all burned out."

"Oh, no, these candles are indestructible. They keep burning even after you die, in the memories of those who loved you."

I can't believe I'm spouting such foolishness and listening to my mother's cheap metaphors.

"Maná, while Juan was suffering the unspeakable because of Tommy's disappearance, I was with another man. That's what I'm talking about, not about your stupid candles or your eternal flames. Don't you realize?" I am shouting now. "While he was trying to call me over and over again, I was at the beach, happy as a lark, fucking my brains out. Tommy realized what was going on; that's why he ran away. Juan also knows. Now do you get it? That's the shit I'm talking about." I look away in order to stem the flood of rage and fear that's drowning me.

Maná looks down and presses her fingers together. I attempt to calm myself. I run the back of my hand over my nose and try to take a deep breath.

"If Tommy ran away, that isn't the reason, not the only reason, at least," she says cautiously.

"How can you be so sure?" I ask.

"Because things are never that simple. They never occur in isolation. Tommy is a very sensitive child, and his father doesn't exactly help much, but he's also been bullied at school."

"How do you know?"

"The mother of one of his classmates, who's in my meditation class, told me. Apparently, one of the children felt badly about it and told his mother what was going on, and that's how some of the other mothers found out, among them the woman I know."

"How come you never told me?"

"I found out only a few days ago. I've been waiting for the right moment to tell you."

"So everybody knows except us."

"I'm sure Tommy doesn't want you to know. It's terribly humiliating."

"What else do you know?" I ask resentfully.

"I know that nothing is ever how it seems, not altogether, at least. And that we do the best we can, even if often that's not good enough." She squints, as if she were about to cry.

"What are you talking about?"

"What I'm about to tell you is not an attempt to redeem myself, OK? But I'd like you to be able to see things from another point

249

of view." She pauses. "Remember your trip to Barcelona? How do you think that came about?"

"You?"

Maná nods. Suddenly, I remember the postcard from Edith that came to the house. Maná must have been the one who told Edith how to get in touch with me and asked her to hire me. She must have met her on one of her adventures before she married my father. So my trip and Edith, the two great miracles that saved my life and that I thought were the result of my own efforts, they were both her doing. A fine web of support was being woven behind my back. I can hardly take it in. All that's left is Juan.

Juan came to the restaurant because someone gave him my name and a review from the newspaper along with his airline ticket. My mind starts spinning over the past and over what I knew of my mother during that period, and I vaguely recall hearing Maná say she'd briefly worked at a travel agency. I take a breath and ask her.

"For a while, yes, many years ago."

"So you sent Juan to Edith's restaurant."

Only yesterday, my mother's revelations would have undermined my foundations, but what does any of this matter now that Tommy has disappeared?

She looks up at me. "Your father and I, what we did and didn't do, the good and the bad, that's the legacy we've given you. Now it's up to you."

"I can't stop thinking about Tommy. I can't stop thinking that he might be suffering, that I don't know where he is. I don't know how to do this, Mama," I confess, pronouncing the unpronounceable word.

"Neither do I. Each of us is alone in that, Alma. You can't imagine how much I'd like . . ." Her chin trembles and the tears begin to tumble down her cheeks. Still she doesn't cover her face.

She's crying for me. Perhaps this is one of those profound changes she talks about. Maná feels less fear than I do in the face of life's ironies, in the face of all the questions without answers.

We both look out at the rectangle of sky we can see through the window. This is how forgiveness arrives, not with a big brass band but sneaking quietly in through a kitchen window.

52⧗

The cold seeps into my bones in this windowless room. I'm waiting for Sergeant Rojas. The outside world has retreated: my father, my brothers, my patients, the hospital, that whole complex life full of rituals that seemed so indispensable. Suddenly, a question pops into my head that makes me tremble: Why did you let the birds go?

It's never occurred to me that Tommy had a reason to do what he did. I should have asked him. I should have listened to what he had to tell me. And then, instead of that nonsense I spewed out in his room, we could have sat together and actually talked. Maybe I wouldn't have liked his answer, maybe it would have angered or upset me, and maybe I wouldn't then have been able to leave his room feeling like I had carried out my paternal duty, but I would now be able to remember that afternoon not as just one more phase of my child's orderly upbringing, or merely one more of many similar conversations, but as an essential and genuine moment.

My cellphone is ringing. It's Yerfa.

"Mr. Montes, I just found a note from Tommy."

"What does it say?"

"It says, 'Don't worry about me. I went to see Mama at Los Peumos. Today is the anniversary of her death. I'll be back on the six o'clock bus. Kisses for everyone, Tommy.'"

"Where did you find it?"

"In the pantry, when I went to get rice for lunch."

"In the pantry?"

"Yes, right there. I don't understand why he would have hidden it like that."

"So we wouldn't find it right away."

"But where is he, Mr. Montes? Where is my little boy?"

"We'll soon find out, Yerfa. Try to stay calm."

Sergeant Rojas opens the door, looking from side to side, as though he's the one entering an enemy camp.

"Thanks, Yerfa. I'll call you later."

Rojas holds out his hand and presses mine firmly. I can feel his rough skin. Even though he looks a bit slovenly in his uniform, there is something tidy about his manners. We go into the hallway full of people waiting to be seen. As we pass, a boy with a contusion on his face looks at me defiantly. We walk in silence. The morgue is at the end.

Sergeant Rojas turns his face away. It is not difficult for me to recognize Tommy in the mangled body. I look at my son's battered cheeks, his split lips, his eyes open and bruised, his swollen thorax and arms. One of his feet has been severed from his leg and is connected to his body only with a bit of cartilage. His thigh bone can be seen under the white flesh. His ears, on the other hand, are intact, as is his neck, smooth and clear. His jet-black hair is still shiny. I run my fingers along his frozen body. Someone laughs outside the door. My lips tremble, and a groan rises from my throat, which I immediately suppress.

The man holding up the sheet asks me, "Are you OK?"

"You can cover him back up," I answer.

53 〰

"What's wrong, Mama?" I hear Lola asking me. She wrinkles her nose and shrugs her shoulders.

We are in her room, and I watch her putting away the toys she took over to my mother's house. Tommy has been gone for thirty-four hours. Lola asked about him as soon as we got home and I told her he had gone out with Juan. She was sorry she hadn't been here to go with them. When we got back to the house, Yerfa rushed to the door, her eyes red and exhausted, and hugged us both tightly. Since then she's kept to her room. I feel like a lonely warrior, hiding behind a bush, waiting for something to happen. I hold Lola round the waist and throw her on the bed.

"What's wrong is that I feel like eating you up, as if you were a little piggy."

"Oh, Mama, but I'm not a little piggy," she argues, holding on to me.

"Yes, you are." I kiss her on the neck, that spot that is still completely and utterly soft, just as it was the day she was born.

"No, I'm not. I'm a bunny, remember that," she says firmly, holding me close.

"I know, but bunnies aren't as yummy."

We roll around on the bed, our bodies pressed together. We get to the edge, then roll over to the other side; our movements get faster and faster, until on one of those rolls we end up on the floor, hugging each other. She opens her eyes, looking quite mischievous, and laughs, imitating a cartoon character. She makes quick, sharp sounds that make us both crack up.

I'm amazed that I am able to laugh like this and still feel what I am feeling. I remember playing like this with Tommy when he was smaller. If Juan found us, he'd remind me to be careful and then close the door. I think he would have liked to have played like that with his son, but he couldn't find the path that led to so many pointless hugs. Now Tommy has grown up and they've both lost out on that experience forever. Maybe Juan and I, without knowing it, are trapped with what Maná called "our legacies," those things we bring from our families, things we don't actually choose. We cling to them, or pieces of them, even though they hurt us, and they define our lives to such an enormous extent that we prefer not to look at them squarely. When we see a fleeting image of what we're missing because of them, our instinct is to look away— shut the door, as Juan would do when he'd see me cuddling his son. Then we can go on deceiving ourselves, believing we are actually aware of the choices we make. I hug Lola even tighter.

I think again of the snake who, after squeezing through the sharp rocks to peel off its skin, finds that the sores are still there. How could I not have realized this sooner: That healing isn't a solitary exercise? We need other people. I see it so clearly now, I feel like shouting it out.

"Aren't we ever going to get up off the ground?" Lola asks.

My cellphone rings in my handbag. I get up and desperately look for it until I find it. Leo's name appears on the screen. It seems like forever since I left him this morning. Lola sits on the edge of the bed and fixes her brown eyes on me, fully aware of my anxiety.

"Wait a minute for me, OK? This is an important call from my work."

She makes a face at me with her mouth open, as if asking me, "Since when do you give me explanations for telephone calls?"

I go into my room. I see my travel bag half open on the floor. The rest of the room is neat and tidy, as if I'd been banished.

"Alma, are you there?"

"Yes."

"Did they find Tommy?"

"No."

Leo is silent for a few seconds. I can hear a car passing by in the background.

"I'm sorry."

"It's horrible, Leo."

"You're home, right?"

"How do you know?"

"I'm outside, in front of your car."

The leafy tree outside my window blocks my view.

"Why did you come back to Santiago?"

"It didn't make much sense for me to stay. I want to talk to you."

"It's not easy for me to come out now."

Leo says nothing. I realize he's not going to give up.

"Wait for me," I tell him. "I'll be out in a minute."

I go back to Lola's room and kiss her on the top of the head and promise I won't be long. Then I knock on Yerfa's door to let her know I'm going out for a few minutes. From the doorway I see Leo across the street. His presence, so close to my house, is disconcerting. I open the door to my car and motion to him.

"Come on, get in before this becomes a scandal."

Leo crosses the street and jumps in. As I drive quickly away from my neighborhood, Leo places his hand on my leg. We remain quiet. I feel utterly exhausted. I drive around aimlessly, avoiding the main avenues. It's warm in the car; I open the window.

"Can we go somewhere?" he asks brusquely.

I can't possibly go to a public place and watch people living their normal lives when Tommy is lost. I stop at a corner, any corner; we get out of the car and start walking. It's a neighborhood full of well-manicured homes, some of them brand new. Further ahead is an avenue lined with newly planted palm trees and several dark office buildings. The vanishing afternoon has the same texture as the glass house: a fictitious world suspended in time, a world I no longer belong to.

"So many things have happened since this morning," I manage to say.

"I can imagine," Leo says. I hear caution in his voice.

We keep walking without touching each other. The silence tightens around us, like a muzzle.

"I'm sorry, Leo." I see the dark shadow that crosses his face. "I'm really sorry."

"You don't need to decide right now, Alma—I can wait." I'm moved by his desolation and humility. "I'm not in any hurry."

I throw my arms round him and press him to me. Leo kisses me. The touch of his skin is painful. I can't stand it. I pull away.

"Is it guilt? Is that what's stopping you?" he asks.

"No. No, it's not guilt. I'll probably regret it, especially when you're settled in Bogota with another woman and I'm alone."

I can't tell him what has happened with Juan.

"Do you remember what you told me when we met at Julia's wedding?" he asks.

"No."

"You said it was enough for you not to feel alone. You don't think the same way now."

"Yes, I still do."

"You feel alone with me?"

The days I shared with Leo seem far away, as if they belonged to somebody else.

"Answer me. Do you feel alone with me?"

"Sometimes."

"And with Juan?"

"Almost always."

"So?"

"What, don't you feel the same way, Leo? Aren't you asking me to live with you because you're tired of your solitude and you have the illusion that together we can somehow alleviate it? Weren't you the one who said that what brought people together was desperation? You made that very clear the first night we spent together, so there wouldn't be any misunderstandings."

"I've changed my mind, Alma. And you know why? Because I don't feel desperate with you . . . I thought you felt the same way," he says, "but I guess I was wrong."

We get to the street with the palm trees. None of this will make any sense until Tommy shows up. Even so, I keep talking.

"Soon we'll both be even more alone. After trying and failing, we'll be more alone than ever."

"Look, Alma, what happens in itself doesn't mean a whole lot. It can be as fortunate or unfortunate as what never happens. The only difference is that when something happens, we can choose to endow it with meaning. That's all I'm proposing, that we give this meaning, for both of us."

Our dialogue seems to me like a pantomime, a parody of reality. I have the urge to run away.

"'Endow it with meaning . . .'" I mumble.

"Exactly," Leo says. A smile breaks at the edges of his lips.

"I'm sorry, Leo, none of this makes any sense right now. I don't even know what I'm doing here. Tommy has disappeared, something horrible could have happened to him, I don't know where he is, and I'm incapable of thinking about anything other than him."

There is silence.

"I understand."

"Everything has changed, Leo," I say, trembling.

"Definitively?"

The darkness creeps up into the sky. We no longer have anything to share. Leo takes my hand and presses it, as if wanting to express a vast and also final sentiment.

54⧗

I look at Soledad's photograph propped up with a rock on her gravestone. Her dark eyes look out to sea, where Tommy must have fallen. He's the one who left it here. Behind her bruises, Soledad has a peaceful, even luminous look on her face. Her pupils shine through the slits of her eyes. A blast of wind swirls around me. I begin to cry. Below, the waves crash against the rocks. I see Tommy staring at me; his gaze burns through me and peels me open. Through his eyes I see a man who is alienated from the things around him, a man who only vaguely perceives reality in brief and fleeting flashes. All my certainties have vanished, even the one I'm trying to formulate now. Tommy. I remember his drawing of the Minotaur, the drawing that always seemed somehow feminine to me. I can see it so clearly, as if it were right in front of my eyes. I enter the labyrinth. I continue through the passageways of Tommy's consciousness, his vast world I never had the guts to enter, out of ineptitude, out of fear of encountering his pain, the knowledge that his mother killed herself. How pathetic my efforts were, how false. I left him alone in his labyrinth, and all by himself he found his way out.

I have to find a way out, too. But how? I look out to sea. The gray waters scratch the rocks, and the clouds spread like blots of ink across the sky. I remember my cellphone in my pocket. I take a picture of the water, and another, and another, trying to capture its elusive splendor. The water that took my Tommy away. Perhaps, by freezing the moment, I can find the gap, the tiny sliver of light at the exit of the labyrinth.

I think of Alma. No, more than think of her; her image appears before me, as if she'd been waiting for the right moment to make herself seen. I remember Tommy's words. She's the only person in the world I can tell that he's dead, that I saw his destroyed body, that something in me is dying at this very moment. She's the only person to whom I could confess that I have never felt so frightened.

I call her cell.

"Juan," I hear her say immediately. "Juan, Juan," she repeats anxiously.

"Tommy is dead," I say.

Again that sense of unreality spreads through me, as if this were happening somewhere else, to another man.

"He died in the ocean," I continue, "in front of Soledad's grave."

Alma doesn't answer. Silence drowns us, a deep silence in which our breathing echoes. I know she is crying; she is closing her eyes, desperate to escape from the horror. That's what I am doing.

"Juan, where are you?" she asks. Her words seem to be creeping along a narrow thread that can break at any moment.

"At Los Peumos Cemetery."

"Who are you with?"

"I'm alone."

"Juan, you'll wait for me, right? Wait for me?"

I cry again. I don't even try to stifle my sobs.

"This is what we'll do. You will wait for me, and in the meantime, we'll talk. Agreed?"

I say yes, I agree.

"I'm not going to hang up until I get to you, do you hear me?

I'm leaving now. I'm in my car and I'm turning on the engine. I'm not going to leave you, Juan. I'm not going to let go of you. I'm going to put in my earpiece, so we can keep talking. Just wait a second. There, I've got it."

I know she's got the window open and that her red hair is blowing in the wind.

"And while I drive, and so I won't fall asleep, you can tell me a story. Whatever you want."

I know that she is rubbing the back of her hand across her nose, back and forth, that she has a determined look on her face, and that her foot is pressing down hard on the gas pedal.

"If you don't want to talk, that's OK, too."

I can see her biting her lips until they hurt.

"Alma," I say finally, "it's just that you are the thread."

"What are you talking about? I'm only a thread? A miserable little thread? Is that all I am, Juan?" I hear her laugh, a hoarse laugh.

"You are all that. You are the thread Tommy left for me to get out of the labyrinth, because I can't do it alone. Do you remember?"